MERCHA

Neelima Dalmia Adhar was educated in a convent school and a reputed college in Delhi and has a Master's in Psychology with a specialisation in 'Personality'. Her first and only job was to teach Psychology to undergraduate students of Delhi University. A passionate 'people-watcher', she is drawn to oddities and thrives on writing about personalities and human behaviour, from the quirky to the mysterious to the bizarre, a subject she does chillingly close to the bone.

She lives in Delhi with her husband, children and two grandchildren.

Other books by the author

Father Dearest: The Life & Times of R.K. Dalmia
The Secret Diary of Kasturba
Radha: The Princess of Barsana

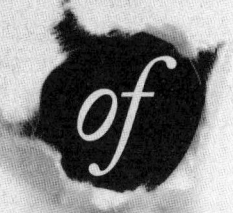

MERCHANTS of DEATH

NEELIMA
DALMIA ADHAR

First published by Har-Anand Publications Private Limited in 2007

Published by westland ltd in 2017

Published by Westland Books, a division of Nasadiya Technologies Private Limited, in 2024

No. 269/2B, First Floor, 'Irai Arul', Vimalraj Street, Nethaji Nagar, Alapakkam Main Road, Maduravoyal, Chennai 600095

Westland and the Westland logo are the trademarks of Nasadiya Technologies Private Limited, or its affiliates.

Copyright © Neelima Dalmia Adhar, 2007

Neelima Dalmia Adhar asserts the moral right to be identified as the author of this work.

ISBN: 9789360458836

10 9 8 7 6 5 4 3 2 1

This is a work of fiction. Names, characters, organisations, places, events and incidents are either products of the author's imagination or used fictitiously.

Author's disclaimer: Several well-known people, mostly politicians, make brief appearances in these pages, but this is a work of fiction and none of the other characters are real. Barring some facts, which are historically documented, none of these events ever happened and any resemblance to any person living or dead is purely coincidental.

All rights reserved

Typeset by Newgen KnowledgeWorks Pvt. Ltd, Chennai
Printed at Nutech Print Services, India

No part of this book may be reproduced, or stored in a retrieval system, or transmitted in any form or by any means, electronic, mechanical, photocopying, recording, or otherwise, without express written permission of the publisher.

To my children
Mrinali, Nishant, Yameer and Sharnamli

And my precious grandchildren
Shyraa, Shauryaveer, Zaavian and Azarius

FAMILY TREE

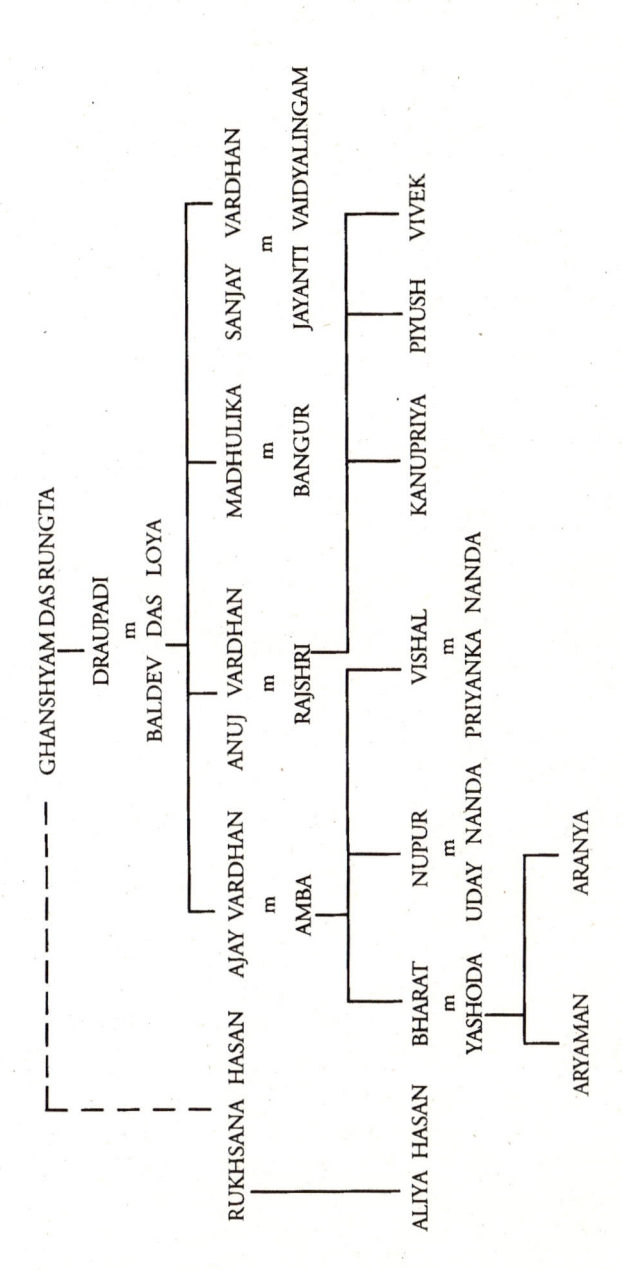

```
                    GHANSHYAM DAS RUNGTA
                           DRAUPADI
                              m
                       BALDEV DAS LOYA
    ┌──────────────────────┼──────────────────────┐
AJAY VARDHAN          ANUJ VARDHAN           MADHULIKA    SANJAY VARDHAN
    m                      m                     m                m
  AMBA                  RAJSHRI               BANGUR      JAYANTI VAIDYALINGAM
    │                      │                     │
┌───┼───┐              ┌───┴───┐            ┌────┼────┐
BHARAT  NUPUR          VISHAL              KANUPRIYA PIYUSH VIVEK
  m                       m
YASHODA  UDAY NANDA   PRIYANKA NANDA
         
┌────┴────┐
ARYAMAN  ARANYA
```

RUKHSANA HASAN — — — — (dashed line to family)

ALIYA HASAN

New Delhi
September 2002

> *He was the husband of his mother and the father of his sister. He was both venerated and despised, the prostitute and the saint, the depraved and the transcendent, the hideous and the resplendent, the one who gave birth and the one who never procreated. He was the fairy tale and the horror story, neither living nor dead—just trapped in the matrix of time!*

Forty-eight year old Bharat Loya was a troubled man. Managing Director of a fifteen hundred crore conglomerate, he sat sunken into a dark leather chair in his office that was furnished with an Emperador marble floor, a Venetian chandelier, a monogrammed Louis XV mahogany table, family photographs mounted on silver frames, an original Picasso, and rare objects of art. He had thin lips that imparted a stern look to his deceptively boyish face. His body language exuded the arrogance characteristic of his breed. He had long tapering fingers that tapped absently on the table in front of him. The meshed gold strap of the Moon-Phase Patek Philippe he wore glowed in the light filtering from a Tiffany lamp.

His stooping shoulders curved inwards towards his chest, as he stared out of GI House at the crawling traffic on Jantar Mantar Road, eight floors below. A mediaeval pink monument deemed to be a ladder for the kings to observe the stars stared back at him with the stern beauty of a nun. He felt a surge of energy flood his senses.

Rising on this snarling commercial street, from the midst of shoddy peanut vendors, paan and bidi peddlers, junk food kiosks and noisy pedestrian bus stands, GI House, the headquarters of Global Integrity Industries, stood in the heart of Connaught Place as a symbol of the changing ethos in the landscape of Delhi, the city that had been ravaged and resurrected seven times, over hundreds of years. Seated on the eighth floor of this state-of-the-art building, Bharat Loya could feel the vibrant force churning the bowels of his domain from where a blueprint of the covert interplay between the powers-to-be and the 'merchants of death' was chalked out and implemented with mathematical precision.

Like all arms dealers Bharat Loya lived in a different moral universe from the rest of the world and even though his work was highly clandestine his identity was hardly a mystery. He had beaten back with panache many challenges in his undercover operations, each one having left him more powerful than before.

With corruption rampant like never before in the Indian ruling circles Bharat Loya knew that he was there to stay. The new mantra 'no middlemen, no commissions' meant nothing to him and the ban that followed only pushed him along with his 'holy tribe' further underground.

The track record of his dubious defence deals, all executed without regard for efficacy or cost had made him the most coveted facilitator for the major arms cartels of the world. With his deep pockets and legitimate facade of hotelier-cum-airline-owner he stood as the uncrowned king of the whole immoral pack. Yet Bharat Loya was a troubled man.

At GI House this was no ordinary day.

On the lower floors, hectic activity was under way. Preparations to celebrate a very special occasion were being carried out. Aryaman Loya, the first born and only son of the MD, had turned twenty-three. There was a palpable air of frenzy in the floors below. There could be no gaffes. The MD behind his deadpan face and misleading mild manner was known to be intolerant of inefficiency. All members of the staff were now assembled in the conference room on the second floor, to enact the ritual for which they had been warming up.

Earlier that day, as Bharat Loya stared at himself in his bathroom mirror, he had noticed the increasing grey in his thinning hair. Some new wrinkles were visible around his darting eyes that betrayed signs of fatigue, and deep frown lines etched the centre of his forehead. He poured liquid soap on to his hands and began to scrub. He had done that several times over that morning. He felt a throbbing pain on the left side of his head. He took a long breath. The pain worsened as thick mucous trapped in his sinus cavities shifted and then trickled back into position. Try as he did, he could not expel it.

'Damn!' he cursed as he turned away from the mirror in irritation. A heavy mental shutter dropped, blocking the annoying whispers from his soul—*'every day in every way, I am getting better and better...better and better...!'*

After a long drive in silence to GI House, he took the reserved lift to the eighth floor. *Aryaman entered the building just behind him.* Bharat Loya was grateful for the solitude that would greet him in his private office, where no one but the summoned could enter. The large, vibrantly coloured painting on the far side of the corridor irked him.

'It should have been in monochromatic tones,' he murmured to himself.

Aryaman followed him to his room noiselessly.

In the conference hall two floors below, on a slightly raised podium stood a square table covered with a white satin sheet. An enormous chocolate cake with a single white candle was placed on it. A silver knife, decorated with a red ribbon, lay beside it. A hushed silence fell upon those assembled there as the MD entered.

Aryaman glided in beside him, holding on to his arm.

With measured steps that made him buckle slightly at the knees, he walked up to the podium, with his son. The distinct chill that emanated from his person should have been enough to freeze the vast hall that boasted of superb air-conditioning and perfect acoustics. Soft notes from a piano began to play, as someone stepped forward to light the candle. With a barely perceptible tremor in his flat voice, the MD began to sing. He voiced the melodious words of the age-old birthday song for his son and heir, to be joined in, by the rest of the congregation. When the singing stopped and the music faded out, a few shuffling feet interrupted the pindrop silence. In a theatrical gesture, the MD lifted the knife and sliced through the cake, cutting a neat triangular wedge.

Aryaman made no attempt to blow out the flickering candle that slowly dripped wax onto the cake.

No one rushed forward to feed him the first piece, but that was because no one had seen him standing there beside his father, clutching onto his arm.

The lone birthday boy wasn't there at all. He had been dead for two years!

1

Calcutta
June 1954

On a hot and balmy night, in a sprawling nine-acre mansion in the leafy Alipore district of Calcutta, Bharat Loya, the son of Ajay Vardhan and Amba, and the grandson of Baldev Das and Draupadi Loya, came into this world, with a silver spoon in his mouth—a spoon that carried with it an in-built curse, that would affect three generations in a macabre manner. The innocuous looking baby with his ruddy complexion, crumpled features and tightly clasped fists, wailing loudly in his cradle, was a miniature imprint of his father. The young ecstatic parents, who were both below twenty years of age welcomed their tiny, five and a half pound son, with pride and joy into their hearts and home. That home would provide him the nurturing and growth within a large joint family of over ten members.

Headed by the grandparents, Draupadi and Baldev Das, and their three sons Ajay Vardhan, Anuj Vardhan and Sanjay Vardhan, and one daughter Madhulika, the clan had indeed been bestowed with the greatest blessing of having witnessed the birth of the first male child in the third generation.

Like most babies belonging to the privileged class, he was to be treated like a precious jewel inside a splendid home modelled on the lines of the palace of Louis XIV at Versailles. A retinue of impeccably attired servants and a stern caretaker, called Adam Wilson, were entrusted with his care. The doting family, photographed, filmed and tape-recorded every single step that the newcomer took to prepare a record of his life, since the moment he had uttered his first cry, after leaving his mother's womb. But unfortunately Bharat Loya was emetic and not too robust and his delicate digestive system was a constant source of stress to his frail and beautiful, eighteen-year old mother.

Chosen for her exceptionally fair complexion and princess-like beauty, Amba had been wedded to his father Ajay Vardhan, in spite of her very ordinary lineage. Her long, silky, tumbling tresses, high cheekbones and curious almond-shaped eyes had transported her into a quagmire of wealth and luxury, and a lifestyle that she adopted, effortlessly.

Like most women of her class and unlike her own mother, Amba suffered from a severe bout of postpartum depression after the birth of her son, which was dismissed cursorily by her dominating mother-in-law, because she hated unnecessary fuss and couldn't understand such modern maladies.

Despite his inability to digest milk and a constantly bleeding nose, the anaemic infant showed early developing milestones. His mother, however, who was small-breasted in proportion to her narrow frame, just could not bring herself to breast-feed him. She found it painful and distasteful, for nothing had prepared her for the fatigue and melancholy that childbirth entailed.

Raised on a fare of powdered milk formula and some home remedies for the first twelve months of his life, Bharat Loya grew up a small, unobtrusive child who caused no trouble other than his health, and at most times went unnoticed. His constantly blocked sinuses, inflamed ears and febrile constitution became a routine, growing-up affair.

His mother took occasional pleasure in the infantile glurks and googles that he emitted from time to time, and his lactose-intolerance and her inability to breast-feed him was soon forgotten. Although he spent most of his time in his nursery with Mr. Wilson and his nursemaids, the brief spells of body contact with his mother that he was treated to once in a while, became the high point of his existence. He was soon to begin his lifelong romance with his mother that would grow into a deep-rooted Oedipal fixation in his later years. It would manifest as a strong attraction for older women with shell-shaped pink ears and fair skins. It would also breed in him, an admiration for women with beautiful hands and feet and slender bodies, a fetish that would dictate compelling codes of conduct in his adult years.

By the time Bharat Loya was a toddler of two learning to speak a few words, there was an addition to the family.

His uncle Anuj Vardhan was wedded to a demure, nubile, pretty, eighteen-year old from the same city, who hailed from reasonably well-to-do Marwari stock. Rajshri, like her elder counterpart, also sailed into the opulent but authoritative matriarchal domain of her mother-in-law, with ceremonial grandeur. Within nine months, she had given birth to her first child, a girl, who was named Kanupriya.

In his formative years, Bharat grew up in close proximity to his grandmother, her two daughters-in-law and the third new entrant into their charmed circle, his little cousin Kanupriya.

Unlike him, Kanupriya was a big, bouncy, fair and large-eyed baby, with a physically strong constitution. Like her older cousin, her life too would be shadowed by the immutable curse of the silver spoon, with which she had been fed the first drop of honey, on the day she was born.

Two-year old Bharat would often sneak up to Kanupriya's cradle and smother her with long, lingering, wet kisses. He would only stop when he was yanked away by his nurse or she rescued by hers. It left him angry and weeping, because he believed Kanupriya was his personal plaything. Sometimes he pinched her overblown pink cheeks that felt like his rubber toys, or made shrill sounds in her ears that startled her and made her scream.

It was his pet game. But the game he liked most was sitting on his mother's lap with his head buried in her bosom, his thin arms wrapped tightly around her, pretending he had fallen asleep. Unfortunately, it was not a game he could play too long or too often, because his mother was impatient and had developed other interests not uncommon to beautiful women in the throes of postpartum blues. The most compelling one being, Prithviraj Jaipuria.

2

Amba's frenzied attraction for her husband's best friend had not developed overnight. Her podgy, short-statured and bespectacled spouse, with his big ears and protruding lips, did not exactly excite her. The unabashed attention from his friend was more flattering and deeply thrilling. She craved for his company. The feeling was new to her and dispelled her gloom.

By then, the Marwari society of Calcutta had declared her the undisputed beauty icon of those days, and her husband the most envied twenty-two-year old. Her delicate frame and translucent skin that served a deserving tribute to the finest jewels that she wore, made him look even plainer by contrast. Her eighteen-inch waist, mocked at his visible pot-belly, making most people treat her with utmost sympathy and him with veiled contempt. Within a few months of their association, the whole of Calcutta was agog with the rumour of the scandalous affair between Amba Loya and Prithviraj Jaipuria.

In a race dominated by small-statured, dark and puny looking men, Prithviraj Jaipuria was considered a classic

Greek hero. Cultured and soft-spoken, the fair, tall, suave and wealthy scion of the hundred and fifty year old house of textile magnates, made no pretence of the fact that he was completely besotted by her. Most believed that his own sexually inadequate, ailing wife Nayantara, who was also a beauty and of high pedigree, was a convenient trade-off to Ajay Vardhan and that kept the perverse harmony of the foursome intact.

For the prudish Marwaris of the fifties, ridden with heavy pretensions of morality, it was a bitter pill to swallow. Even though it was no secret that incestuous relationships, illicit affairs, sexual liaisons with available or desirous in-laws and carnal links with employees and staff were rampant in Marwari homes, such scant regard for public sensibilities was a source of grave outrage. Immoral affairs were best kept within the four walls of a home and the occasional scandal that did worm its way out of a closet would find its perpetrators doomed to ignominy. Within these rotting hypocrisies, discretion was warranted and normally observed. But the rich lived by different rules.

The wife-swapping stories of the prurient foursome rocked the city of Calcutta, but the four were neither ostracised, nor discredited, because they were positioned too high up on the social ladder. In fact, their mystical enigma was magnified enormously as a result.

In any case, the head matriarch of Loya House, Draupadi, was also a trend-setter who lived by her own rules. The eldest child of Ghanshyam Das Rungta, a controversial Marwari industrialist of international fame, she had inherited a huge chunk of her father's empire when she married her tutor, Baldev Das, who hailed from a humble family of the small town of Shikohabad.

Brought up like a true blue-blooded princess, she was a woman well ahead of her times. Her fiery temper and rebellious manner had made her distinctive among her peers, most of whom were shackled by their orthodoxy. Her style of entertaining reflected her class and breeding and her parties became legendary. Her banquet table overflowed with exquisite crystal and silver and the choicest wines and liquors accompanied the varied and exotic vegetarian cuisine. Her gatherings triggered off a scramble amongst those who tried in vain to ape her. Haughty and arrogant, she thought nothing of cavorting and publicly romancing with any rake who caught her fancy, from budding poets, to handsome young bureaucrats or promising politicians. In the famed *baithaks,* the soirees, that were frequently held in her ornate reception halls, with their select Persian carpets and rich interiors, she held forth, gambling, singing and dancing till the small hours of the morning, with the who's who of the city joining her in her wild revelry.

Draupadi had a dark complexion and thick features. Like most Marwari women, she was robust and big-boned. She displayed the unmistakeable confidence that comes with wealth and good fortune, and never considered her plain looks to be a handicap. She had been pampered and spoilt by her father and she carried an air of obduracy about her. Her scandalous elopement with her tutor had caused an uproar in the staid society those days, but her doting father had set aside every moral protest to save her from social disgrace. No one ever questioned her conduct thereafter.

Her short-statured tutor gained an entry into the elite and coveted class of the rich and famous by virtue of his marriage. Under the tutelage of his father-in-law he learned the skills of managing the vast business that had fallen into his lap thereof. He soon understood that theirs would be a woman-dominated Marwari home, with a clearly demarcated pecking order. Taking his height to be not merely a symbolic acceptance of his wife's supremacy he succumbed to a life of bullying, never to interfere in her day-to-day existence.

Baldev Das belonged to the trader bania community by birth and came from humble stock. He had crude facial features, small eyes, a bulbous nose and an incongruously fair complexion. These genetic characteristics would translate their imprint firmly, into all the four products of this mixed marriage. All four would be short, dark and predisposed to coronary disease. In a cruel and chancy process of natural selection, none would be bestowed with either the fairness of their father's skin or the towering height that their mother possessed. So in a society governed by clear cut biases in favour of fair skins, their appearances would be rated as below average.

By this time, the Marwaris began to understand that since they controlled the industrial and financial world, they had the power to execute a radical change in their genetic strain by introducing fair-skinned and beautiful women into their bloodline. As money power determines and alters social rules, it was not difficult to begin a systematic drive to root out these disagreeable handicaps and many matrimonial alliances thereafter were decided on the lightness of skin tone rather than by the quality of their class or stock.

By this transition, many rich eligible men procured beautiful (read fair) and malleable brides from ordinary backgrounds and with them, other related and inevitable maladies like early boredom and conjugal ennui. As a result, sexual gratification often found opportune outlets in covert extramarital relationships that were manageable on the sly.

Amba and Ajay Vardhan by that analogy were not the only or even the first ones to publicly violate the prescribed moral code. Draupadi too, had had her share of scurrilous, sexual associations that had faded quickly into obscurity, as age, ill-health and thirty kilograms added to her girth incapacitated her, forcibly diminishing her libidinous appetite. She donned the respectable mantle of a Tsarina of culture and became a patron of the arts, still pursuing the finer things of life with elegance and aplomb.

3

By the time Bharat celebrated his eighth birthday, he had acquired two more siblings, a girl who had turned four and a boy who was two years old. His little brother, Vishal, inherited his mother's complexion, but not her looks and his puny looking baby sister, Nupur, turned out to be a spitting image of their father. That thwarted any attempts the family may have made towards improvement of their bloodline by marriage.

The silver spoon, tied by the invisible karmic thread, wove its malefic pattern into each of their lives as they flourished, blissfully unaware of the doom it portended. During those years, Kanupriya also acquired two younger brothers, Piyush and Vivek, who grew up in their ostensibly harmonious home in which the cracks had formed, but were not yet visible.

Kanupriya's father, Anuj Vardhan, was an indiscriminate and star-struck womaniser. He had experimented in every form of sexual adventure by the time he had turned sixteen. His amorous pursuits had included making love to two sisters in the same bed and progressed through an extraordinary array of models, small-time starlets and a widowed cousin, who was five years older. He firmly believed that celibacy, more than rich food, ruined a healthy constitution, so even as he had been fathering his three children, he continued his old habits of frantic gambling and the pursuit of carnal pleasure. He wooed the objects of his lust with intense fervour and grandiose gifts, which included mountains of orchids and diamonds from Tiffany. He treated his women to extravagant holidays abroad, with a style that could humble the richest of tycoons. His sharp business acumen drew him laurels from his associates and elders, and he found himself catapulted into fame and prominence when he accomplished a clever takeover of two extremely lucrative textile mills in Kanpur, at the age of twenty-three. That placed him beyond reproach and above social censure. Any bliss, that might have been present in his marriage, soon dissipated.

His miserable and neglected wife, burdened with the arduous task of child-rearing, sank into a deep depression from which she never recovered. She resorted to psychiatric treatment for her chronic condition and began her long and desperate dependence on drugs. As a result, her three children became mute and unhappy witnesses to their father's profligacy and mother's gloom.

A few years later, mindless of the damage he was inflicting on his family, Anuj Vardhan moved Chaya Devi, the ace siren of Bombay films, into a luxurious flat in the swanky neighbourhood of Malabar Hill and made her his full-time mistress. For the time being, it seemed that she had managed to curb his insatiable, sexual appetite, and had him tied down to a life of forced fidelity.

Sanjay Vardhan, the youngest of Draupadi's children, did not have either the flamboyance or the intelligence of his elder brothers, nor did he possess the mild manner of his older sister Madhulika. Having received very little of his mother's love and father's attention, he deviated onto the path of least resistance that lured him to the safe and secure world of drugs. By the time his parents discovered his malady, it had seeped deep into his veins and they gave him up as a lost cause. He remained most of the time in his illusory world, or in the company of his servants and maids, who provided him with a ready supply of prostitutes for sexual experimentation. He grew up a fat and lonely teenager with mildly homosexual preferences, condemned to a life of isolation, within the walls of his home. His social handicap became the city's worst kept secret. It led to a vicious round of rumour-mongering that he had been deliberately introduced to drugs and rendered mentally infirm, so that the elder brothers could divest him of his rightful share in his father's wealth.

If Draupadi had any misgivings about the state of affairs within her home, she made a good job of hiding it. Most perceived her bravado as a camouflage of her own prurience. Some years ago, an old personal chambermaid had discovered her in a compromising position with a handsome young poet from Bihar, who was subsequently awarded a berth in the Upper House of Parliament, quite clearly on her decree. The story was passed around like an unending chain of Chinese whispers, but Draupadi Loya was above remorse or reproach. The young and hot-blooded poet continued to enjoy her benevolence as she entertained him in her customary style. Most such evenings, her husband was away on conveniently arranged business tours and she had him solely to herself. Never did her confidence waver or her control slip. The only time that she heard a member of her staff gossiping about her libertine conduct, she had him sacked on the charge of theft.

Her husband remained her doting and servile companion, seemingly unaffected by her serial infidelity and she stayed strapped firmly in the driving seat, till the day she died.

Baldev Das suffered from no complexes about his small-town origins, nor did his dumpy stature pose an impediment to his phenomenal rise. At forty, he was enjoying the prime of his life. The owner of a colossal industrial empire that he had inherited from his father-in-law, his industries spanned a limitless stretch along the entire north-eastern belt. With strategically located headquarters in the commerce capital at Calcutta, his interests covered every conceivable area of manufacturing and finance. The list of his companies included jute, textiles, heavy metals, rolling stock, cement, ship building and a chain of ammunition and ordnance manufacturing units.

Baldev Das now reigned supreme, as a master manipulator and unchallenged despot of power. He found himself greatly elevated in social and political circles. With that commanding position, the Prime Minister and his senior cabinet colleagues became his personal friends and he, the extra-constitutional king-maker. With the leverage to interact with top-level politicians and bureaucrats, he flourished in his private world of high intrigue, low cunning and casual scruples.

Baldev Das had no personal political ambitions. He rejoiced in the role that his astute business acumen had accorded him. Able to avail of classified information straight from the Finance Minister's desk before fiscal budgets were announced, he opportunely exploited markets to his advantage. By retaining a number of parliament members permanently on his pay roll, he created a new breed of puppets that redefined the paradigms of corruption and bribery. His intensive and fine-tuned information system in the political arena kept him alive to even the slightest tremors in the financial market, which he skilfully manoeuvred to his benefit. That kept him miles ahead in the race. His crafty technique procured for him the combined power of several cabinet berths and positioned him far beyond the reach of the laws of the land.

Predictably, such a lifestyle lured the best of matrimonial proposals for his plain-looking daughter Madhulika. The orthodox Marwaris, who subscribed to the *stork-exchange* belief of choosing class and wealth above looks, would find ideal marriage material in her. Just a few weeks before her sixteenth birthday, the grandson of the reigning monarch of paper and steel, a doyen of the classic and elite House of Bangurs, a quiet, self-effacing, eighteen-year old was engaged to her. The glamorous engagement ceremony presented only a tiny flavour of the forthcoming wedding. In the next six months, grand preparations were carried out to enact a royal panorama, akin to that of kings and queens.

Her splendid dowry included an array of jewels, set with rare gems, ranging from Golconda diamonds, Burmese rubies, Colombian emeralds and Basra pearls fashioned by international jewellery houses, and hall-marked silver and gold tableware to be complemented by priceless Czechoslovak crystal. She would also get an emperor's collection of Chinese porcelain, jade and ivory carvings, paintings by Old European masters, life-size statues of Italian marble and exquisite antique carpets from the looms of Persia.

On the auspicious day of the wedding, the guests were received in the vast, ivory and gold banquet hall that was decorated with exotic flowers, specially flown in from Thailand. Under a Venetian chandelier, glittering with one hundred and eight candle-bulbs, five hundred wedding guests were served a fifty-six course banquet, on a silver service, on which gold sovereigns had been kept for each of them, to take away as mementos.

With the heritage that she had been gifted by the privilege of her birth, Madhulika left her mother's home for an equally opulent one in the city. She moved away from the shadow of doom that was to hover around timelessly, over the other inhabitants of her parental home. Stories of her grand wedding filtered down the streets of Calcutta and were lapped up by the locals, who were ever hungry for exotic dreams.

The Loyas had set impossible standards and shattered the Gandhian myth of high thinking and simple living, that was the hitherto practised decree of most Marwaris. Such an audacious display of wealth was to be rated among the few that would precede or survive the changing tides of Bengal. The Left Naxalite's movement, extreme and bloody, that would assume its menacing face in India in the mid-sixties, would compel most business houses to begin an exodus, to the safer and distant havens, of Delhi and Bombay.

4

But the Loyas were still in Calcutta as Bharat Loya was growing up. Sickly and puny, Bharat was an overprotected child. His first interaction with other children began when he was sent to a playschool, run by an English woman, near his home. Most of the time, he sat at the desk closest to his class teacher, deeply absorbed in her dress and face. He soon developed a strong affinity for the first adult woman he had encountered outside his family.

Kelly Robins was a perky little Anglo-Indian who had long painted nails and tiny feet. She wore bright lipstick, short dresses and pointed high-heeled shoes, all of which showed off her comely figure. Bharat slowly learned to relax in the company of strangers, never straying too far away from his cardinal attraction, Miss Robins. He climbed onto her bony lap on the slightest pretext to feel comforted, and was soon addicted to the strong perfume she wore. Kelly Robins too was fully aware of the star status of her ward with his freckled 'Georgie-Porgie' countenance, so she treated him with extra care and overt favouritism.

Bharat was a quick and quiet learner. He memorised dozens of nursery rhymes, faster than any of his classmates and could write alphabets and numbers in well-defined characters, a feat that put him notches higher than the other four-year-olds of his group.

At the end of each day, stern-faced Mr. Wilson had to drag a wailing Bharat home, because he couldn't bear to leave 'Pretty Miss Robins' behind, and get back to his boring life.

Miss Robins became Bharat's obsession. He carried tiny gifts for her from his collection of miniature cars and stamps and even painted an oversized card for her on her birthday. The special attention she gave him instilled in him a new feeling of confidence. He overcame his irrational fears of heights and fast-moving swings and competed with all the tougher and bigger children in his class in sport-related activities. At a school play, he sang the national anthem in a solo performance in his off-key and feminine voice, never for a moment conscious of his abject inability to sing. Indeed, the little preschool ward swept by his love for Miss Robins had crossed all barriers of timidity.

On passing-out day, a farewell party was organised for the outgoing students. The school was decorated with brightly coloured streamers and festoons and there was an air of joviality.

'This is for you Miss Robins,' Bharat said shyly as he held out an expensive and beautifully wrapped bottle of perfume that he had taken from his mother; 'and can you please sign my autograph book.' He could barely look into her eyes.

'Yes of course my dear.' Miss Robins planted a kiss on his cheek.

Bharat went home teary-eyed and sad clutching his autograph book close to his heart, leaving behind his little kingdom, better prepared for the next and less guarded phase of his life. He touched his cheek several times and did not wash his face till the next day.

Pretty Miss Robins, autograph book and all, would soon become a distant memory, till the amnesia of growing up wiped her out.

At the first grade in school, Bharat Loya had come into his own. Skilfully adept at recitation and reading, he attained a kind of distinction among his peers, who maintained a safe distance from the 'bespectacled swotter.' Sailing smoothly in his class, he was more comfortable in the world of his books. In addition to his school curriculum, he was treated to the obligatory privileges of the super-rich pack. He went on frequent trips abroad with his parents, and the permanent fixtures in their lives, Prithviraj and Nayantara Jaipuria. That widened his perspective and exposure infinitely. On the occasional times that Kanupriya accompanied them, with her nanny, it was an added bonanza. The other siblings, Vishal, Piyush, Vivek and Nupur were too young to be taken along. They would have to wait some more years to join the adult gang.

If there was anything odd about the liaison between Amba and Prithviraj, it escaped Bharat's notice. The extra attention given to Nayantara, with her persistent dry-eyed syndrome, by his father did not unsettle him either. Unlike the primal sight of a sexual encounter between parents that rattles most children, the unnatural affinity between them never disconcerted him.

Since most boys found it difficult to befriend the overprivileged brat, Bharat's closest friend was his cousin, Aditya Daga. A couple of years older, he became his confidant and role model. Aditya was self-assured and taller and had all the trappings of the privileged set. He introduced Bharat to his exciting world of *Playboy* magazines that he had hidden safely, in a box under his bed. He even presented to him a glossy pin-up poster of Marilyn Monroe, sitting astride provocatively on a chair—her nude breasts in full view.

He took him on regular jaunts to roadside vendors and made him taste the forbidden joys of street food from hawkers.

'If you think you are ill you will be,' he taught him in his bravado, and dispelled some of his ingrained hypochondria.

Bharat admired the confidence that Aditya exuded and strived to emulate him. In the privacy of his over-guarded bedroom, he soon discovered the pleasures of his newly awakened libido and the accompanying pubertal changes. At the age of ten, Bharat experienced his first nocturnal emission. At first it frightened him, but he gradually learned to accept it as a pleasant and natural occurrence. It kept him zesty through the day. But Kanupriya, who was experiencing her own growing-up changes, still enjoyed first place amongst Bharat's favourites. He often roughed her up and played boisterous games with her. He felt a weird connection between his private bedroom sojourns and her.

As he progressed to middle school, Bharat immersed himself deeper into his books. He acquired the complete collection of P G Wodehouse, Charles Dickens, and *Tales from Shakespeare* and with them, a finely honed appreciation for English literature. At thirteen, he was writing poignant verse and beautiful essays, quite unlike other boys of his age. It also awakened another dimension in him, a subtle sense of humour and a newly discovered self-worth.

Bharat often lay on his bed surrounded by his books. He aimlessly thumbed through *Alice in Wonderland*, a beautifully illustrated publication that he adored. He could recite lines and verses from all Lewis Carroll's works to perfection. They stirred his imagination. Nonsense rhymes and limericks were his all-time passion and no one was spared his impromptu recitals. Anyone who would resist his verbal regalia was finished! They had to play dead on his command *off with your head*... or else face dire consequences.

As he prepared for his weekly home-theatre, rehearsing the lines from his most-loved poem one afternoon, a graphic image of a walrus and a carpenter came to his mind. A few hours later, he would subject a captive audience to his solo-theatrics in his inimitable style and off-key soprano voice, on the makeshift stage in the hall downstairs. He remembered the peals of laughter from

Draupadi, the appreciative applause from Amba and Ajay Vardhan, the indulgent pats on his back from the eternal *other couple,* Nayantara and Prithviraj, the unabashed admiration from Kanupriya and the standing ovation from his servants. It transported him into his fun-filled, fantasy world, and blocked out all else except the words of his poem that he rattled off in a sing-song voice to himself.

The Walrus and the Carpenter
Were walking close at hand:
They wept like anything to see
Such quantities of sand. ...
... 'The time has come', the Walrus said.
To talk of many things:
Of shoes—and ships—and sealing wax
Of cabbages and kings. ...'

And then, trailing the along vast sandy shore with the oysters, hating the sun for being a spoilsport, sympathising with the moon, for her dreary plight, feeling sorry for the cruel betrayal of the fat and tired oysters, helpless in the middle of nowhere. ...

The imagery beguiled him. It pleased him, delighted him. He thought he was the walrus or perhaps the carpenter, laughing as the oysters wept, experiencing the ultimate ecstasy that was not solely sexual...

He forgot that he was small, sickly and underweight, as he dozed off into blissful slumber.

5

Aditya Daga, Bharat's only friend, had managed to worm his way around Mr. Wilson with his easy charm. He spent most afternoons and weekends with Bharat playing indoor games, entertaining him with his ribald jokes and perfected card tricks.

Bharat felt a twinge of envy for his older cousin's popularity with girls. He derived a sadistic pleasure on the rare occasions that he could beat Aditya at anything.

On a usual weekend, Aditya arrived at Bharat's home, looking forward to an amusing afternoon. He went straight to his bedroom on the first floor, calling out to him as he ran up the stairs. He had planned to take him to see a film and with great difficulty Mr. Wilson had agreed to let him go.

Aditya knocked on Bharat's door wondering why he had bolted it from the inside. After a few minutes, he saw him nervous and shifty-eyed, looking out through the half opened crack.

'Come in quick,' Bharat whispered.

Merchants of Death

Aditya slid in and he bolted the door again. Aditya felt a creepy chill go down his spine. The room was dark and the curtains were drawn. The fan had been switched off.

Bharat placed a finger on his lips to silence him.

'Shhh. Sit quiet Aditya. I have to take my medicine. Don't make a sound. There should be no noise or movement. All windows have to be closed. Light burns it and air blows it away. Don't move. Just sit still.'

Aditya slumped on to the wingchair near his bed.

Bharat emptied something on a silver teaspoon that he was holding between his thumb and forefinger. In a quick movement, he raised the spoon to his mouth and swallowed it in one gulp. His eyes were shut and nose had wrinkled up in disgust.

'There it's done,' he said. The relief in his voice was evident.

'What the hell is this Bharat?' Aditya exploded.

'It's called atom medicine. My mother says it's good for me. It'll take away my nosebleed and fever. It will make me healthy and strong. But it flies out of the window, if you are not careful.'

Aditya gaped at him. He felt a weird sense of discomfort. Something was odd—it was not taking the medicine in the darkened, airtight room, it was not the crazy dumb charade, not the mysterious atom medicine, not even his established and loony hypochondria. It was something else.

'But where the hell was the medicine dammit? I didn't see anything in the spoon.'

'That's because you can't see atoms stupid!'

Aditya felt spooked out. The pantomime disconcerted him immensely.

He felt a chill go down his back again.

The Loya House swimming pool was a magnificent structure, lined with Italian marble tiles in many shades of ocean blue. It was enclosed on all four sides by tall glass doors that afforded a scenic view of leafy trees, flowering bushes and exotic ferns, all around. Slanting over it were sheets of clear glass through which the play of shadows created a magical effect on a moonlit night or a rainy day. Above one side was a row of cabana rooms, with square windows overlooking the courtyard and the pool below.

Often Bharat and his cousins would position themselves by these windows to view the happenings at the pool side, during the frequent parties that were held there. They would titter and laugh like a bunch of monkeys and dart out of sight if someone spotted them.

Amba Loya's pool parties had become a regular feature that gave her a sort of envious status among Calcuttans. Perceiving herself to be a true rebel, she enjoyed shocking society by flaunting convention, to show that love and morals had more dimensions than ordinary people dreamed of. She revelled in the seductive power of her looks that had never failed her. Although Prithviraj Jaipuria was the pivot of her amorous desires, she had widened her ambit to accommodate newer conquests of all ages. A rabid control-freak, she treated each new addition to her list as a reinforcement of her faith in herself, not stopping at even young boys, little older than her son.

Her spirited wildness made her the cardinal attraction at the frequent parties held in her home. These riotous orgies by the swimming pool lasted till the early hours of the morning, sometimes spilling over into the next day. At these dos, she invited all the glamorous people of the city and a select number of screen idols, to provide fodder for libertine star-gazers. The prescribed dress code was a tireless and playful display of her imaginative skills.

Dressing like an elusive siren herself, in sheer French chiffon saris, shaded in vibrant colours that silhouetted her toned body, she let her long hair hang loose provocatively down to her hips, pinning one side over her ear, with a fresh flower. She knew her pale skin, visible from under the gossamer fabric of her attire, afforded more titillation, than if she were to be completely disrobed and she fully exploited the impact by being an inveterate tease.

Underneath her saris, she sometimes wore a tight bathing costume with a plunging neckline in the front and at the back. She would incite someone to toss her into the pool when the party was in full swing and coo in mock protest to watch the guests jump in after her, deeply amused at the storm she had caused.

On the fourteenth wedding anniversary of his parents, Bharat was awakened by loud music that streamed into his room, well past midnight. Boisterous laughter reverberated in the hallway. He stole down the stairs to cross over to the cabana rooms on the other side, to get a better view of the happenings by the pool. He positioned himself at his favourite window and peered down below. A large number of people seemed to be having a riotous time. Some men and women were dancing closely around the pool and many had thrown off their clothes and jumped in. They were splashing water noisily at each other and the din of music and laughter had drowned all other sounds.

Bharat squinted behind his glasses, trying to look for his mother. In the melee of faces, shadowed by dim lights, he could not see her. In a secluded corner, he saw his father dancing with Nayantara. Both his arms were around her and her head nestled on his shoulder. He was rocking her gently back and forth in rhythm with the music.

A little closer to the pool, on the dance floor, he saw a small group, doing a lively, Scottish twirl. Just then, one woman tripped and fell into the water and a few men dived in amidst peals of laughter, as if they were lifeguards.

As his gaze travelled towards the shallow end, he spotted his mother. She was wearing a silver blue bathing suit that he remembered, from a fancy boutique on the Champs Elysees, bought earlier that year. She stood in waist deep water, very close to a man who had his back to him. It was not Prithviraj. He had seen him standing near the bar with some other woman.

The man was holding his mother by her waist and she had placed both her hands on his shoulders. Her head was tilted to one side and she tossed it up, laughing in response to something he said. He saw him hold her chin upwards and then kiss her. He saw him reach his hand around to the small of her back and bring her closer. Bharat felt the rhythm of his pounding heart getting louder and faster. He saw his mother wrap her arms around him. She had allowed the strap of her costume to slip off her shoulder, exposing her lily-white breast, on one side. He saw the strange man move his head down to her breast...

Bharat felt a giddy sensation wrack his body. His heart felt as if it would burst out of his chest. The sight of her naked breast excited him. Like a silent voyeur, he stood in the shadows watching his mother, ardently making love with a stranger. He felt himself float down into the pool, into the body of the strange man, who stood locked in a passionate embrace with his mother. He felt himself reach hungrily for her soft breast, to quell a longing she had denied him as a baby, but was offering to him now, in this magical moment. He felt her kisses on his mouth and face, on his neck and chest, small and light like falling snowflakes, ruinous and marvellous all at once. He couldn't stop the sharp, warm spurt inside his pyjamas. For a long time, he stood there savouring the delirious adult sensation that had him transfixed. He would come back for more.

6

March 1971

With an oddly distorted view of life, morality and sexual fulfilments, Bharat and his two younger siblings, with their three cousins and extended family, grew up as part of a value system, where licentiousness and perversions were infinitely glorified. With all the trappings of royal luxury, free access to limitless funds abroad, from numbered Swiss accounts, they cruised along the surface, living from moment to moment, gathering the speed that serves to detach mind from soul.

In the winter of 1970, Bharat had finished his Senior Cambridge with a second division. His hypochondria had assumed manic proportions, making his earaches, bleeding nose, blocked sinuses and fever as much a constant in his life, as his school books.

A few months after Bharat's final examinations, the guards of Loya House were roughed up by some fierce looking, armed men. They spoke in a crude, Bengali dialect threatening to kill them, if they did not let them enter the premises.

A timely alerted police van had sent them scurrying away. The security was tightened outside, and two special policemen deputed to guard their gates. A high alert was declared in the city the next day. A week later, an anonymous letter written in blood was delivered to Draupadi. It threatened to kidnap her grandchildren and wipe out the rest of the family. Similar incidents were reported by some other prominent families of Calcutta, and sporadic violence rocked vital parts of the city.

The same day, a group of unidentified men broke into the godowns of the Loya Defence Systems and decamped with a sizeable quantity of weapons and ammunition from the arsenal and all the cash from their office vault. The napping government swung into action and set up an inquiry into the incident. Rumours of there being a collusion between the management and the Naxalites ran rife, but no arrests were made.

A chill descended on Draupadi and Baldev Das. After long discussions they decided that it would be unwise to stay in Calcutta any longer.

They moved to Delhi, into a three-acre house on Prithviraj Road, with their three sons, two daughters-in-law, six grandchildren and a battery of servants and attendants, leaving behind their treasured palace in the care of their permanent staff.

A few months later, tragedy struck, when Baldev Das suffered a massive heart attack. He passed away in his new home, in the early hours of a cold winter day, without getting even a last glimpse of the home in Calcutta that he had so loved.

On Baldev Das's death, the whole of the Marwari society plunged into grief. A thirteen-day period of mourning was observed by the family and his offices shut down, as a mark of respect. Sponsored by GI Industries, special supplements were issued by all leading national dailies to highlight his achievements and commemorate the passing away of the established doyen of the industrial world, and the founder of the illustrious House of Loya.

The funeral was held on the banks of the Ganga in Benares where his private jet ferried the family and a special flight was chartered for the other grieving relatives and friends. It was a deserving farewell to a renowned Hindu of his social strata.

Because the upper class maintain a stoic dignity in death, and grief is best observed in private, there were no public outpourings of shattered emotions.

Although Draupadi never needed her husband's moral or emotional support, now widowed, she mellowed down into her role of Queen Mother. That did not, however, diminish her ego, nor the size of the diamonds that she wore. She continued her cultural and literary pursuits and remained in the mainstream, constantly connected to scores of scholars and writers, who wanted favours from her.

After Baldev Das's death, Ajay Vardhan stepped into his father's shoes. Anuj Vardhan, who was by then ruling his own independent domain, expressed his desire for a family partition. His estranged and hopelessly drug-dependent wife, Rajshri had resigned herself to the life of a doormat.

The family business was divided smoothly, without any squabbles or disagreements, even though there were murmurs of it being unfair. Each brother was given the industries that he had been looking after, and since there was ample on the family salver, no one really protested.

The north-eastern industrial belt, and the Loya Defence Systems and Loya Arms and Ammunitions with their head offices at GI House in Delhi came to Ajay Vardhan and Anuj Vardhan was given the manufacturing concerns that spread over Rajasthan. Maharashtra and Gujarat, his mainstay being textiles and cement. He bought a one and a half acre corner house, also on Prithviraj Road for himself, and moved out.

Sanjay Vardhan, who had always been *persona non grata*, posed no problems. His share got clubbed with Ajay Vardhan's and that kept him in a limbo for the time being, making Ajay Vardhan the *de facto* owner of over two-thirds of his deceased father's estate.

Anuj Vardhan razed his newly acquired house completely to the ground. A team of French architects and interior designers were flown in to build a Moroccan style villa, with a terrace swimming-pool, a Chinese style garden, a lotus pond and a climate controlled hothouse to grow his favourite orchids. The entire ground floor was covered in pink Italian marble. A wide sunken area in the centre of the drawing-room was redone three times over, because the exact shade of pink was not available to the eccentric owner.

It was finally completed in a span of two years—the unnecessary delay attributed to the changing fantasies of its whimsical owner. The grand villa would host the most coveted and entrancing celebrations every Diwali and Holi. Anuj Vardhan's parties to celebrate the exotic festival of colour in spring awash with the colour of *tesu* flowers, fragrant with the scent of jasmine and rose petals, with enormous vats of opium-laced almond sherbet and varied cuisine, would become an annual orgy of visual and sensual delight, in the society calendar of Delhi—quite a novel experience for the more staid and less spoilt populace, dominated by Punjabis.

Anuj Vardhan was designated the most generous host of the decade, to make his presence felt even beyond the boundaries of the capital.

Perhaps by moving out of Calcutta, the descendants of the dynasty had insulated themselves from the wrath of the bloodthirsty Naxalites, but not quite from the diabolic curse of the silver spoon.

7

New Delhi
April 1971

Afflicted with the inherent maladies of the upper class, Bharat Loya came to Delhi, an incurable romantic, vulnerable to all the follies of growing up. His passion for English literature and love for Victorian poetry turned him into a curious oddity, quite different from his peers. His social interaction with women was limited. He was comfortable with older women his mother's age and deeply admired female beauty and glamour. The loss of Kanupriya's company had become unbearable. He felt lonely without her and sought solace in his books and poetry. Never having been too close to his younger sister and even further away from his brother, he missed the erstwhile pleasures of living in a large joint family and yearned for his days spent in Calcutta.

He became part of a card-playing group of boys with his cousin Aditya Daga who had also moved with his family to Delhi around the same time. He spent the weekends with them, feeling quite out of place with their ribald humour and male ribbing.

Bharat enrolled for the first year, undergraduate English Honours course in St Stephen's College, at the Delhi University, in the summer of 1971. He was to begin his expedition into a fantasy world that had been just outside his reach till then, led by Aliya Hasan, an alluring young woman who belonged to his own gene pool.

Inhabiting a secluded world, far away from the flashy House of Loyas, Aliya Hasan was a tall and slender young woman of nineteen years. She was the outcome of an illicit affair between two people, who could not have come from more antithetical backgrounds. Her father G D Rungta was an unorthodox, Marwari billionaire with a typically atypical lifestyle. He had turned the pursuit of pleasure and seduction of women into a religion. What attracted most women to him was the hint of scandal attached to his name. He had gained the reputation of being a profligate and gambler, who broke all the rules of God and man. Most people liked to exaggerate his wickedness for dramatic effect. He had sired more than a dozen offspring from his three legally wedded wives, before polygamy was banned in India.

Like most Marwari men, Rungta believed that the finest form of sexual pleasure could only be achieved by constant change. Since nothing indemnifies so completely against social ostracism as success, he had attained a sort of charisma and invincibility, which made him a curiously attractive package. Women fell victim to his charms, his quick turnover earning them the dubious sobriquet of 'season queen.'

Aliya's mother Rukhsana Hasan was a gentle, fair, soft-spoken woman, with a full body and sensually curved mouth. She was a theatre actress with ambiguous origins, but her velvet voice had made her the singing star of the decade. As her fame spread to the homes of the rich and the famous, fate had thrown her onto the path of the sixty-year old tycoon, with whom she had conducted a frenzied affair.

Tantalised by her noble Persian manner, her limpid eyes, her enchanting voice, and her initial aloofness, G D could hardly pass up the challenge she posed.

The new sexual awakening had driven him to a point of insanity, and he had begun the single-minded pursuit of the fresh object of his lust in his customary style. Rukhsana had stood no chance against his relentless, emotional bombardment and had finally succumbed to him. They had drifted into a passionate relationship that had caused the usual uproar in Delhi, and had thrown her life into complete disarray. It also brought her onto the highly visible platform of the city's celebrities, not as a performing artist, but as their respected equal.

Within one year, Rukhsana had borne G D a child and had met with the fate of all her predecessors. The newborn girl, with her large eyes, mother's complexion and family genes could do little to restrain her father's wanderlust. Before she turned three, Rukhsana in a last-ditch effort gave birth to a male child who was autistic, after which G D had ruthlessly ended the affair. He wanted no responsibility to shackle him and adequately compensated her for four years of the life she had given to him. He bought her a comfortable house in the old quarter of the city and deposited a sizeable amount of cash for her in a fixed deposit account. She was allowed to keep the jewels that he had given her and provided her with a tidy, monthly income, generated from another property, that he transferred onto her name.

Rukhsana was abandoned to bring up her two children as a single parent, with all links with their father permanently snapped. He did not care if his paternity was disclosed to her children, because he had freed himself of all moral guilt, by not leaving them penniless.

His family rejoiced at the collapse of *the Rukhsana factor* and never acknowledged the presence of her children even privately. Rukhsana took to a secluded life on the outskirts of the city, making no attempt to connect with her past, thereafter. Even though the father of her children kept popping up in the newspapers as a powerful luminary in political and business circles, she never allowed herself to get trapped in self-pity. She had a lot to be grateful for, she consoled herself, thanking Allah for his benevolence.

Aliya grew up an attractive young girl, with long lustrous hair, large smouldering eyes and a fiery kind of appeal. She moved with a grace and agility that betrayed the best traits of her divergent cross-breeding. She also possessed an astute sense of survival.

Headstrong and wilful, she was free of the illiberal bindings of her native legacies, Hinduism and Islam.

Having received the best education in the city's most elite convent school followed by a famous college in the university, she maintained a brilliant academic record, acquiring the confidence and finesse of a true urban sophisticate. Even though she was aware of her father's identity, she never felt the need to be recognised by him or his family and did not harbour any lurking resentment against him. She was content in her art, books, music and the company of her unfortunate younger brother and indulgent mother, and she never let her mind wander unnecessarily. The rare times that she felt a gnawing awareness of her bloodline, across an invisible boundary that divides the virtuous from the immoral, she learnt to ignore it. It amused her that her father's family tree was spread over an uncharted territory, that was much deeper underground than over the surface, and that the eldest daughter of her father's legitimate descendants had grandchildren her own age.

Aliya loved life and was too free-spirited to be dampened by her nefarious origins. She was proud to be just who she was.

8

The three most powerful forces that are known to motivate human behaviour are sex, money and revenge. Seventeen-year old Bharat Loya stood on the brink of an inviting world, quite unprepared for these mysterious energies that would lure him onto the next phase of his life. Unaware of the peculiar, magnetic field that surrounds blood relatives, Bharat strayed into Aliya Hasan's orbit. In the transient nature of life and relationships, this was bound to happen.

Seated adjacent to each other in his college auditorium at an inter-university music festival, something compelled the two strangers to strike up a conversation with each other.

'Hi! I'm Aliya Hasan,' she said. 'What's your name? Can't stop admiring your fancy watch.' She pulled his hand towards her and peered at it.

'Thank you. I'm Bharat Loya,' he said awkwardly.

For the slight and shy Bharat, who was tongue-tied in the presence of women, Aliya presented an alluring package. Her high cheekbones, long hair, easygoing manner and infectious laughter drew him to her.

Within the first few days of their chance meeting, both discovered their common lineage, which did nothing to undermine the pull that they felt towards each other. Bharat felt a pleasant rush. A familiar stirring of his mind and soul. For some reason, he was reminded of Kanupriya. Aliya perplexed him. It was like a floating dream. He wanted to touch her, to not let it pass.

The fact that Aliya reciprocated his feeling, no doubt added to her list of charms. Although it would take a while for it to alter into something tangible, their romance had taken off with a velocity that was unstoppable.

Bharat's satirical wit, punctuated with his ever handy Victorian verse and naughty limericks, dominated a great deal of the time they spent together, and Aliya too was treated to his favourite poems which she lapped up in delight.

Bharat Loya was in love, or perhaps in love with the idea of being in love. Driven by a deep pleasure-principle, he discovered the taste of forbidden fruit. The unpleasant rider of sexual guilt that creeps alongside did not burden him just yet.

Aliya's unthinking assent to cruise along dispelled the apprehensions that had initially troubled him. She dominated his life and thoughts and all else seemed insipid by contrast.

When Aliya could no longer bear the burden of her deed alone, she told her mother about the breach that she had committed. Her mother, naturally shocked by her transgression, was speechless. The violation of her unwritten diktat that no one could ever trespass into the forbidden fortress terrified her. This vile friendship was sure to infuriate the father of her children, and condemn her to a life of greater misery, if he were to find out.

Aliya's reckless streak was nothing new to her, but this was unforgiveable.

'I beg of you Aliya, give up this dangerous friendship. You don't know anything my child. We will be destroyed by the powerful forces from the other side. Please listen to me. Give up this boy. In the name of Allah, please I beg of you. You will be the death of me. *Ya Khuda, Ladki tu merijaan legi kya?* What should I do? What should I do? This girl will be the death of me.' Rukhsana's voice quivered. Her hands were trembling and she had tears in her eyes.

Trapped by her genetic heritage of daredevilry, Aliya was unfazed. Inside her surreal world, she filtered out all the sounds that could dilute her verve. She had long realised that trying to make her parents turn into the mother or father, she would have preferred, was a waste of time. She had tapped into an immortal, energy source within, and was hardly going to be scared into a life of submission by her timid mother.

9

Aliya believed that man's destiny runs parallel to nature, which is not merely the creator of beauty, but also its destroyer. Destructive impulses, therefore, have to be obeyed in the same way as gentle ones. She became addicted to her role of 'carer' that had made Bharat cling to her. Deep down inside, she felt slightly vindicated. A perverse satisfaction at the divine retribution. She had been placed in a position of control. It helped to exorcise some of the phantoms, deeply interred in her.

With Aliya, Bharat discovered the way to begin a lifelong affair with himself. He felt male and virile. He began to look upon himself as a whole, new, beautiful person.

'It's okay to enjoy sexual attraction Bharat. Sexuality is a vital part of our being,' she cooed. 'Approach life as if it were a work of art. You should know that it is possible to be criticised and feel loved at the same time. There is no single *right way* my dear Bharat.' There was enticement in her words.

Bharat Loya was in another world. He felt freed from the matrix that had bound him, since the time of his conception, in his mother's womb. He felt mature and loved despite all his imperfections.

Aliya played along with the charade. She felt clearer about her present and for her the taste of forbidden fruit was intoxicating. Aliya also was in love with Bharat, her father's great grandchild who was short, slight and two years younger. The perversity of it, like all immoral liaisons, was exciting. She often mused about the fallout it would have when his family found out. The danger was delectably sensuous.

Quite naturally, the two grew extremely close and like a perfect and committed lover, she moulded herself to suit every need of her younger boyfriend. She dressed in the colours he loved and kept her hands and feet perfectly groomed, conscious of his paramount fetish. She washed her thick, long hair with fresh lime, till it was squeaky clean, and brushed it till it shone like a skein of silk, letting it fall straight down to her waist. She darkened her eyes with a kohl pencil to enhance their devilish sparkle that synchronised with her laughter. Like a consummate courtesan, she fine-tuned her taste in books, poetry and music to his. She could even recite verses from his all-time favourite, Lewis Carroll.

Aliya carefully studied Havelock Ellis' *Psychology of Sex,* the revolutionary *Kinsey Report,* the works of Shakespeare and the philosophy of Jean Paul Sartre. Never sidetracking her own subject, she read to him from Sigmund Freud's teachings and spent hours, interpreting dreams. Her bedside Bible became the best-selling treatise called *The Sensuous Woman* that listed methods of how to turn into the perfect object for male pleasure.

Together, Aliya Hasan and Bharat Loya discovered the erotic pleasures that could be enjoyed in everyday life.

'You have wasted yourself on me Aliya. I can never marry you. You should have worked on my uncles Sanjay *Chacha* or even Anuj *Chacha* instead, my gorgeous,' Bharat rued.

'In some other lifetime Bharat, not this one. It's you that I love,' she whispered in his ear.

'You have the most beautiful, shell-shaped ears, my Aliya,' he said softly as he ran his fingers through her silky hair, breathing in the fragrance of her lime shampoo.

She kissed him passionately, crushing her mouth to his and let his tongue glide deep into her throat.

They stayed locked in each others arms—Aliya the dominant female *Shakti* and he the infant at her breast. The feeling was more profound than the act of actual copulation.

10

Call it the incongruity of fate or nature's safety valve that inhibits most illicit relationships, by giving them a short life span. The most infamous quadrilateral between Ajay Vardhan, Nayantara, Prithviraj and Amba, was also to die its natural death. Amba had acquired the status of a cult figure in the company of her new found fan following, from the populace of Delhi that was starved for glamour and riches. Prithviraj, for the time being, was left footloose and fancy free. Nayantara lapsed into a prolonged spell of an idiopathic disease that confined her permanently to her bed. Ajay Vardhan's attention shifted to a conveniently located cousin's wife, Devyani, living in Bombay, where he frequently traveled. The amorous wife of his paraplegic cousin, eagerly reciprocated his lustful overtures, and no one questioned the realigning polarities, which were treated as routine.

Ajay Vardhan perceived himself as an industrialist. He laboured hard to maintain his corporate image and indulged in highly publicised philanthropic activities to enhance his social standing.

Among all his companies, Loya Defence Systems and Loya Arms and Ammunitions were of very little importance in his agenda, and their running was left entirely to his administrative officers. That gave them a kind of supreme autonomy, whereby they could manage them as their personal fiefdom. The administrative department was answerable to and closely monitored by the Chairman, and only rapped if the balance-sheet showed a negative figure. They were adept at providing the Chairman with a constant supply of cash by evading excise duties and selling raw materials, scrap and certain finished products in the black market which was highly profitable and illegal. As long as they maintained an uninterrupted and sumptuous cash flow, all else was overlooked.

It was during this period that a Saudi Arabian billionaire Omar Al Fayed was befriended by Ajay Vardhan. Fayed was well known for his extravagant spending and glamorous lifestyle. Driven by a ruthless predatory instinct that lay hidden beneath his polished and suave veneer, he had built his vast empire around war and destruction to become one of the most feared men in the arms trade. He had brokered several controversial international sales and was connected to almost every shocking event that had occurred in the western world in the last two decades. Positioned at the intersection of a medley of social networks he was also believed to have links with some dreaded terrorist outfits and stakes in the Sicilian drug-running mafia.

Ajay Vardhan had found a toe-hold in the grandiose and lucrative world of the arms trade. He soon got into the loop of its Indian chapter. His established links with the power hierarchies helped to turn him into the chosen facilitator to promote their interests.

On the personal front, rumours of Ajay Vardhan's affair with his cousin's wife filtered into their home, but it did little to rattle Amba. Prithviraj and Nayantara having outlived their utility in her life, she moved into another realm. Her ageing and widowed mother-in-law kept ill-health and she comfortably marginalised her.

Then she turned to the one tiny irritant in her life that would take careful planning to weed out. It was not the absence of an indulgent lover with an overworked libido that irked her. It was Sanjay Vardhan who would need shrewd and careful handling. Amba had time on her hands while Ajay Vardhan continued his reckless jaunts to exciting new destinations abroad.

11

London
May 1972

Ajay Vardhan Loya was a hard-nosed Marwari with his family arrogance ingrained deep in his veins. He had no qualms about flashing his wealth and connections and lived his life to the fullest, indulging in every passion to cater to the compulsions of his flesh and spirit. His wide array of friends in top political and military circles had been highly advantageous for both his personal and business needs.

Lounging in his four thousand square feet penthouse apartment in an expensive part of central London he looked every bit the debauched and powerful wheeler-dealer that he was deemed to be. He felt a surge of energy spiral up his back. He took a deep breath inhaling the crisp summer air and let his lungs expand till he felt they would burst. He slowly exhaled to the count of ten as he heard the doorbell.

'Mr. Fayed to see you Sir.' The butler announced the visitor whom Ajay Vardhan had been eagerly awaiting.

'Show him into the library James and bring us some black coffee please.'

Fayed was ushered into the library that overlooked a vast expanse of Hyde Park. It had floor-to-ceiling windows from where the thick canopy of trees in shades of green, brown, ochre and gold could be seen around the Gothic architecture of the Imperial city of London. His armed bodyguard took position near the wall by the entrance.

'Khushamadeed! My brother, my friend. It is so nice to see you.' Fayed greeted Ajay Vardhan as he spread his arms wide to embrace him and settled into the plush sofa near the fireplace.

The butler wheeled in an ornate silver service of the Tudor dynasty and poured out the steaming liquid into Minton china cups. The aroma of freshly brewed coffee filled the air.

'You have a beautiful place here my friend. I can see that you also have excellent taste in paintings and interiors.' Fayed's soft deep baritone rang sincere.

'So let's get down to business shall we? What are the developments at your end?' Ajay Vardhan said as he glanced at the coarse man by the door totting a Kalashnikov as if it were a toy.

'Ah yes Brother, this is a good time for all of us. The Soviet Union has made steady inroads into your country. Your Prime Minister is quite favourably inclined towards them. The KGB has deposited two million dollars for a very senior Indian politician in a secret account in Switzerland. The Soviets claim to have over two dozen members of your Parliament on their payroll. They say that they have managed extensive penetration into those layers of the armed forces that are responsible for procurement of military hardware. Your last Prime Minister, the one who mysteriously died in Tashkent some years back. You know what happened there Ajay don't you? You were also part of that delegation. There was something unnatural about that death and even though there were some murmurs of the KGB's involvement no one ever found out the truth. And now with the new regime in place there cannot be a more opportune time for us.'

Ajay Vardhan was listening intently, conscious of the menacing stranger looming in the corner. He had never forgotten that morbid winter day when the sudden death of the Indian Prime Minister in Tashkent had shocked the country and as part of his delegation he had brought the body home. 'Yes, you are right,' he said. There is a massive exercise now to modernise the armed forces and huge budgets have been allocated to the Defence Ministry. Our government has only woken up to this after the drubbing we got from the Chinese.'

'See, that's what I mean. Everything is in place. You must continue to lobby hard with your friends. You must also expand your circle as fast as you can. We must not let any contract get past us. It is my dream my Brother that by the time your son is ready to take over the business, every little nail and screw that has been bought by your Defence forces shall have been routed through us *Inshallah!* The stakes are very high and we won't get a chance like this again.' Fayed rolled his r's and softened his t's and d's as he spoke in his characteristic middle-eastern accent. 'You know what I want?' A tenderness had crept into his voice. 'I want you to become for India what the Kandujas were for the Shah of Iran. And believe me we can make that happen my friend.'

Ajay Vardhan laughed as he absorbed Fayed's words. 'Omar a lot of ground has been covered by our strong network of liaison men. The concerned ministers are old friends and have a high regard for our family. I foresee no obstacles in our path. Tell me, has the money been sent to our account in Zurich? We cannot go forward unless that is cleared. These guys back home are greedy bastards and we can only score if ours are the most tempting packages in the offing.' Ajay Vardhan had lowered his voice.

'Here take a look at this Brother.' Fayed waved two stapled sheets of paper at him. The familiar logo of a bank statement was visible near the folds.

Ajay Vardhan squinted at the figures. A contented smile played on his face. 'Voila! This is good news,' he said jubilantly. 'It's time for us to celebrate.'

'Yes my friend. I'm looking forward to Kanduja's party tonight. He has the most luxurious yacht I have ever seen. And those twin sisters from Thailand that are flying in today. He swears they're fifteen-year-old virgins. As smooth as they come. Oh yes, I saw a whole entourage from Delhi at the Dorchester last night. Two or three of your cabinet ministers and their, how-you-call them, *chamchas* and a big group of parliament members all here in time for Kanduja's birthday bash. And even that top man from the Air Force. What's his name, that burly guy with a scar on his face? He's asked for a Rolls Royce to pick him up at the airport. The randy bugger wants a big-breasted woman to escort him. They are all here and tonight promises to be full of fun.' Fayed was squeezing invisible breasts in the air. 'Is your gorgeous wife here too my Brother?'

'No she's coming in from Paris tomorrow. But I have something else for you. You'll meet this sexy woman with me tonight? She's that Admiral's wife remember? The big-assed one who wears nothing under her dress. She's world class Omar. Gives the best blow-job you've ever had. You have to try her for my sake. Trust me you'll keep asking for more.'

The two men, one a lusting, ravenous Marwari whose first passion was wild sex with another man's wife, and the other an ageing Arab whose fetish for deflowering virgins had not diminished with age, slapped each other's backs with an easy bonhomie that penetrated far beyond the brief of their business, while the decks had been cleared for the 'death merchants' to close in.

12

New Delhi
March 1973

Moving into her grand new home in Delhi didn't change anything for Rajshri Loya. She was in the throes of an acute depression, the kind of stupor that traps the mind into a dark abyss, with no escape hatch. She had spent eighteen years of her life battling with mental cruelties, inflicted on her by her philandering husband. Her debilitating condition and severe drug dependence had turned her into a recluse. She stopped going out altogether and hardly ever dressed up. She even felt disconnected from her children. She did not encourage them to spend time with her. Their noisy chatter unsettled her. It pierced the wall that she had built around herself.

Seventeen year old Kanupriya was growing up with an attractive charm. She tried to get close to her mother with her sad, searching eyes. Rajshri was afraid that she would sense the turmoil that was simmering below the surface, and turned away from her. The fragile bond between them was systematically eroded, ultimately proving disastrous for both.

Almost two and a half years after the family had moved to Delhi, early one morning, Rajshri woke up from her disturbed sleep, on the four-poster bed in her room. She felt a dull ache around her temples. That had become a permanent feature with her. The room was dark as she never drew back the curtains and had become sensitive to strong light.

She fumbled out of her bed and entered her dressing room. She stepped out of her white, satin nightgown that dropped onto the marble floor, in front of a full-length mirror. The person that stared back at her was a stranger. Tangled tresses framed the sides of her head. Dark circles outlined her sunken eyes. Her dilated pupils had an abnormal glaze over them. She felt the image go hazy in front of her. She rubbed her eyes. Her hands trembled annoyingly. The square, six-carat diamond ring, felt like a constriction on her fingers. She tried in vain to pull it off, and gave up. The diffused light in the room reflected off the mirror surface and hurt her eyes.

She strained hard and looked at herself again. Her flabby stomach had dozens of stretch marks that radiated diagonally from below her navel, on to both sides of her lower abdomen. Her thighs were dimpled with unsightly blobs that gave them a rough orange peel look.

Rajshri squirmed. The image frightened her. What had become of the waif-like little girl that had left her mother's home eighteen years ago? Where was that petite and innocent woman, who had her virginity taken by a strange man in a wild night of scary antics? What had transformed her into this hideous mass of quivering flesh?

She turned away from the face in the mirror. She heard a faint sound of piped music, echoing in her ears. She felt drawn to it. It dispelled some of her anxiety. She stepped into her shower cabin and stood under the spray of water for a long time moving her hands gently all over her body, till she felt cleansed and her skin tingled. She stepped out of the shower and dried herself vigorously. She sprayed a generous amount of her favourite perfume onto her body, till her total perception became one single sense of smell. Her long hair fell in straight wet strands that stuck to her breasts, dripping water onto her skin. She felt light-headed. Like a phantom, she floated into her dressing room and opened her wardrobe. She pulled out a bright red sari that she had worn on her wedding day and in slow and deliberate movements draped it around herself, folding the pleats. She removed her wedding jewellery from the chest of drawers and put on each piece, just like she had done the first time she had worn them.

She heard the sound of the *shehnai* and revelry getting louder. The drum beats had galloped to a frenzied rhythm to welcome the approaching bridegroom. They filtered into the room, making everything around her vibrate.

She put a vermillion *bindi* on her forehead and pencilled her eyes with kohl. She pinned a jewelled pendant onto the centre of her parted hair. A round diamond nose-ring, dangled provocatively from her nose. She felt a sense of joy that she hadn't experienced in a long time. The pleasing image before her eyes was now her own. She felt an ecstatic out-of-body sensation.

She took out a long red *dupatta* from her drawer and looped it twice around her neck. It felt soft and sensuous on her throat. She tugged at it and hooked the other end over the ceiling fan. She tested the knot. It should not be loose she thought. The wedding knot should be eternal. If it gets undone, it will be a bad omen. She tugged at it again. Satisfied, she climbed onto a stool, placed near her bed.

'I must not be late,' she mumbled, as she closed her eyes in joyous surrender. The last thing she heard as she kicked the stool from under her was the sound of the drumbeats and the music fading away. Her eyes rolled into her sockets and darkness engulfed her.

Eighteen years ago, Rajshri had entered the gates of her new home to cohabit with the stranger whom she married. She timed her exit in a macabre coincidence, exactly on the same day, her eighteenth wedding anniversary.

Rajshri Loya's name was consigned to an insignificant black-bordered, square obituary, in the local newspapers. Her hasty funeral was attended by just the close family. Her body was cremated in the clothes she wore when death embraced her, minus her jewels.

The thirteen-day mourning was a private affair. The cause of her death was announced, matter-of-factly, as sudden heart-failure.

Anuj Vardhan's life did not change with Rajshri gone. He finally felt freed from the yoke that had burdened him all these years. It pushed his children further away from him and Kanupriya into a deeper despondency. 'It's my fault,' she thought as uncontrollable tears rolled down her face.

It was still too early for anyone to have sensed the morbid curse of the silver spoon that had claimed its first victim.

Two years into Aliya and Bharat's affair, Draupadi succumbed to a massive heart attack in a private nursing home in Delhi. In an out-of-turn departure, she predeceased her seventy-nine year old father, who was broken with grief, over his beloved daughter's death. Her surviving relatives, headed by Amba, would enact yet another grand pantomime at her funeral that would be attended by the who's who of the country.

Draupadi Loya was dressed in death as she had in life. Always adorned with expensive clothes, she merited similar treatment to prepare for her final departure. Her body was wrapped in a beautiful, seven-yard shahtoosh shawl that had been gifted to her by her father. Stripped of the famous gems she always wore, she embarked on her last journey, leaving behind all worldly possessions to her daughter-in-law, who quickly moved into the void left by her.

Aliya felt no grief at the death of her half-sister whom she had never known and reacted with cold apathy. Although Bharat did not show any distress either, at the death of his grandmother, he was a little surprised when she told him she wanted to attend the fourth-day mourning ceremony, because she thought it was the right thing to do.

Unlike most mothers, Amba had chosen to ignore Aliya's presence in Bharat's life. She was not going to be beaten by the frivolous daughter of a whore. The crafty little schemer was no match for her.

'How's your new girlfriend? She's quite a looker *haanh!* Have you slept with her yet Baba or is she just leading you on? She joked with Bharat.

'Oh Mama! How can you say this? I only love you my beautiful mother.' Bharat nestled his head onto Amba's lap slightly embarrassed by his mother's nonchalance.

Aliya on her part believed this to be a mild acceptance from the ever-benevolent Amba.

When Amba heard of Aliya's desire to attend the mourning ceremony, she said, 'Oh! that's so sweet of her. Get Aliya on the telephone for me, will you?'

Her voice was syrupy. 'Thank you, Aliya, for your caring. I really appreciate your gesture. But my sweet child, you know there are certain family norms that we cannot break. You cannot come to this house but we will definitely meet somewhere outside, another time. Please don't misunderstand, Aliya, I could never tolerate anyone insulting you.'

Bharat felt giddy with a heightened adulation for his utterly bewitching mother and Aliya was completely disarmed.

In one stroke Amba had rendered both powerless. Confident, that Bharat's Marwari blood was stronger than his passing fancy, she would wait patiently for Aliya Hasan to fade away.

For now, she had to attend to a more urgent matter—Sanjay Vardhan should be easy to handle.

Draupadi's death had caused a tiny ripple inside Sanjay Vardhan's secluded world. He felt the impenetrable cloud of anaesthesia around him, give way. He experienced an unfamiliar sensation of pain, a sort of anxiety that was unsettling. He saw his dead mother, lying wrapped in her shahtoosh shawl, covered with fresh red and white flowers. Behind her closed eyes, he sensed her piercing gaze on his face. His eyes misted over.

A long line of mourners filed past, placing flowers at her feet. Somewhere in the room, Amba was icily conducting the ceremony. He stood beside his mother's corpse with his head bent down, and then lowered himself to touch her unyielding feet. He burst into tears. It felt weird. Whom was he grieving for? A mother who had never cared for him or a life snuffed out?

'You lived your life Mother. I still have to suffer mine. Good-bye till we meet again.' He mumbled.

He moved away from the inanimate object that lay on the floor. He was the only one from whom there had been a visible outpouring of anguish, and all eyes were fixed on him, as if he were an uninvited tramp.

That night, Sanjay Vardhan took a mega-dose of his daily fix. It was more than four times the usual strength. It should act fast he thought, as he felt a thick, purple, velvet cloud permeate his senses. It soothed his eyes and caressed his face. With each ticking second, the dull pain he had felt, ebbed out.

The heavy anxiety began to lift. He saw a beautiful woman, dressed in a black robe, smiling at him. She held out her arms wide, beckoning him. He knew she was the all-comforting death. It was a feeling of intense bliss. He slipped into a deep, comatose sleep, on a fluffy, luxuriant bed, of purple smoke. ...

Sanjay Vardhan was discovered in a dangerously unconscious state by his valet, the next morning. He alerted Amba who had him immediately transferred to a private nursing home, under the care of the family physician. They administered the antidote that pulled him back from death's door. He would get the dose right someday, to meet his seraphic angel on the other side, he thought.

Sanjay's misdeed made Amba swing into action. She decided to employ a full-time nurse to look after him. After interviewing a few women, she settled on a qualified, young Tamilian, who looked efficient and energetic. Through her, she was confident of being able to keep him hanging on life-support permanently. She instructed the nurse to report directly to her and adhere to the rules laid down for the rest of the staff.

'Keep him happy, but don't let him step out of line,' she instructed. The implications were clear. She had given her the license to bring him to a level of sanity, till such time that she could devise a plan to completely eliminate him.

13

Jayanti Vaidyalingam was an experienced nurse, who came from surprisingly good stock. Orphaned in a road accident at the age of five, she had been brought up by an old aunt in a sleepy village near Madras, who raised and educated her, with high moral values and a staunch belief in God. To ensure good job prospects, she had made her take a course in nursing, because she lacked the means to send her for a degree in medicine. Jayanti specialised in psychiatry and drug de-addiction, and found a promising job in a hospital in Delhi. Stricken by the pain of parting when Jayanti left Madras, her old aunt died, leaving her niece alone, to fend for herself, in a cruel world.

One year after she moved to Delhi, Amba's family physician offered Jayanti the chance to work as a private nurse for an attractive salary, and because the job came with free accommodation, she agreed to present herself for the interview. Amba put her through a grilling half hour session, before approving of her for the post. Although there was something unsettling about her, Jayanti found Amba, charming—the kind you just couldn't help but like. Satisfied that she was going to live among cultured people, Jayanti accepted.

Ruled primarily by a sense of duty and compassion, she struck an easy rapport with Sanjay Vardhan. She saw the neglected child inside him, crying for help and reached out carefully, not wanting to frighten him back into his shell.

With her association, a churning process began for him. Never having been in such close proximity to any woman, and never having experienced maternal love, the wall of ice around him began to melt. Something pleasant began to filter into his mind. He stayed awake a little bit longer than before. He wanted to eat and bathe and wear clean clothes. He even heard himself laugh, after a very long time. A perceptible change overcame him. He felt the heaviness gradually lift off his shoulders, and he could breathe freely once again.

For Jayanti, it was not that simple. She knew that the pathway out of his treacherous hell would not be easy for Sanjay. It would take patience to guide him out of there and the failure rate was morbidly high. He also would need intense counselling.

Every morning, Jayanti reported to Amba with his progress report. Every morning, she was interrogated with the same intrusive questions that she assumed stemmed from both duty and love.

'I hope you are not breaking the rules Jayanti and you are not going to end up pregnant,' Amba said. 'Remember you will be dealt with very sternly if you do.' Her voice was menacing and curt.

'Go and have one of those birth-control things inserted if you haven't already, and don't you dare slip up. You can take the money from the office if you want...'

Indignant that Amba had presumed sexual concessions as part of her job, Jayanti decided to put in her resignation, for no amount of money was worth this humiliation.

She spent a sleepless night, weighing her options. Her heart went out to Sanjay, the unsuspecting victim of his sister-in-law's greed. She could not bear to leave him to the wolves.

She had never heeded the gossiping household staff with their unending tales about Amba's serial-adultery and Ajay Vardhan's depravity. She had never paid attention to the scandalous talk that transpired daily, between the thirty-odd members in the staff room, after work. Maybe, all of it was true. Maybe, Sanjay Vardhan had been pushed onto the path of self-destruction, by the very people he trusted. Maybe, his vilest foe was his own beatific *Bhabi*. May be she had plotted all along to destroy him.

It struck Jayanti that Amba Loya, behind that sugary manner, was grossly evil. The rumour that Amba and her son shared a sinful, incestuous relationship could also well be true. Indeed the greatest benefit, if Sanjay stayed single and mentally incapacitated, would come to Amba. Jayanti had been made a pawn in her vile game-plan. She had been roped in, to provide him with an outlet for his carnal gratification. By ensuring no more additions to the family, Amba Loya would rid herself of any claimants to Sanjay Vardhan's inheritance.

Jayanti decided to hold on to the tottering man and nurse him out of his hell.

As the days went by, Sanjay's appearance changed and so did his life. With the nursing and love that he was getting, he felt a sense of happiness that he had never known before. He followed Jayanti around like a little puppy, never wanting to let her out of his sight.

'Don't ever leave me Jayanti,' he said, 'I have been wandering aimlessly for so long. Lost in the wilderness as it were. You have brought me home, and given me back my life. Promise me you will never leave me, like they all did—my mother, my brother, my friends. They all deserted me. And poor Rajshri *Bhabi*. She escaped. She must be in heaven. I felt bad when she died, but good for her. She found her peace and I found you...' His voice trailed off. 'Don't ever leave me Jayanti, or leave me with the lady who waits on the other side of the purple cloud, if you have to go. She eludes me each time. She beckons me and then runs away. She is a tease Jayanti—not like you. Don't ever leave me.'

Sanjay placed his head on her lap. She ran her fingers through his hair, softly. She saw the anguish ease from his face as she caressed his brow. She planted a tender kiss on his forehead. He had fallen asleep like a little baby, comforted and secure. Creeping alongside, Jayanti felt the unmistakable tug of a strong, sexual arousal.

Jayanti hummed a tune as she cooked her evening meal. The words of a Tamil song her mother had sung, when she was a baby, came into her mind. She felt vital and alive, with a spring in her step, and a tingling in her body. She heard *Akka's* melodious voice in the distance. She heard the wind rustling in the palm trees, to the rhythm of the tune from her distant past.

The imagery associated with innocence and love came flooding into her senses, like the big waves that came rolling onto the shore, in her native village where she had grown up. The huge waves that symbolised power drowned her solitude—they eased the ache she felt when she thought of her mother and father...the waves filled up her sand pit and washed away her sand castle. They drenched her skin—the nostalgic seaside smells—the swaying trees, the dancing pebbles and the enticing shells on the sandy shore—she lay in the shallow, rocky water for a long time. After a while, when the roaring stopped she ran into the thatched hut where *Akka* waited for her with her meal of hot *idlis* and *sambar* singing the same song. It wafted into her ears, louder and louder, till she was transported into her innocent childhood days. She knew *Akka* was smiling at her from heaven, telling her that her *idlis* had been done. It felt good to be cooking for him.

'I love him,' she told herself, 'and he loves me too.'

Jayanti spread a clean, white, starched tablecloth on a little round table in Sanjay's room. She filled a crystal vase with tall-stemmed, red roses that she had picked from the garden. She placed it in the centre with two candles in a silver stand, on either side. She laid the table with a set of shining, silver cutlery. She put her favourite music cassette of

Ravi Shankar's sitar into the system on the wall cabinet. She was all set for a cozy, candlelight dinner.

She showered and dressed in a traditional red silk sari with an intricate gold pattern, woven along the border. On each wrist, she wore six gold bangles that had belonged to her mother. She pinned a string of fresh jasmine flowers onto her long-plaited hair. She felt beautiful and regal as she led Sanjay by the hand, into his sitting room and seated him on the chair. She sat across him and stared into his eyes, as the soft notes of the sitar filled the room.

They finished the meal of the finger-licking South Indian delicacies, relishing each morsel and hanging onto every moment. Neither of them wanted the evening to come to an end.

Jayanti followed Sanjay into his bedroom. The music had stopped. She heard the roaring sound of waves rolling in at high-tide, the wind rustling in the swaying, palm trees and the melodious words of Akkra's song.

She felt herself melt into Sanjay's arms. She closed her eyes as he kissed her, gently at first and then passionately, bruising her full parted lips. Then he moved hungrily down her throat, savouring each spot, lingering on and then moving to the next. He undressed her, layer by layer and eased her onto his bed. He stepped back to stare at her naked body. In the diffused light of his room, she looked like a perfect statuette of a *Yakshi,* the goddess, from the temples at Khajuraho. Her dark skin glistened, with of tiny beads of sweat.

'You are beautiful my beloved,' he whispered in her ear as he kissed her again, on her lips. He moved down her mouth to her chin. He cupped her soft and full breasts in his hands, putting his mouth to them in a gentle sucking motion, then moved down to her navel, over her pubis, below her thighs, over her knees and down to the soles of her feet. Jayanti trembled with a sensation that racked her whole body.

Sanjay Vardhan made love to her, a passionate and languorous session, where Jayanti surrendered to him, fusing her identity with his. Sanjay felt a violent and sustained multiple orgasm for the first time in his life. He weaned off his drug-dependence in exchange for the greatest of highs known to mankind—that of true love.

Jayanti Vaidyalingam and Sanjay Vardhan were married in a quiet ceremony at his home, six months later.

14

Deluded into a false sense of security after Draupadi's death, Aliya and Bharat carried on their affair, perceiving Amba's silence to be tacit approval. Aliya's mother reconciled to her daughter's bull-headedness and her own fate, praying for it to come to a peaceful end. She had long given up her lectures on immorality, but could not stop worrying about a fearful backlash from her children's estranged father. Gradually, her fears dissipated, as over two years had passed, without any cannons being fired at her from the other side.

Just before his final examination, Bharat went to Calcutta for a brief holiday. Without waiting for a reaction from her mother and in reckless disregard of her chronic whining, Aliya took the first flight to follow him to the city of his birth. She was delirious with the anticipation of spending a weekend with him, away from the prying eyes of people she knew.

Aliya stayed with an old school friend to avoid unnecessary complications.

As her taxi pulled up on the ivy-covered porch of her dead sister's domain, she felt an eerie sense of *deja vu*. It all seemed so familiar from Bharat's description of his growing up years. Peals of laughter and loud notes from a piano, playing songs that she associated with her own childhood resonated in her ears.

She entered the lacquered doors that were inlaid with mother of pearl, coral and lapis lazuli, feeling dwarfed by their enormity. Those doors held inside them secrets of a cursed, dynastic tomb. She felt that they would close in on her and she would be trapped inside forever. An icy chill gripped her as she was ushered into a library, by a faceless, mute, uniformed doorman, who did not even look up at her.

The library was a plush room with Persian carpets, dark wood panelling, Queen Anne furniture and a rich Victorian interior. The walls were lined with rows of neatly stacked leather-bound books with gilded borders. An antique Venetian mirror accented a wooden fireplace that had been decorated with a pair of tall candelabras, and several silver frames with pictures of the family in varying sizes. Bright silk cushions picked up the colours from a rug that was spread in front of the fireplace. A pink crystal chandelier enhanced the glow from a pair of Tiffany lamps. Aliya sensed a faint aroma of tobacco mingled with leather—a pleasing blend that enchanted her.

She settled nervously on the sofa. Her palms were clammy and her throat felt parched. She was a felonious intruder in her deceased sister's home—a sister who had been haughty and conceited and would never have let her in, had she been alive. The pounding in her chest grew louder. She almost expected Dracula to come sweeping into the room, with his long black coattails and unnerving manner, but the perverse gratification she felt, took the edge off her fear. She felt herself float out of her body into the dimly lit corridors that led to nowhere cutting into different time zones. She morphed into the characters of Rebecca in her white gauzy wedding gown, trespassing the conjugal rights of a dead wife, and then, Tess of the Dubervilles, Queen of Sheba, Cleopatra, Delilah, Helen of Troy, Lady Chatterley, on and on she continued to move, from century to century, era to era, heaven to purgatory, till she could fly no more and she snapped back into her body, just as Bharat entered the room, smiling warmly at her. She knew she had done the right thing by being there.

'You look absolutely gorgeous Aliya,' he said as he held her in a warm embrace and lead her to the two-seater near the fireplace.

The evening stretched lazily into the night, as the two sat beside each other holding hands, inhaling each other's breath saturated with pheromones. The acute vulnerability of sexual arousal was bound to lead to its imminent conclusion. As if it was a sacred ceremony Bharat slowly drew Aliya closer and unbuttoned her shirt. He peeled off her clothes gently urging her to do the same to him.

'Let me just look at you my goddess,' he whispered in her ear kissing her on her neck till she was completely undressed. For hours, they lay naked in each other's arms, all vanities and pretensions between them evaporated before they made intense and passionate love.

The consanguine pair finally surrendered their virginity at the altar of a powerful deity called eroticism. The culmination of Bharat's Oedipal dream sank into the recesses of his mind like a sleeping serpent. Like Oedipus Rex, who had rejected the sinful prophesy of the oracles, he too would be blinded by an all-consuming guilt later, but for now, he shared this mystical moment with his loving Aliya that lingered on all night.

Aliya too felt a strong sensual contentment, but the disconcerting feeling that someone had been watching her did not go away.

Bharat and Aliya returned to Delhi and to their daily lives. Both appeared for their final examinations to earn their graduate and postgraduate degrees, respectively. They would part as lovers and friends, never to meet again.

Before leaving from Delhi in the summer of 1974 to join the family business in Calcutta, Bharat Loya gave Aliya a signed card inscribed with two lines that read,

Isn't it ironic?
It was once platonic

This may be a final good-bye Aliya,' he said to her wistfully. 'I don't know when we can meet again.'

Aliya, in turn, painted a cute teddy bear on a card. She had written four words inside.

I still love you.

Bharat retuned to Calcutta where the Congress government by then had quelled the Naxal militancy and the fear psychosis had largely abated.

Aliya Hasan sank into obscurity. The violent storm that had blown her off her feet settled down. She missed Bharat immensely, but took solace in the fact that she had helped him become the chrysalis that was ready to take off as a butterfly in the world beyond. Carrying the bittersweet memories of a romantic interlude that had a predetermined outcome, she had come back to her starting point.

Her own, oft repeated words, *love emanates from the soul but cannot be chained to it,* afforded her no consolation.

15

The decade that preceded Baldev Das's death in 1971 was one of great turmoil, within and outside the House of Loya. It was the decade in which the country witnessed two assaults from China and Pakistan on its soil. It was the decade that saw the death of Jawaharlal Nehru, the first Prime Minister of independent India, in harness in 1964. It was also the decade during which the Nehru-led Congress government, in an overt populist stand, lashed out at the black market economy, which like a venomous cancer had spread deep into the vital organs of the young republic, scuttling the policy implementation of the planning pundits.

The counterparts of the Jewish community of the West were the Marwaris of India, who had traditionally been associated with profiteering and black marketeering in essential commodities like wheat, sugar, newsprint and cement during and after the Second World War. The tag of Dirty old Marwari had stuck to them like an unsightly scar, ever since.

However, people had begun to condemn this organised white collar crime that was being perpetrated by powerful Marwari businessmen who owned closely-held industrial concerns with their parallel economy that was estimated to be several times greater than the entire budget of the country.

Sensing the climate of favourable opportunities, Nehru resorted to stringent public measures to check the rot, despite his own dependence on these very sources for funding and support. Some highly controversial Marwari industrialists were prosecuted and imprisoned, and aviation and coal were nationalised in a run-up, just to prove to the poor that the government was sharply pitted against anything that blocked the path of their progress.

Even as he indulged in his passion for the finest French wines and highly priced 555 State Express cigarettes, Nehru pulled out all stops to establish, that no matter how big or influential he be, no one was above the law of the land. These punitive methods would reach a point of hysteria in the following years of Congress rule.

Expectedly, the dragnet closed in on Baldev Das Loya, early in 1963, after one of his own employees blew the whistle on him.

S J Billimoria was a moderately built, straightforward man, with some Japanese blood in his predominantly Parsi genes. As manager of Loya Defence Systems since 1957, he possessed a sharp mind that could cut through trivia to get to the root of any issue.

Billimoria sat at the head office of GI Industries staring out at the gigantic gnomon that was the royal gateway to the stars, built more than two hundred years ago.

Much like his own mental state, the pink monument was also enveloped by a blanket of pollution of both earth and spirit. Billimoria felt uncomfortable stirrings in his soul. Repelled by the anti-national activities transpiring right under his nose, he could no longer tolerate this blatant indictment of his ethical values.

The debauchery of his proprietor's family, the scandalous tales of their licentious depravity and their reckless disregard for society had all but ravaged his senses. From the office of Loya Defence Systems, he was mute witness to the unchecked flow of information and of the ill gotten lucre that was being accumulated by his bosses. He was particularly revolted by the shady men and undesirable women that were often seen at GI House. His conscience was seized by an uncontrollable guilt at being a spectator to the unscrupulous practices going on right under his nose.

In a spirit of self-redemption, he and the company secretary, Jai Narain Sanghi, shot off a letter to the Prime Minister to complain about his errant Chairman's misdeeds. That served to appease him and force the government to constitute a commission of inquiry to investigate the alleged irregularities of the GI management.

Nehru, perceiving that prompt action would serve to divert public attention from the drubbing that India had suffered following the Chinese aggression in 1962 that had left him reeling with a mild cerebral stroke, immediately ordered the setting up of a four-member investigation committee that comprised a retired High Court judge, two heads of public sector companies and the chairman of a national bank. Baldev Das Loya was made to step down from his chairmanship; an autonomous board of directors was appointed to manage the company affairs; and they were issued a show-cause notice why their licences should not be cancelled.

The family lost its mafia-like grip over the running and management of the company and found itself in a hostile confrontation with the power hierarchy. Airtight methods were set in place to plug their illegal cash inflow. It sent Baldev Das running for cover to all his allies in the political and bureaucratic circles whom he had been nurturing for this kind of an eventuality. Even though he shared a close relationship with the Finance Minister, he could get no reprieve from him and many more cases cropped up.

Billimoria retained his position as general manager, much to the chagrin of his employers, and Jai Narain Sanghi became the extra-constitutional authority to mock at their impotence. This status remained till the committee was dissolved with a change of guard, when Indira Gandhi took over as the first and most ruthless woman Prime Minister of independent India in 1966 in what would set the trend for a long dynastic succession.

16

Unaffected by the turbulence in the company affairs, Ajay Vardhan Loya, the willing cuckold, and Amba, the authorised courtesan, continued their peccadilloes and their lavish jaunts to overseas havens. Their diverse holiday destinations, selected from luxury travelogues, in the company of their 'new recruits' continued, as did their extravagant shopping sprees in the most fashionable boutiques of Italy and France. For these there was an unending supply of foreign exchange from their secret Swiss accounts. Their bills were settled by an employee who most often accompanied them, and no one suspected that this indiscretion would become Ajay Vardhan's ultimate undoing in the near future.

The two recent entrants to this charmed circle were a former army officer, Brigadier Harish Mehta, and his ravishing wife Rashmi. They had both been overwhelmed by the Loya lifestyle and got totally sucked into it. True to his army habit, Mehta began to maintain a dossier of all the vouchers and bills of expenditure on these holidays, whenever he could lay his hands on them. His

Merchants of Death

blackmailing instinct, coupled with an innate jealousy would some day earn him a killing. Besides, he was in no hurry to encash his look-the-other-way policy, when he leased his wife for the industrialist's pleasure.

Unaware of the mole inside his baggage, Ajay Vardhan carried on his escapades with his 'merry wives' and consorts, and Mehta tucked away the eggs into his basket, pretending to be the classic wimp, who gladly allowed his wife to accord sexual concessions to his benevolent friend.

In the meantime Mehta had been granted premature retirement from the army and Ajay Vardhan appointed him as Executive Director, in a newly acquired trading concern called Todd Martin and Company, for a generous salary, attractive perks, a fully furnished house and an equity holding in his name.

Rashmi acquired the status of the most favoured diva in Ajay Vardhan's coterie, pushing Devyani down to second place. She also became Bharat's new fancy, following a distinct pattern in his life, whereby he fell in love with all his father's inamorata but, unlike his father, he never let his mother slip from first place.

The current calamity brewing at home, however, threw them somewhat off their feet.

Baldev Das Loya urgently summoned the family for a conference to manage the crisis. The only workable solution centred around nailing Jai Narain, since Billimoria was untouchable, and approaching the other members too risky. At first, they toyed with the idea of letting their in-house *femme fatale* Amba loose on the traitor. She was to offer him five crore rupees to retract his statement and get them off the hook, and in return for that, his family would be given an amnesty, should he be prosecuted. Their strategy hinged on the time-tested tenet that once you establish the sell-out price of any man's soul, all you need to do is to make him an offer that exceeds it.

The Finance Minister was caught in a bind. As a close friend and ally of Baldev Das Loya, he felt it was his duty to bail him out of his mess. But in the office he held, he had a reputation to protect and the Loya scam was too hot to touch, because it was being monitored directly by the Prime Minister's office.

So, the only hope they had was pinned on Amba, which came crashing down, when Jai Narain Sanghi not only declined to meet her, but also put in a complaint to the members of the committee, that the Loyas were trying to intimidate him. Having tasted failure for the first time in her life, a snubbed Amba Loya began hatching the next plot with the rest of them to nail the insolent blackguard. They would have to devise something more forceful to bring him to an end, for having double-crossed *the holy trinity!*

A few months later, the country's best criminal lawyer filed a petition in the Calcutta High Court, alleging that Jai Narain Sanghi had fraudulently retained a bag of jewellery, worth over five crore rupees and some *benami* properties belonging to the Loyas that had been entrusted to him for safekeeping, during the Naxalite-trouble days.

The petitioners demanded an immediate recovery of their belongings and attached an annexure, with the petition that described each piece of jewellery in detail ruing privately over the loss of their *benami* properties that they had no way of getting back. The matter was immediately lapped up by the press and public.

Jai Narain Sanghi was well versed in the high-handedness of his employers, and even though he had not anticipated this move, he understood that they were capable of resorting to desperate measures to break him. The subsequent trial opened a can of worms that led to vicious mud-slinging on both sides. Jai Narain fought back, spurred on by the power of truth. The conspiracy to cast aspersions on him turned out to be a blank salvo.

The trial dragged on, with half the people convinced that the mighty Loyas had been done in by a lowly employee and the other half gloating over their humiliation. As the hearings lost their initial hysteria and the newspapers relegated the reporting of the details to the back pages, both parties resigned themselves to the outcome.

Jai Narain Sanghi got his much-awaited and deserving reprieve, as the case was thrown out of the Calcutta High Court, and the crestfallen Loyas had to let the matter rest. He continued as a symbol of authority, mocking their might and they beat a hasty retreat with their tail between their legs.

In the summer of 1964, Jawaharlal Nehru succumbed to his second cerebral stroke, to die as the first Prime Minister in harness. Fortunately for him, he departed at a time when his popularity graph had touched an all-time low and death accorded him a timely exit.

An unobtrusive five-feet-four-inch tall Kayastha from Uttar Pradesh, Lal Bahadur Shastri, who was then Home Minister, was sworn in as Prime Minister to rule over the country for two years, long enough to witness the first war between India and Pakistan in 1965. He would be the second to die in harness, albeit under mysterious circumstances, in the USSR, just after signing the Tashkent Peace Pact with the warring Muslim neighbour.

The presence of Ajay Vardhan Loya as one of the few businessmen who accompanied the Prime Minister as part of his delegation would raise a few eyebrows back home because of his links with a dubious international arms dealer and some senior politicians. However, the whispers and conspiracy theories soon died out and were forgotten.

It was only in 1966, when Indira Gandhi became Prime Minister that the stars shone favourably on the Loyas, and Baldev Das managed to worm his way back into the corridors of power. The Loya scam vanished from the notoriously short public memory, and the matter stood finally resolved. Billimoria was sacked, and Jai Narain Sanghi was cast aside to die peacefully of old age.

The Loyas were firmly back in control by the end of 1967, free to propagate their undercover operations in alternative areas of the dark market. Their other industries that had been adversely affected by the post-war recession limped back to normalcy.

Baldev Das died in 1971, after seeing Indira Gandhi elected as Prime Minister, twice over. He did not live to see her imposition of the ill-omened Emergency in 1975 that brought about her ruin, two years later.

17

Soon after his father died, Anuj Vardhan's affair with his old-time paramour, Chaya Devi, also came to an end. He now had his sights trained on a gorgeous, twenty-one year old Muslim woman, Zaira Ali Khan, who was the reigning national beauty queen. His wife died during this affair and within six months of it he had moved Zaira into his home. His three children were rescued by their despairing grandmother, who brought them under her guardianship, for a short while, and then left them in the custody of an unwilling Amba, when she followed her husband to the grave, two years after him.

Sanjay Vardhan and Jayanti, having discovered a beautiful new world together, were working out their own plans, so they demanded a legal separation from the existing set-up.

A partition deed was drawn up by their lawyers, wherein, two defunct jute mills in Calcutta, a small five-hundred square yard house in Delhi, and a ridiculously small amount in cash, were allocated to Sanjay Vardhan's share. Adamant to get out, they relinquished all their claims in favour of this partisan division, without as much as a whimper of protest.

They sold the two mills in Calcutta, at a throwaway price, and flew out of their dreary nether world, into the serene idyll of Austria. They bought a beautiful country house in the mountains, where they lived happily, and Jayanti gave birth to two boys, in the following years.

All contacts with the family at home extinguished, they had finally been accorded an amnesty, from the malefic silver spoon. The dreadful shadow now fell on three unsuspecting victims, Kanupriya, Piyush and Vivek, who were being tossed back and forth, between an uncaring father, and a hostile Amba *Tai*.

Amba's practised control-games acquired manic proportions by the time her mother-in-law died. Having superbly handled the Aliya Hasan affair, she spent most of her time shuttling between Calcutta and Delhi. She conducted the orientation of her son into the business, while allowing her husband the fashionable licence to stray within a circumscribed radius.

Early in 1975, a modest gold-rimmed invitation, addressed to Bharat Loya, arrived in Delhi. It announced the forthcoming wedding of Aliya Hasan to a Muslim, by the name of Javed Abdullah. Amba tossed it into the dustbin, dispelling the last of her anxieties about Aliya's lurking presence in the shadows. She was content that Aliya Hasan was buried in history at last. She would learn later that Rukhsana and her autistic son had migrated with her daughter to the United States where Javed Abdullah was a professor of Psychology at some university—a safe distance, too far away, to pose any hazard in her son's life.

Trapped in her own web of loneliness and confusion, Kanupriya floated along like a drifter as she lived through her teens, fantasising about secret romances with famous people, taking her pin-up poster adulation to psychopathic levels. Inside this make-believe world, she grew very close to her younger cousin, Nupur. They shared the intimacy of friend and ally, together seeking solace in the unreal drama, that life had drawn them into. Kanupriya always suspected that her aunt, Amba *Tai*, was not particularly happy about the time Nupur spent in her company, but her cousin, who was oblivious of the undercurrents, never relented.

Back in Calcutta, Bharat Loya, with his wild streak of youthful arrogance and appetite for sexual adventure, had let himself loose on a society that gladly imparted him his star status. His youthful excesses marked a depraved ruthlessness and he revelled in the power of his new office, as the eldest son of Amba and Ajay Vardhan. The veneer of his graduate degree and the licence to act without moral reservations had cast him into the mould of *most eligibles*.

He could fall madly in love within fifteen minutes and a woman who caught his fancy, would have to wait no longer than a few seconds for him to make his first move. His greatest charm was his sharp wit and his disdain for middle class conservatism.

Shuttling between his father's offices dotted all over Calcutta, and factories spread over Bihar, he often sat in the head office of the East India Jute Mill, in his deceased grandfather's chair that was flanked on either side by two large portraits of his regal-looking grandparents. He spent hours in that chair, letting his mind wander. He remembered a cartoon strip in the *Playboy* magazine. A little toddler sat astride the lap of his grey-haired, bespectacled grandmother who was knitting sweetly like all grandmothers do; he looked up into her eyes and said,

'Tell me a story grandma about the time you were a whore in Chicago...'

Convulsed with uncontrollable laughter, he would drift into another equally impish reverie.

18

Dehra Dun
July 1975

The year Bharat Loya turned twenty-one, far away from Calcutta, in a city nestling in the foothills of the Himalayas, a young woman was celebrating her eighteenth birthday. She was a highly strung girl of great beauty, fair skin, large luminous brown eyes and a wide forehead that had been marked with a terrifying future. The elder of her parent's two children, she had been named Yashoda. Her father, Shrikant Bansal, was a small-time, unsuccessful businessman, addicted to alcohol. His wife, Sucheta, after years of mental abuse, had resigned herself to her husband's failings, and the rearing of her daughter and son. She had small aspirations, to marry the girl into an educated middle class family and settle her son into a secure job, so she meticulously tended to their education, to fulfil her duties as a single parent.

Yashoda and her brother, Chand, had been sent to the best schools of the city to imbibe all the finesse needed to fit the bill of her moderate dreams.

Yashoda finished school with the polish of a convent education, and an impeccable English accent. She was well versed in all the old-fashioned accomplishments of prospective brides like cooking, embroidery, flower arrangement and interior decoration. With all these and an exceptionally fair complexion, her mother calculated that she was comfortably placed in the marriage market. She began spreading the word among their friends and relatives to find the right match for her daughter, oblivious of Yashoda's private plans, that had another direction altogether.

Suket Kumar Singh was a strapping, nineteen-year old youth of mixed origins. His grandfather, a retired Indian Civil Service Officer of the British Raj and old-time resident of Dehra Dun, retained his lifestyle, living in his world of fruit orchards and lazy Sunday lunches that were well attended by other old residents of the city.

He aspired to send his only grandchild to the coveted Indian Foreign Service and provided him the education that would prepare him for his ultimate dream. Suket's father was a senior manager at a government owned tea-estate and his mother, from whom he had inherited his looks, was an attractive woman of British descent, who taught English in an elite convent school.

Yashoda and Suket had known each other since they were ten years old. They had travelled in the same bus to their respective schools, long enough to strike up a friendship, which blossomed into a sweet, teenage romance between them. Suket felt the natural stirrings of his adolescent love for her, and she a special rush in his company. She began dreaming of a life with him, in his cozy little haven, with his English breakfast of scrambled eggs and freshly baked muffins, with home-made strawberry jam for tea. Suket's family took to the affable, meek Bansal girl, allowing her to spend much of her after-school time in their home.

Heady with the success of his new-found identity in Calcutta, Bharat Loya had let himself loose on a host of nubile women of all ages, willing to grant him favours. Initially, there were a number of marriage proposals from Marwari parents of prospective brides, which were turned down by his mother, for various reasons. She wanted only the best for her first-born. However, as his reputation became that of an inveterate womaniser, with a crazy turnover of women, his allure in the old-fashioned, matrimonial market diminished. The rumour mills began to work overtime to entertain the city spectators, and a particularly, scandalous tale of Bharat's affair with a stunning Bengali woman, ten years older than him, ruined any remaining chances of getting him a high class match. The woman, with her fair skin and dazzling green eyes was constantly spotted with him, and because she lived with her husband, who was employed by the Loyas, in a two-room outhouse, appended to their main building, the affair was comfortably manageable. She remained his prime fixation for a short while, after which, predictably, he moved on to his next pick.

The class of women, who attracted him, revealed the genetic compulsion of Bharat's preferences. Much like his philandering uncle Anuj Vardhan, he only mixed with small-time starlets, aspiring models and permissive airhostesses, who found his bank balance more attractive than his looks. His wild parties, that reverberated with music and dancing through the night, and most often ended in the swimming pool, were similar to the orgies of the Ajay Vardhan and Amba days, and typical of her, his mother let him flourish in his fantasy world, for she knew she could pull him back any time, by the leash that she had tied around his neck.

On a chance visit to Dehra Dun, Amba Loya spotted Yashoda. Within the first hour of their meeting, she decided that the demure and fair-skinned girl would be the ideal match for her son. She took off the diamond ring from her hand and slipped it on to Yashoda's finger, lilting characteristically.

'*Yeh aaj se hamaari bahu hai!*' (She will be my daughter-in-law.)

Her words pierced through Shrikant Bansal's drunken stupor and he fell at her feet, as tears of joy rolled down his face. He fumbled for words of gratitude, but could not speak. Sucheta too stood rooted to the spot, overwhelmed with awe and disbelief. It sunk in after a while that she had been relieved of the burden she had carried on her shoulders all these years. Even her son had been shown the door to a rosy future, she thought, as her voice choked with tears of joy.

As the quiet Bansal household went into overdrive to prepare to give away their daughter, Yashoda was in deep anguish. She was being plucked out of her peaceful and ordinary existence to be laid down at the feet of the reigning empress of the Calcutta Marwaris.

She was being pushed by her parents into a dark, blind alley, without her consent, and it terrified her. She had not even seen the man they wanted her to marry and she could not bear the thought of never meeting Suket again.

She could not allow herself to be sold like a prize heifer at a cattle fair; to be judged by her height, skin, looks, body, fertility, udders and capacity to produce milk. She stole out of her bed at midnight, to head straight into the arms of the only person who, she believed, could save her from ruination.

In the winter of 1977, Bharat Loya and Yashoda were married in Calcutta. The entire city celebrated what was perceived to be the enchanting resurrection of Cinderella's fairy tale.

Predictably, Yashoda's attempt to run away with Suket had been aborted, and her foolish dream shattered. Suket's parents beat a hasty retreat, not wanting to disturb the peace of their small, happy family, and Suket forgot about his schoolboy's infatuation with passing time.

On her nuptial night which followed the grand panorama of the wedding, where all the country's celebrities showed up in their finest regalia and expensive jewels, Yashoda entered her bridal suite, exhausted and numb.

The gnawing pain of separation from Suket persisted within her. The idea of being despoiled by a mousy-looking, bespectacled stranger, made her ill. Weighed down more by her apprehensions than her attire, she sat down at the edge of her bed and wept.

Bharat Loya was a patient and gentle lover. He undressed her slowly, down to her skin. The lust for new flesh, her lifeless surrender, the background music, her soulful eyes, her dishevelled hair, compounded with the hype that surrounds, what is believed to be, the most magical moment tabulated in the history of sexual evolution, Bharat Loya consummated his marriage. He took the virginity of his unwilling bride—the carnal release strangely, did not procure him the joy of his first sexual encounter.

Yashoda lay crumpled inside her body, impregnated with her husband's seed. She did not even merit the bona fide pleasure of her conjugal union, in a forced and painful surrender.

As they turned their backs upon each other to drift into their separate worlds, Bharat fell asleep filled with visions of Aliya Hasan, and Yashoda stifled a sob as she remembered Suket's sunken eyes and stubble beard.

She had become a mere number, in the statistics of over seventy per cent Indian women who never experience an orgasm, in their entire married lives.

19

The second War between Pakistan and India in 1971 which led to the creation of Bangladesh ushered in desolate winds of change. A severe economic recession hit the country. Anuj Vardhan's reckless lifestyle and insane spending habits had taken their toll. Zaira, who had a high boredom factor and even higher survival instinct, had cut her losses and quickly moved on to another Marwari, a soft-drinks bottler, who had fallen madly in love with her. This set off a chain of events and one by one, Anuj Vardhan suffered blows to his life and business. His two textile mills were running huge losses and the labour unions were on strike. He was forced to declare a lockout that made thousands of workers jobless. Rumours were rife of the twin jinx of his Kanpur mills, and no one wanted to touch them.

Like the synchronised crumbling of a tall tower in a virtual reality game, the vital organs in his system packed up one by one and he found himself caught in a nasty tailspin.

As his borrowings mounted and the government became serious about recovery of dues, his beautiful house on Prithviraj Road was attached by the income tax authorities and he was forced to move out. Deserted by the most elusive of his companions, Lady Luck, he was completely friendless. He lost his feel for cashing-in on opportunities that had at one time been his greatest strength. His social cheering-squad, that had earlier exalted him, turned their backs on him. The ultra-potent aphrodisiac in his goblet, the elixir of wealth and success having run out, he was left looking like a fool, clinging on to his fast-dwindling bank balance.

A middle-aged exporter, one of the few who stood by him, took a fancy to him, and he moved into her home and married her, shortly after. She gave birth to a girl the following year, but their marriage did not see her through the third year and he moved out again into a rented two-room terrace apartment, to live the life of a lonely and bankrupt recluse—a shunned and despicable loser, whom even his relatives didn't want to know.

With Anuj Vardhan's collapse, people began to talk about a curse that had trailed him. They had not connected it to the dynastic jinx, just yet.

Kanupriya too was going through her own struggles. The stepmotherly treatment from Amba *Tai* was getting worse. She could turn to no one. She was two years younger than Bharat but he was in Calcutta. Her cousin Nupur was in college at seventeen. Her two younger brothers were not old enough to afford solace, or provide answers. There was a deep frustration breeding inside her. By 1975 she had severed all links with her father and was watching him nosedive in his self-created disaster. She sought the easiest way out, by making herself available to men. It was the amazing anesthesia that freed her from pain. It made her feel sensuous and desirable. It gave her the power to recognise herself as a passionate and hot-blooded woman, and helped to soften the hostility of her environment.

She found herself mostly drawn to middle-aged men. She found them to be more mature, more gentle, and utterly arousing. Her long repressed desire to be loved by her father had found its natural outlet and dominated her fixation. Like a skilled geisha girl, she honed herself to become an object of lust for men over forty. She spent hours, making up her face in front of her bathroom mirror, plucking her eyebrows, pouting her lips, pinching her cheeks, padding her breasts, to feel like an adult.

She would paint her full mouth with dark glossy lipstick, and line her eyes with kohl. It changed the shape of her face dramatically, and the blush highlighted the hollows beneath her cheekbones. She practiced her facial expressions—pouting, kissing and smiling wide, cocking one eyebrow up, to look like a flirtatious streetwalker, prancing in high heels, upon her bedroom floor.

Kanupriya, the textbook embodiment of Electra, the epitome of an overgrown Lolita, the highly charged nineteen-year old, just couldn't bear to be in the company of fumbling teenaged boys. She went to bed with her make-up on, sleeping on her back, so as to not mess up her face. She was to begin her short-lived and arduous journey into self-damnation, riding piggyback on a fractured dream.

20

Yashoda and Bharat left for their two-month long honeymoon around the world, to stop at their last destination in Hawaii. In the last leg of her trip, Yashoda felt ill and nauseous. Presuming it to be exhaustion of their hectic schedule and long flights, she never for a moment suspected that she was already carrying Bharat's child. Bharat's effort to be the perfect charmer did little to ease her. She showed no keenness to shop at luxury stores, or go sight-seeing to new places, which her newly betrothed husband was so enthusiastic about.

At night, she slipped into her chiffon and silk negligee to prepare for their usual sex, which was as mechanical as if she were having her dinner. Even though Bharat was loving and tender, she had not got accustomed to his nudity, and the sight of his thin arms and spindly legs disconcerted her.

A few days before they were to return, Yashoda missed her period. Her nausea had worsened and the mere sight of food sent her retching. She resigned herself to her role as the receptacle and carrier of her family's progeny that had revealed its stamp of finality. It depressed her. She longed to be with Suket, and felt an aching emptiness, as she thought of the shape her life had taken. *Love is so short, and forgetting is so long,* she murmured to herself and wept.

As Bharat Loya undressed himself to get into bed beside her, she felt a strong wave of bile rise in her throat. She ran to the bathroom sink and threw up.

When they reached Calcutta, Yashoda discovered she was pregnant. Having discharged her ultimate duty as a woman, she surrendered herself and her unborn baby to Amba, who subjected her to a meticulous schedule and diet. She was not allowed to eat or drink anything without Amba's approval. Her breakfast consisted of five shelled and soaked almonds and a glass of milk with Rooh-afzah sherbet, to make the baby's complexion like peaches and cream. Tea and coffee were taboo, as was alcohol and even her thoughts were to be sanitised, as per Amba's orders. Her room was filled with big, coloured posters of cute and chubby babies from Mother Care catalogues, and taped chants from the scriptures, or soothing *bhajans* and hymns were played all day. Since her body was the abode of the divine child that was growing inside her, she had to be given the appropriate *sanskars,* according to her mother-in-law's decree.

Amba Loya, who had become Ma Amba in her new incarnation, donned saffron saris and a long string of *rudraksh* beads around her neck. She had begun the process of worldly renunciation that was to be completed in a few years. She proclaimed that a divine child was on its way, to lead civilisation to supreme bliss and considered it her privilege to nurture him, as she had done her son. She became an ardent disciple of a spiritual woman called Bhagwan Guru, listening to her religious discourses with sincerity. She trailed her, as part of her entourage all over the country and ended her pilgrimage in Haridwar, at the head ashram, where she would go into silent retreat for a few days every month.

Believing that she had attained supreme knowledge and had been elevated to an extraordinary spiritual plane, she began conducting her own discourses every day, during which the doors of her plush, drawing room were opened to all fellow *satsangis,* who came in droves to listen to her—or to be treated to a prime display of what she excelled in—hypocrisy. She talked to the devotees of detachment and renunciation with emotional rhetoric, accompanied by teary outbursts, to convey to them, that wealth only brings pain, and worldly desires are the root cause of suffering. The gaping *satsangis,* all but fell in love with the beautiful and beatific Ma Amba, bowled over, by her humility and her simplicity.

In keeping with her preachings, Ma Amba did renounce her jewels, but she never let go of the reins of power she held over her domain—nor did she hand over the keys of her coffers to her successor.

21

When Aryaman Loya was a five-week-old rudimentary mass of fast growing cells inside Yashoda's womb, he measured only a few centimetres in length and his beating heart was no bigger than the size of a pinhead. He had tiny vestigial limbs and a thick tube attached to the middle of his stomach, through which he was continuously fed. He was encased inside a sealed sac, filled with a watery fluid that was at a soothing temperature.

Aryaman did not know that he was a boy. He did not know that one out of the several hundred million spermatozoa, swimming in his father's ejaculatory fluid, had fused with the ripe ovum in his mother's womb, to create him. He knew nothing about the odds that brought together the X and Y chromosomes from his parent's genetic junkyard, to determine his sex at conception. He did not know that neither of the two organisms that had fused together, to produce the activated nucleus of his being, could have selected the traits that he would possess, when he was born. He only knew the feel of a spongy wall that he could bounce off, inside the temperature-controlled sac of amniotic fluid that would be his home for forty weeks. He did not know the sensation of light—he knew only darkness. Both those gifts of sight and light would come to him after he was born.

'Why after he was born. He was already born, wasn't he? Alive and kicking?'

By the time Aryaman began to hear, he was a fourteen-week old foetus. He had gained more strength and was bigger. He could somersault and flail his arms about, knocking his mother's insides with his knees or his elbows. He could sing and dance and laugh and cry. He could gurgle and regurgitate and pee and defecate. His brand new body was equipped with the perfect mechanism to produce more of his kind. He talked to himself, and to God. He asked God to come and play his darkroom games—to touch his tiny ears and nose and hands and feet and then one by one, he would will them to sleep.

The frisky little embryonic mass had no idea that each move of his was being translated into a sharp sensation for his mother. In her third trimester, overweight and twisted grossly out of shape, she had begun her countdown for his arrival. Till then, he could frolic all he wanted to in his uterine world, till he became too big to stay there, and the natural and arduous process to expel him would commence. His mother's abdominal muscles would begin short and painful contractions that would become longer and more frequent, as her cervix dilated to accommodate his head, push him down the narrow passage and eject him out of her body. The force of the blood, plasma, body fluids and degenerating afterbirth would rupture the tender skin around her vagina, after which his umbilical cord would be clamped and then cut off.

The biological laws of nature and survival would become operative for two separate individuals thereafter, leaving them connected by only a moral filament, bound by mortality.

Aryaman spent eighteen agonising hours in a perilous journey as he travelled head-downwards, to finally burst into a labour room, flush with bright lights, at the Bellevue Nursing Home in Calcutta. There were several phantom-like masked figures moving about as someone held him by his ankles and spanked his bottom. The pain made him yelp weakly like a whining animal. The sound of his cry startled them. There was a frenzied jubilance in the people around him as someone shouted, 'It's a boy.'

The nurse who was holding him upside down, wrapped him in a sterilised sheet and handed him to the woman who was his grandmother.

Bharat Loya stared at the slimy, wet, guinea pig-like form covered in blood, from a distance, feeling squeamish, but proud and virile at having sired a son. He patted his listless wife on her head for having accomplished the glorious deed and went home.

Yashoda lay on her hospital bed, completely drained after the long ordeal. The searing pain of her contractions ceased after a torrent of hot, melted butter had gushed out of her vagina. She heard a long wail of a newborn baby, drowned in her own screams before she passed out.

She did not see Amba inspect the child's genitals officiously, before he was taken away by the nurse. She did not even hear the doctors announce the sex of the child, or congratulate her. She would only come round after a few hours, when the newborn infant would be put to her breast, to be suckled by her, but before that, Amba Loya would make him lick a few drops of honey from a silver spoon.

There could have been no greater reason for the inmates of Loya House to rejoice. Amba, the new religious sensation of Calcutta, with her flair to do things differently, prepared for the fortieth day celebrations on the birth of the newborn prince. Playing out a pagan script with an artist's precision, in a world where the miraculous and the terrible coexist, Amba Loya, the born-performer, the consummate artist, the intimate provocateur who flirted with the gods and fluently orated the gospel, planned to tap the emotions of the city's smart set, with an effusive display of her skills. A display that would not mar her spiritual sensuality, despite her worldly renunciation in full throttle. It was to come wrapped in saffron, the colour of the sages, to awaken the mystic romance trapped in the hearts of all those who would emulate her, to flatter her.

Two weeks earlier, a parchment cut-out in the shape of a *peepul* leaf had been delivered to hundreds of expectant invitees. It was embossed in gold letters, and a single word 'saffron' in the left corner, specified the dress code. It was an invitation to the privileged set, to come and witness a divine miracle under the auspices of Ma Amba.

The preparations for the grand *yagna* were supervised by Amba herself. A huge saffron and red *pandal* was erected on the lawns of Loya House, to accommodate one hundred and one pundits, who would chant in unison, *shlokas* from the Vedic scriptures. Another similar *pandal* came up on the other side of the lawn for spectators and guests. Thousands of oil *diyas* lined the pathway. Huge shallow terracotta urns filled with water and floating candles were placed in the centre of floral *rangolis* in prominent positions around the garden and the swimming pool. Orange and yellow marigolds formed a floral sheath over both the sitting areas. Marigold strings trailed in asymmetrical lengths from the branches of all the trees that had been lit up with fairy lights. They were wound around the pillars and colonnades, and a gigantic platform decorated with roses, jasmines and paan leaves, was constructed between the two *pandals* to seat the mother and the child.

On either side of the entrance, coconuts and conch shells were placed on top of a silver urn, as symbols of fertility and prosperity, without which no religious Hindu ceremony is complete.

The *pandal* filled up with men and women dressed in various hues, ranging from red to saffron. Amba greeted them at the entrance by handing each of them a string of *rudraksh* beads that had a pendant, pasted with a photograph of Ajay Vardhan. They were requested to wear it before being seated to watch the ceremony.

Amba herself had worn a flaming orange sari in keeping with the prescribed code. Her fragile beauty was that of a classic film star, gracefully renouncing the world, in a well-rehearsed film script. A string of *rudraksh* beads with her husband's picture was prominently visible around her neck.

As the sun set, painting the sky with the warm hues of red wine, the oil lamps lit up, and the priests raised their conch-shells to their mouths. The hundred-odd shells created a powerful resonating sound like the rolling waves of an ocean, and the dancing flames of the lamps, mingled with the colours of dusk to transform into an incredible *son et lumiere* show.

Amba rose from her position and the priests began their powerful chant. She disappeared into the house and was seen soon after on top of the main building. She stood with her arms stretched upwards towards the sky, with her eyes closed. The chanting and invocation rose to a hysterical crescendo and all the onlookers closed their eyes to join them in their prayers.

Amba sat down on a floral crane-pulley holding a little baby wrapped in saffron, wearing a gold crown. Lowered by the chain-pulley that was also decorated with strings of marigolds and roses, she descended from the sky like a celestial being, calling out to the awestruck spectators to raise their hands in the air, to be blessed by her. When she landed on the ground, she handed the baby to Yashoda and signalled the chanting to stop. Then she turned around to the audience to speak.

She invoked the blessing of the Lord for all her listeners, thanking him for his gift of benevolence to the Loyas, the gift of a divine child that glorified their status, because she believed he was an incarnation of the Lord himself.

Chants of *Jai Shri Ram* and *Har Har Mahadev* rent the air as the crowds broke into applause after which they were ushered into the area where a sumptuous vegetarian feast and exotic fruits and desserts had been laid out. Bharat Loya also dressed in saffron like a sadhu, moved about, mingling with the guests, beaming with pride, at the impact that his mother's novel idea had created on the spectators.

Yashoda stood by herself in one corner, wearing her wedding nose-ring and an ornately embellished, bright yellow *odhni*, ritually awarded to the mother of a male child, over her head. The baby had been taken inside by the nurse. Her maternal emotions oozed out of her swollen, lactating breasts that ached as if burning hot barbed-wire had been tightened around them, as she thought of her little boy.

The guests left after dinner, feeling satiated, but spooked out. Word was out the next day, that Amba Loya had gone stark mad. Some even rued that something terrible was going to befall on the Loyas. The freakish and ill-omened pageantry would not augur well for them.

For Yashoda Loya, life took on a pace that made her feel totally out of control. She had resigned herself to the rearing of her son, believing it to be the cardinal purpose of her existence. An irrational fear had taken root in her heart—an anxiety that forewarns of something bad, that was to happen. She did not like society gatherings and found it a drag to converse with stupid socialites. She was in an acute postpartum depression.

Amba too was unhappy with the state of affairs in Delhi. She had been disturbed by her daughter's increasing dependence on Kanupriya, and despised her for the role model she presented for Nupur. With no one to control her, Kanupriya, now twenty-two, was cruising at top speed. She and Nupur had formed a close foursome, with a thirty-year old Punjabi hotelier and his younger brother, who were both addicted to marijuana.

Every night, the two men would fetch their dates and proceed to Tabela, the popular discotheque of those days at the Oberoi Intercontinental Hotel. The four would smoke pot, drink and dance all night, in the dark hall, filled with intertwined bodies and loud music. They would indulge in all the daring adventures, common to young people their age. Most of the time, they would end up in their boyfriends' home, where they would make out separately, or sometimes jointly, to enhance their levels of fun. Their inordinate licentiousness, the yearning to be loved and the passionate desire for sexual fulfilment, had led them into this wayward life and accounts of it soon reached Amba's ears. She decided that it was time for her to step in.

22

Amba Loya needed to get Nupur away from Kanupriya as soon as possible and decided to send her out of Delhi. Kanupriya and her two brothers would remain at the house in Delhi in the care of her staff. She cut down their expenses to a bare minimum and sharply curtailed the use of the cars and other amenities for them.

Kanupriya was devastated at being separated from her cousin, but was too terrified of Amba to protest. Sensing Nupur's discomfiture at the unexplained breakup, Amba began gently counselling her.

'Half-baked knowledge of sex is dangerous Nupur. Kanupriya is encouraging you towards the wrong kind of men. I'm your mother, I understand your needs, my baby.' Tears welled up in Nupur's eyes.

'She's a very bad influence on you my child. I wish I could just send her away somewhere. Ever since her mother died she's just gone wild. I'm your mother and will choose only the best for you. Don't feel shy, you can come to me for anything,' she said. 'Have I ever stopped you from going out with boys? But you cannot have sex with just anyone. I'm not going to allow that vile Kanupriya to corrupt you and lead you to hell.'

Nupur began to cry. She was upset at the insinuations against her cousin but she could say nothing to her mother.

'Why don't you go to the Rajneesh ashram at Poona? That should be good for you. Their initiation and orientation programme shall help you get rid of all your problems. I know you will find everything you want there.'

Bhagwan Rajneesh's ashram was infamous for its wild sexual orgies and the clandestine intermingling of its members, from all over the world, to practise his preachings of free sex.

So Amba assumed that her daughter would be distracted enough to keep her mind off Kanupriya and snap her dependence on her. She wanted Nupur to travel up the spiral, from sex to superconsciousness, as evangelised by Osho himself and retain her control on her, permanently. Nupur had no choice but to sail along with her plan.

Meanwhile, an old benevolent aunt suggested a very handsome, Marwari match, for Kanupriya—a well-settled young man from Bangalore, and even though Amba did not particularly care either way, she agreed to the engagement.

Ranjan Goenka turned out to be better and much more than anyone had expected. The twenty-eight-year-old, who hailed from a well-established industrial family, was a qualified MBA from an Ivy League American college. He had been working with his father in their pharmaceutical business since he had returned from the United States two years ago.

Amba was greatly astonished by his looks and confidence, and his ready acceptance of Kanupriya irritated her. Even though the thought of palming off her liability to him once and for all was tempting, she felt a twinge of jealousy—a horrible feeling, that she was losing control. Kanupriya for her part was delirious with joy. At last she had found some anchor in her crumbling world and the escape hatch that would deliver her from the clutches of vile Amba *Tai*. She began dreaming of a life far away from her in the South, even planning to take Nupur with her, sometime in the future.

Amba hosted a dinner for Kanupriya's prospective groom and his parents in Delhi. The two exchanged rings to formalise the engagement. Bharat and his brother were called in from Calcutta to attend the ceremony, but Yashoda stayed back because she did not want to travel with her baby. Amongst those who also played host were Nupur, Kanupriya's younger brothers, and her father Anuj Vardhan, who put in a fleeting appearance. Ajay Vardhan was on a business visit to Bombay and could not rearrange his tight schedule.

At dinner, Amba seated herself at the head of the table, with the newly engaged couple on either side of her, and she turned on her charm for the future son-in-law. As the evening drew to a close and the guests were getting ready to leave, Kanupriya noticed her fiance looking a little flustered. She went up to him, but before she could speak she heard Amba call out to her.

'Kanupriya what are you doing? Go and see your mother-in-law to the car. You really don't know the first thing about good manners. God knows what you are going to do when you get married. You will surely bring shame upon us,' she grumbled.

Amba's reprimand offended her but she dismissed it from her mind as her routine standoffishness that would soon come to an end.

Kanupriya and Nupur stayed up that night, chatting till the early hours, totally captivated by the newcomer's looks and charm.

'Hey *didi,* did you see the way *jija* looked at you all evening. God! You are so lucky! He's so dashing and you two together will make the whole town jealous,' Nupur gushed.

Kanupriya caressed the flawless, round, five-carat diamond that sat on her slender ring-finger, filled with visions of a brand new and exciting life with her new-found mate. But fate had reserved its final irony for her in the next turn of events.

Ranjan Goenka left Kanupriya's house visibly disturbed. He had found her vivacious and attractive. He loved the way she pouted her mouth, before she broke into peals of infectious laughter. Her sparkling deep-set eyes, lined with kohl and her well-formed body was a sensual delight. But that Amba was odd. His initial liking for her was marred within the first hour of their meeting. Even though she was sugary and pampering and beautiful and elegant, he found her manner highly contrived. The sharpness that crept into her voice each time she addressed Kanupriya did not escape him. Such treatment to an abandoned child was common, but something else was odd about Amba. He had sensed her come unnecessarily close to him, too many times that evening. He had felt her eyes linger on him, for uncomfortable lengths of time. She had brushed his arms with the tips of her fingers while she spoke a bit too often. She embarrassed him.

He recalled the events of the last evening with disgust…

'Come on Ranjan, you are not eating anything. Don't you like the food? Your plate is empty,' she had said. She had piled some rice onto his plate and picked some up with her fingers.

'Here, won't you let *Tai* feed you?' she had stretched her hand towards him forcing the rice into his mouth, her fingers lightly brushing his lips.

Ranjan had looked around him feeling weird.

'Thank God no one had noticed!' Kanupriya was engrossed in conversation with Nupur. Then he had felt Amba's foot upon his. He looked up at her, and saw a teasing smile on her face. He felt her toes curl in and out on his ankles again and again. He froze.

'What the hell was she up to?' he thought. He glanced up and saw Amba munching away at her food, with a fervour that matched the tempo of her shameless footsie game.

Ranjan had lost his appetite. He had wanted to leave that instant. He would have to tell his mother everything when he got home. He had been utterly revolted by Amba's vulgarity. He began to feel apprehensive about Kanupriya as well. What if she turned out to be anything like her *Tai?* He decided that he would have nothing more to do with this lot. Ranjan Goenka called off the engagement the next morning.

23

The incident had a nasty fallout. Amba came down heavily on Kanupriya, blaming her for some breach that had brought about this unexpected disaster.

'Nobody is ever going to marry you, you foolish girl. What the hell did you say to him? Such a good match I had found for you. God! What will I do now? I am fed up of teaching you social graces. And now there will be a bad name on us all.'

Kanupriya, who was already in a state of confusion and pain, packed her bags and moved out with her brothers. She begged her father to let them stay with him, weeping piteously at his door. Anuj Vardhan had no choice, but to take them in.

Kanupriya had reached the end of her tether. For the life of her, she couldn't figure out what had gone wrong. Her fiance had seemed so taken in by her. Why this sudden turnaround in just twelve hours? His abrupt rejection had thrown her off her feet. It left a gaping wound inside her—a pain that just would not go away: She reacted by going on a wild, male-poaching spree to assuage her bruised ego. She moved around freely, with a host of married men her father's age who were only too willing to take advantage of the attractive young woman with easy morals and a delightfully high level of permissiveness.

After a brief stint with two middle-aged Marwari industrialists of the city, she settled on Raghu Hari Jaipuria—a forty-four-year old nephew of Amba Loya's erstwhile paramour, Prithviraj, who lived in Bombay, but travelled frequently to Delhi. Expectedly, Raghu Hari's involvement with Kanupriya became the biggest scandal to hit the scene. Kanupriya savoured the voyeuristic delight of being paired off, decimated and ripped apart by gossip-mongers, from within and outside her clan—most of whom condemned her as an immoral sexual predator.

Driven by a torment that carried her beyond her social identity, she experienced her sweet and sour moments that were at once erotic, ecstatic and deviant. She was hooked onto the secret excitement of sharing her mid-forties lover, with his insipid heavy-hipped wife and two children, who were almost her own age. She revelled in the feeling of supremacy, of being better. She gloated in her own sexual prowess that included extra dollops of oral sex, a finely honed skill that she knew most men hanker after, but seldom get at home. Clearly, she was at an advantage.

Raghu Hari Jaipuria however, was the classic Marwari male. For him social facades and traditional family structures were as important as outlets for carnal gratification. The safety of his boring marriage was no substitute for the thrill of forbidden sex. He played the field like a skilled juggler, between two airtight compartments that separated his wife from his mistress and did not wish to upset the apple cart, needlessly.

Even though she was the last to find out, Raghu Hari's wife eventually did and the usual drama followed which altered the arrangement only marginally for him. It made him adamant to not let go, but he also became more discreet to avoid a repeat of domestic hysterics and sustained emotional third-degree.

Kanupriya was left feeling perversely stronger. She capitalised on the exposure by foisting herself with greater fervour in her extra-constitutional position. She reiterated what had trickled down into her head from her environment, over the years, that sex is a significant though not crucial part of a marriage. She was happy to let Raghu Hari's wife keep the nomenclature, as long as she would let her keep the man. What she did not confess to was that she had begun secretly dreaming of becoming the wife of the man who loved her effusively, paid her bills, took her on sinful sojourns abroad and pampered her with gifts worthy of his status.

Once in a while, in his weaker moments, Raghu Hari had said to her, that it pained him to end every meeting with parting, and he would change all that some day by marrying her. Each time he went home to his wife, however, Raghu Hari still struggled with his identity that was neither conservative nor liberated, but heavily chained to self-doubt.

Would women rule the world if treaties were made in bed?

Expectedly, the entire Marwari community ganged up against the defenceless twenty-five-year old, condemning her depraved genealogy, blaming her errant father and ostracising her from their social circles. Her paramour and equal partner-in-crime, not surprisingly, was absolved by them, as a privilege of his gender.

Amba Loya got the chance to wash her hands off Kanupriya.

'This foolish girl will surely destroy all of us. She just can't stay out of trouble. I won't have any more of this nonsense. She is making a spectacle of us. Why did that wretched Rajshri have to dump her baggage onto me?'

Once again, her immediate and extended clan were subjected to a display of puzzling attitudes on permissive sex, where all that is taboo is implicitly acceptable, as long as it is not explicit.

A few months later, as nature's safety valve came into play, Raghu Hari Jaipuria fell off a horse while riding and had to be hospitalised in Bombay for a broken rib. That kept him forcibly in the care of his wife and suspended his travels to Delhi indefinitely. Kanupriya made several attempts in vain to contact him. The sudden break in their meetings depressed her. Her inability to be with him was becoming unbearable and she did not know how long it would be, before she could see him again. She was getting desperate.

Kanupriya did just what she ought not to have done. She boarded a flight to Bombay, in abject defiance of the unwritten diktat that all mistresses are obliged to follow. She did not know that she had put herself on a fast track to death row.

24

Aryaman Loya had comfortably crossed the normal milestones of his first nine months. He kicked about happily in his cradle, in his blue and white boy's nursery, decorated with big colourful replications of Disney characters. He had learnt to recognise a few familiar faces that appeared around him. Sister Mary in a white cap and Mummy and Papa. He had learned the feel and smell of his mother. He was taken to her, each time he felt hungry. By instinct he knew how to suck her breasts and he could defecate too. Both pleased him immensely. He knew only two sensations—pleasure and pain.

He would wail at the top of his voice when he was hungry, or wet, or cold, or if his tummy ached. He knew it brought about frantic activity and immediate attention. When he was happy, he lay quietly in his crib, sucking his thumb, staring up at a colourful contraption that was suspended over it. It moved up and down and round and round. It emitted musical chimes that soothed him and put him to sleep. The curly pattern on it sent him swirling back into the sac of fluid that had kept him warm, inside his mother's womb.

Aryaman had been seeing objects and colours. He could see shapes too. He could differentiate smells and could hear sounds. He knew the sweet smell of the talcum powder that was dusted over him, many times every day. He felt happy when his Mummy picked him up and cuddled him close. He loved the feel of her skin, the sound of her voice, her eyes, her smile and the touch of her breasts.

One day, Aryaman woke up feeling wretched. He was very restless. His heart beat rapidly and his body was burning hot. He could not stop shivering. Sister Mary wrapped him in a thick, soft blanket. The shivering just would not stop. She took him to his mother. He sucked her breasts for a while, but it did not make him happy. The milk rushed back up his throat and he vomited all over her.

He felt restless again. His eyes felt heavy and even in his mother's arms he did not feel any better. Sister Mary touched his forehead. Her palm felt cold, he winced. He wailed loudly, but this time it did not work. Nothing worked. Sister Mary stuck something into his armpit. It felt icy cold and poked him. He wailed louder and would not stop crying.

'He has a fever. 103° degrees, Madam.'

Then another flurry of activity.

'Call the doctor.'

A harried voice.

'He's got high fever Doctor. Can you come to see him. Please?'

'What's a fever? Why don't you take it away?'

Aryaman felt terrible. His crying had not stopped. He felt worse when they put him down. His lungs were tired and his mouth ached. He felt a pounding in his ears.

They did not put him down till the doctor came.

The doctor was a fat man in white. He had a funny snake around his neck. He pressed a flat, cold, metal thing onto Aryaman's chest. He wailed again.

'Go away fat man. Take fever with you.'

The fat man looked at him. He shone a light down his throat. He pulled open his eyelids and then let them go.

'Ouch that hurt.'

Aryaman turned away.

'Go away fat man. Take fever with you.'

He saw him scribble something and hand it to Sister Mary. Then all was quiet. He did not have the energy to cry. It was not helping anyway. The fat man had gone. He had left fever behind. He still felt restless.

Then his father came to him. He smiled at him and stretched out his arms.

'Come to me, my son.'

He touched his forehead with ice-cold hands.

Aryaman squirmed. His father took him into his arms from Sister Mary.

She handed him a spoon. She shook something vigorously and poured a red liquid onto the spoon.

His father held the spoon close to Aryaman's mouth. A sharp smell hit his nostrils and he began to cry again.

'I don't want this, take it away.'

Someone held his head and someone else pinched his nose.

His father prised open his tiny mouth and emptied the foul, burning red liquid, down his throat. It almost gagged him. He shook his head from side to side and screamed.

'What are you doing to me?'

He felt the liquid rush back up into this throat, out of his mouth and onto his father's clothes.

On a dark, dreary evening, as the shadows of a gloomy night lengthened on Loya House, a worried Bharat paced up and down the nursery, holding his sick and shivering child.

The doctor had come and gone.

'It's a viral fever. Very common nowadays. Nothing to worry about. Just give him half a teaspoon of pediatric Crocin syrup. It's paracetamol. The fever will come down in half an hour. Nothing to worry about. The shivering is normal. You should also give him a preventive for malaria—just in case. Just a precaution, will do no harm. This weather is tricky and malaria is common too. He'll be fine. Don't worry.'

Bharat, Yashoda and Sister Mary, each took turns with the baby, rocking him in their arms, pacing up and down in the nursery, but nothing worked. He had not even kept the Crocin syrup down. How would the fever go away?

Bharat decided to administer another dose, combined with the anti-malaria Pyraquin this time, *just for safety*.

He had made a fatal error.

Aryaman was exhausted and half asleep. His eyes were glazed. His head fell listlessly to one side on his mother's lap. Sister Mary had cleaned the vomit from his hands and face with a soft sponge. She had dusted him with the sweet, scented Johnson's baby powder, but the foul smell of curdled milk and vomit, hung in the air. It made him want to throw up again.

Aryaman was shaken out of his weary stupor by his father. The bright lights from his room hurt his eyes. The colours from the contraption mingled together and began to swirl.

The spoon was brought close to his mouth again.

'Another try?'

Again the sharp smell hit his nostrils. This time it was worse. Both the syrups had been mixed together, *just as a precaution*.

Then the same drill.

They prised open his mouth, pinched his nostrils, and shoved it swiftly into his throat. This time it stayed down.

Aryaman was drained—too drained to even cry. He lay lifelessly in his crib, staring at the curly pattern above him. Sleep eluded him for a long time. Then all of a sudden, the lights went out. He blinked in the dark till he fell asleep.

25

At the Bombay hospital it was a routine week day. Raghu Hari Jaipuria's deluxe room on the fourteenth floor, that was used for important patients, had been cleaned, vacuumed and sprayed with a freshener that smelled of pine. The window, near his bed, gave him a bird's-eye view of the busy street below. The hum of the air-conditioner drowned any unwanted sounds that filtered through. He had been sponged and changed and was wearing blue hospital clothes that were given to convalescing patients.

The fall from the horse had been nasty. Raghu Hari was a superb rider and had never had an accident before. Luckily, he had fallen on his side and had suffered no injuries to his head or spine. The orthopaedics department at the Bombay hospital was the best in the country.

He knew he was in safe hands. More than three weeks had passed since his accident. Raghu Hari was in a better mood. The driving pain in his ribs had subsided and he could sit up without help. Like a loving and devoted wife, Charulata had not left him alone for even a second—not even to go home to take a shower. He would have liked to call Kanupriya if only he could have but it was impossible. He felt guilty. He knew Kanupriya would go mad worrying about him. She would be deeply upset. He would make it up to her, when he was well. He would take her on a holiday to his home in the south of France. He had been promising to do that for a long time....

The hospital waiter entered, carrying his breakfast tray, followed by his two sons. They touched his feet by bending over double, waist downwards and settled on either side of his bed, chattering pleasantly. Charulata rose to pour out the tea into the cup.

All was well. They made the picture-perfect family, a pretty foursome, a loving mother, convalescing father and two pampered sons.

Kanupriya took a taxi from Santa Cruz airport and headed straight to the hospital. She rode in silence, staring out of the window while her thoughts played havoc with her. She could not think straight. She was dying to see Raghu Hari and would deal with all else when the time came. She knew he would be furious, but he would forgive her. Her intentions were pure but her rationality had been defeated by her recklessness. She knew nothing else.

Kanupriya entered the hospital lobby with trepidation. A life-size statue of Lord Ganesh, in black granite, stared at her from behind a trail of incense smoke. There was a garland of fresh, red roses around his neck. After making preliminary inquiries at the reception, she strode

Merchants of Death

up to the elevator and punched the fourteenth floor button before the door closed. She walked down the steel and grey corridor that smelled of mountain dew, her heart pounding wildly. The thought of coming face to face with Raghu Hari's wife made her chest go tight and she could barely breathe.

She stopped outside his door and studied a small square white card, that had RAGHU HARI JAIPURIA scribbled untidily on it. She did not linger there for fear of a last minute panic attack. She turned the knob and walked in.

She saw Raghu Hari Jaipuria sitting propped up on the bed with a breakfast tray clamped across his middle. He looked shaven and bathed. The fragrance of his familiar cologne hung in the air.

Kanupriya felt a wave of remorse. She felt like she had been betrayed. There were no signs of the anguish she expected to see on his face—no stubble beard, no dark circles around sunken eyes. He looked cheerful and content in the company of his family.

She saw his two sons, lazily sprawled on either side of his bed, watching a mindless Hindi film on the in-house movie channel. She saw Charulata leaning over him, feeding him cereal from a bowl. She noticed the large, diamond studs on her ears, the printed chiffon sari that partly covered her head.

As she moved forward, everything froze. It was as if the pause button on a TV screen had been pressed and all of them had turned to stone!

Kanupriya blanked out all else as she came face to face with her adversary. The wronged wife of Raghu Hari

Jaipuria against whom Kanupriya had no grouse, except that she was married to the man whom she loved and who loved her. She folded her hands to greet her. Charulata hurriedly put the bowl down. She pulled the free end of her sari close around her head and stared back at her piercingly.

For Raghu Hari Jaipuria, the most dreaded nightmare of a man in his situation, that of a confrontation between his wife and his mistress, had come true.

He began fumbling for words that refused to come to his rescue.

Just then, like a raging bull, one of his sons charged up and stopped Kanupriya in her tracks.

'You bitch, you cheap two-bit whore,' he roared. 'How dare you come here? Get out this minute or I'll throw you out of here,' he was frothing at the mouth like a rabid dog.

Kanupriya did not know what happened next. She felt a rough hand grab her by her hair, jerk her head backwards and push her out of the room. Her eyes filled with tears of humiliation and pain. She looked one last time at Raghu Hari, but her vision was blurred by her brimming tears, as she was dragged out and the door slammed in her face.

Kanupriya scrambled into the lift. She did not stop crying till she reached Delhi.

The pretty postcard family of the Jaipurias suffered a minor set-back. The raging and frothing progeny of Charulata had just demonstrated his might. The might of a moral policeman who expelled his father's mistress, while his father watched him in silence, too feeble to protest.

Kanupriya was devastated, more by her lover's impotence than by the brutal humiliation she had suffered at the hands of his son. She had erroneously expected a great deal more from him.

Back in Delhi, Kanupriya dressed up in her finest party clothes, put on her best make-up and rounded up a group of her friends to drown her sorrows at her old haunt, Tabela. She wanted to live up the night, as if there was no tomorrow. The incident that had plunged her into a deep pit of gloom had to be expunged from her soul immediately. She felt a familiar aching void creep up within her, like a dark force. She downed a few shots of vodka and took long drags from a freshly rolled joint, that some one handed her. She danced with carefree abandon continuously, till the early hours of the morning in the swish nightclub, not caring who stood beside her. Her friends, all of whom were stoned by the end, never suspected that the next time they would see her, there would be no laughter, no cheer, no clinking glasses, no music and dancing, there would only be quiet murmurs as they filed past her dead body, that betrayed none of the indignities inflicted on her, or her five-month old unborn foetus, before she died of suffocation.

Kanupriya was found hanging from the ceiling fan of her room at noon the next day.

The fragments of the pretty, picture postcard family of the Jaipuria's had been scotch-taped together again.

26

In Calcutta, the doctors at the Bellevue Nursing Home were worried. Aryaman Loya had been admitted four days ago. He had been running a high temperature over ten days. He had become frail and dehydrated. They kept him under observation. The tests showed nothing.

Aryaman couldn't understand why they were doing this to him. He still felt sick. Painful needles were jabbed into him, several times a day. He screamed each time. He hated them. He hated this strange dark place.

He could hear voices that were familiar. Sister Mary, his mother and his father and many other strange new ones but he could not see them, or anything else.

Why didn't someone put the lights on? He felt afraid of the dark. Didn't they know that?

Only one narrow sliver of light shone from the corner of his left eye. He blinked and tilted his head to that side, but it went away—then there was darkness again.

He wanted to go home.

On the fifteenth day, Aryaman's fever came down. He was going to be taken home.

Thank God! He rejoiced.

He would be able to play in his crib and watch his moving mobile with its colourful swirls. He would be able to kick and turn on his blue and white sheets, and stare at the coloured pictures of big creatures on his walls. His bright nursery made him happy.

Thank God he was leaving this dark, gloomy place that smelled awful. He remembered this smell. It was there when he crawled out of his uterine sac into the tight, dark, tunnel that he thought would never end.

But then it did. And then, he had ejected into the brightly lit room, where he was born. And then, he was roughed up and turned upside down, and spanked and made to howl. And that smell took a long time to go away. But now it was back.

Aryaman Loya would never see any of that again. He did not know that his mother looked sadly into his eyes, as he lay in the car on her lap. He felt the moving car. He felt her hand on his forehead and then he felt her kiss him tenderly.

It was his mother for sure, but why couldn't he see her?

Maybe because it was night?

Nothing changed when Aryaman came home. The same cradle, the same singing mobile sounds, the same smells of baby powder and the same darkness.

What was wrong?

It took him a long time to understand what was wrong, to know the difference between darkness and light—that it was only the absence of light that was called darkness—that light dispelled darkness and changed its length to create colour—that light travels faster than sound, but would not for him—that *light years* is a unit of distance and not time—but before that, he would learn that the gift of sight had been snatched away from him, nine months after he was born—for no fault of his.

His parents had learnt that the foul tasting liquid, the evil miasma, the mixture of paracetamol and pyraquin, *only a precaution,* had adversely affected his optic nerve. The nerve that carries light energy to the optic centre of the brain had been impaired by a virulent reaction to the anti-malaria drug administered, *just for safety,* and that it could not transmit light signals to his brain any more; that it was an occurrence that happens one in a million—a remote chance—a far-fetched possibility; and that it was he, who had been chosen by the hand of fate to be that unfortunate, remote one in a million, *just by chance.*

Specialists from all over the world, after a battery of tests and highly advanced investigative procedures, would come up with a grim diagnosis that Aryaman Loya, the son of Yashoda and Bharat, the grandson of Amba and Ajay Vardhan, the great-grandson of Draupadi and Baldev Das, and the great-great-grandson of G D Rungta would never see again.

He had been blinded—by a sliver of light,
A light that would not show him the way,
Yet if that light went away,
He would see only darkness.

And that would never change. Not for all the money or expertise in the world.

Aryaman's sense of loss would deepen as he grew older, so would his father's guilt and mother's helplessness.

Bharat's heart seized up. He looked down at his hands, the hands that had held his tiny, helpless baby, pinned him down and forced the deathly potion into his mouth. The baby had gagged and retched. They had forced it into his mouth again. The innocent looking syrup—an everyday happening in everyday life—had corroded the tiny nerves, somewhere inside his tiny little eyes that were threaded to his tiny little brain, by a strand, that had a singular, predetermined function. To transmit light signals up and down the pathway, to illumine his world. He stood in the wreckage of his thoughts, enveloped in waves of remorse and smashed his fist on the wall. He was unable to stop his tears. He slid to the floor with his hands tightly clamped into balls, as the finality of the dreadful truth seeped into him. A poison that invaded his consciousness, a guilt pressing down on his heart for having sinned.

Like a continuously moving cinema, the fast-changing images on a circular screen, fading and resonating waves of noise, screeching howls from the oracles that portended doom, the agonising screams of Oedipus Rex gouging out his eyes, stirred the depths of his soul. Thousands of sleeping serpents raised their heads, hissing and spitting, accusing him of what he had done. The real horror was unchangeable and was there to stay. Its holocaust was very different from the truth that he had learned; that the line which divides the hideous from the sublime was not murky and blurred and could not be rubbed out and redrawn at one's will. The truth was, that the blood on his hands would never wash out. Never! The overwhelming guilt drowned out all else. He wrapped his child tightly inside a sheet and held him close to his chest. He lay down on his bed with the baby, but the sinister truth, defying sleep, tugged at his mind. It dragged him back into the deep recesses of a life gone by. The whispers from his soul deafened him. He tried hard not to think of Aliya Hasan.

The year began inauspiciously for the House of Loya. Bharat moved back to Delhi in the winter of 1982, with his wife and family. GI Industries in Bihar had been registering huge losses. There were lockouts and strikes from disgruntled labour unions and The East India Jute Mills had shut down. Bharat Loya arrived in Delhi to take charge of GII, after his unsuccessful stints with jute and the industries in the North-east that were facing serious labour problems, Yashoda had delivered her second child—a girl who was named Aranya.

Amba Loya, who had philosophically accepted her karmic decree, sank deeper into religious evolution and continued to sample different gurus. Nupur had long completed her initiation into life and truth at Osho's Ashram and was back under the tutelage of her mother. Ajay Vardhan suffered his first angina attack in Bombay and was being nursed back to health by his paramour, Devyani. Rashmi Mehta had been banished from his inner coterie and was licking her wounds.

In the Calcutta High Court, a matter of cheating and fraud had been filed by a Brigadier Harish Mehta of Todd Martin and Company against his partner and Managing Director, Ajay Vardhan Loya. Kanupriya's death had been forgotten like an amputated limb, and she had become a small, black-bordered, faceless obituary, in the dusty archives of history.

Yashoda Loya was again in acute depression, a torpid entity who trudged along like a headless phantom, ripe and vulnerable for an affair.

Aryaman had been assigned to the care of an experienced and gentle pediatric nurse from the United States who was specially trained to look after visually challenged children. And the best doctors from all over the world had finally given up on finding a cure for his disability.

27

The Foreign Exchange Regulations Act was amended in 1973. There was hardly any businessman in India who did not at some point fall to the temptation to a breach because a payment even as little as fifty dollars made or received in foreign currency without the prior permission of the Reserve Bank of India was illegal. Violation was a serious criminal offence and punishment was severe.

The Directorate of Enforcement had been vested with the absolute power to interrogate offenders and order arrests. The act terrorised the big and mighty taking into its sweep most everyone. But, more dreaded than the act was the fear of interrogation in custody. Chilling stories of third degree methods used by enforcement officers to extract confessions, some deaths in custody and even one suicide of an accused who jumped from the thirteenth floor of the Enforcement office building, had rattled the toughest of men. Marwaris were not reputed to be tough in such matters—in any case.

Ajay Vardhan Loya had committed two breaches. The first breach of FERA was not uncommon, understandable and to some extent manageable. The second was a grievous error of judgement—misplaced trust in Brigadier Mehta.

Brigadier Mehta was not a man in a hurry but he was an incensed man seeking revenge. Having stockpiled his armoury for years with weapons that would come in handy, his neatly folded dossier, that contained incriminating evidence of FERA violations by his Managing Director and partner in Todd Martin and Company, was ripe for harvesting.

Todd Martin and Company had been registering alarming losses for a period of time, long enough to make him feel cheated. His equity holding too had been diluted by a crafty manipulation technique. His cash flow threatening to stop permanently, Brigadier Mehta decided it was time to press his reserves into service.

Ajay Vardhan Loya's fancy for the Brigadier's wife Rashmi had slackened considerably with age, disability, boredom or all three. He was being nursed back to health by his sister-in-law in Bombay, quite oblivious of the plot being hatched against him.

With Rajiv Gandhi heading the Congress government at the centre and an absolutely incorruptible erstwhile ruler of a small-time state of Uttar Pradesh, Vishvanath Pratap Singh, as Minister of Finance, there was a concerted drive to clean up the rot and the hatchet fell on all FERA offenders. It was scary enough that the draconian law was to be used with great impunity under Mr. Clean, but what was more terrifying was that the office was headed by a man of unimpeachable integrity who, woefully, could not be managed at any cost—not even by the direct intervention of the Prime Minister who also would fall under the hammer of his own decree!

Time had caught up with Ajay Vardhan Loya.

The Calcutta High Court having taken cognizance of Brigadier Mehta's complaint issued a directive to the Enforcement office at the centre to investigate the alleged irregularities of Todd Martin and Company. Simply speaking, they had been directed to ascertain whether Ajay Vardhan Loya was in the possession of a staggering one hundred and fifty to two hundred crore rupees in a numbered account in Switzerland that had been illegally transferred out of the country.

By the time Bharat Loya landed in Delhi to take charge of GII, after his unsuccessful stints with the industries in the North East that were facing serious labour problems, Yashoda delivered her second child—a girl who was named Aranya.

His two younger siblings, Vishal and Nupur, had just begun to crawl out of the woodwork. When he was not living in his elder brother's shadow, Vishal was an unrecognized face who had set his eyes on a nubile, sixteen-year old, dusky, long-haired girl of Punjabi origin.

Priyanka Nanda, an intensely attractive young woman, was the daughter of an army officer. For the sheltered younger sibling of Bharat, with a newly discovered identity, she posed an irresistible challenge. His pursuit, that culminated in marriage, paved the way for two major events in the House of Loya that were to alter their lives, permanently.

It brought her hitherto non-descript brother Uday into contact with Nupur, whom he would marry after a courtship of two years. The Nanda family, that were the relatives of a well-known politician, were to become firmly entrenched into the lives of the Loya brother-sister duo. Both Priyanka Nanda and Uday would be dragged into their marriages which were in themselves peculiar, because the exchange of a daughter for a daughter-in-law, was not generally looked upon as favourable.

The second one was far more significant. If the coming events are said to cast their shadow, then the stage had been set for an exercise wherein the veteran politician, by a quirk of fate, would find himself elevated to a top cabinet post some years later and would be forced to do everything in his power to protect Ajay Vardhan, to help him escape prosecution and arrest. The political arm twisting, however, would not come to a desirable end, because of a stickler for the rules—one R.K. Lyndoh who headed the Enforcement Directorate.

Lyndoh had learned all his moral science lessons at school. He had learned to live, speak and practice the truth—but life was about to teach him another lesson in survival.

28

In the distant idyll of Mauritius, a land of supernatural beauty, enchanting backwaters, exotic flora and fauna, and sun-kissed beaches, a six-foot tall and exceptionally handsome shipping magnate had been raised like a majestic monument—in the lap of luxury and wealth.

Jaywant Mallya was a light-eyed, fresh-complexioned Konkan Brahmin, considered to be a Don Juan of his breed. He was also witty and kind, known for his courtesy and untiring vigour. Love to Jaywant was an absorbing game, in which emotions took second place to sexual urges—more so, after being in a ten-year old staid marriage, with the gentle mother of his two children. Then fate sent him an antidote.

The annual music and dance festival held in Bombay was a three-day glamour event sponsored by the GI Industries where the entire world of art and cinema congregated every winter. For fellow Indians who are known to be notoriously star-struck, the Loyas had the instrument to not merely mingle with the star-set and oblige aspiring wannabe's for personal considerations, but they could also oblige star-gazers by inviting them to their special enclosure to witness the grand ceremony which was followed by lavish cocktails and dinner for the participants and select invitees of the city. It was the high-powered networking ground for GII where lusty politicians and bureaucrats were entertained and accorded all kinds of favours.

It was at one such evening, while Bharat Loya mingled with his guests and Yashoda stood alone in a corner looking tired and bored that Jaywant Mallya, who had specially flown in for the festival, first set eyes on her.

'Hi! I am Jaywant Mallya. Who are you pretty woman? Why have you eluded me all these years?' Jaywant extended his hands and held her by her waist pulling her gently to him. He pecked her on her cheek brushing the corner of her mouth tenderly with his lips and looked deep into her eyes and said,

'I ne'er was struck before this hour,
With love so sudden and so sweet
Your face blooms softly like a flower
And steals my heart away complete.'

A bit startled by this bold and deft move Yashoda stiffened. Jaywant pressed on.

'I never saw so sweet a face
As that I stand before
My heart has left its dwelling place
And can return no more...

Don't be afraid beautiful, I won't bite. Just tell me who you are for no mortal can be as beautiful as this. Who are you?'

'I am Yashoda Loya. Bharat Loya is my husband,' she blurted out nervously.

'Say no more pretty woman,' he said placing his hand lightly over her mouth to muffle her words. 'I want to spend the rest of my life just looking at those gorgeous eyes, no I want to drown in them.' Jaywant's deep and soothing voice touched a chord somewhere in Yashoda's heart. She wanted more. The man had charm. He was flirtatious and irresistible. She had not heard such words in a long time.

It was Yashoda's compelling beauty that had not been ravaged either by her personal torment or her stifling marriage that drew him to her. His quizzical good humour, dominating voice and magnificent dress sense was equally attractive and the situation was tailor-made to turn into a not uncommon tale of permissible adultery between them. A liaison that highlighted once again the attitude of the upper class that spelt a different code. A belief that love and fidelity were mutually independent entities and could coexist separately and without conflict forever. Their volatile chemistry would soon find Yashoda Loya swept off her feet, to be wooed to a point of insanity, by the incredibly handsome shipping tycoon.

In a sense, the dulled ache of Yashoda's personal strifes, the inadvertent casualty inflicted on her first born, and the distant memories of unrequited love intensified her longing to become a whole person again. Jaywant

Mallya had ignited the dormant woman inside her. She found new feathers sprouting in her clipped wings and from the depths of her soul, a little girl screaming to break free.

Jaywant Mallya was indeed riveted to her. Her eyes revealed a sense of loss that he wanted to take a lifetime to understand. The invisible creases of a tragedy that had still not etched her youthful skin began to fade away. Broken shards of glass were shining light into her from the outside—telling her to give that love to the living. Lust moved hotly in her veins. A rare restlessness stirred up inside her. This time it was not encased in fear or desolation—it had the. thrilling quality of adventure.

29

Aryaman Loya was the first to sense his mother's anxiety. Having been divested of a vital one of his five faculties, his sensory system was working overtime, to magnify the stimulus receptivity of the others. Aryaman began to hear colours, touch light, feel shadows, taste hues and smell shapes and forms. He could discern objects and people from an incredible distance and his perception of smell became keener than that of an animal.

For Aryaman, his mother's restlessness was not new. He had felt it when his baby sister was born. His American nanny Paula, with her heavily accented English, had comforted him immensely.

He learned to accept the newcomer who would be sharing their lives and that his mother would have much less time for him. But then he had Paula, his security blanket, his warm comforter, his bean bag, his giant teddy bear. She never let him cry. She never scolded him and he listened to her. He followed her around, clutching her elbow, weaving skilfully, in and out of the corridors of his grey world, heeding approaching and receding sounds. The sound waves computed accurate distances in his ever-active brain and he rarely stumbled or walked into an object. Then all of a sudden, there was another rude intrusion.

His mother was being pulled further away from him. He had barely adjusted to Aranya, but who was this other entity? He tried to conjure up a form. It disturbed him. He ran to Paula and jumped into her all-enveloping arms. The nagging feeling of something wrong, stayed with him, long after.

On Aranya's fifth birthday, Aryaman, a gawky nine-year old, stood awkwardly in the sitting room. Like a plant that tilts its stalk towards the rays of the sun, his head had tilted to one side, from where a sliver of light played hide and seek inside his brain. He felt a constriction in his throat. He had been feeling it for some time. His mother had been dismissive about it.

'You fuss too much,' she said.

He would tell Paula. She listened to him.

Aryaman sensed a strong current between his mother and a stranger in the room. The noises of shuffling and running feet of the dozens of children around him had faded away. He felt uncomfortable, like he had been shut up all by himself, in a cylinder made of one-way mirrored glass. Paula was not there. Only his mother and the other person and him, behind the phantom screen.

He could sense it. His mother's hair was covering half her face. He heard her giggle. She did not do that too often. Her eyes flashed like a schoolgirl's. She sounded different. This was not the mother who had given birth to him.

Then silence.

A smile had crept up his mother's face and brightened her eyes. He knew his mother had jumped across the line that had segregated her, from the rest of her sorrowful world. The stranger pulled her into him and kissed her on her mouth. Her body tensed, and then slackened, and then turned into a limp, lifeless object in his arms. She reached up and took his hand onto the gauzy fabric of the breezy, pastel-coloured chiffon sari that covered her breast.

Aryaman turned away and called out to Paula. How strange it felt that those who had sight could not see. A deep painful envy engulfed him. He despised the alien who got the better kiss and the longer time from his mother. His throat constricted as he called out to Paula, while Yashoda Loya had begun to breathe freely again.

30

Omar Al Fayed's cartel had reasons to rejoice. They had indeed zeroed on the right man. With his established links to the Indian ruling elite there could not have been a better person to represent them than Ajay Vardhan Loya. The cartel that looked after the interest of a Russian conglomerate that manufactured military aircraft also represented an Israeli and a French company that manufactured advanced fighter jets and air-to-air combat missiles. Loya had proved beyond doubt that he was capable of moulding opinions to their advantage and therefore worthy of their patronage.

Undoubtedly India had became the most lucrative market for arms with its multi-billion dollar defence budget and these merchants of death who spent billions of dollars on their research and marketing were going to stop at nothing to peddle their wares. It was no secret that arms procurement in India had a great element of farce and in the garb of national security acquisitions were rarely made public. In this cutthroat race, bribery and kickbacks were rampant and commissions that often ran into millions of dollars were being poured into secret overseas accounts of those who decided purchase and planned future acquisitions.

India's long-winded judicial procedures, its rubber-stamp parliament and its apathetic public had made the executive supremely powerful. Parliament had turned into a mere debating society with no control over ministers and bureaucrats and hugely tempting packages were being doled out by defence agents to a very thirsty government where there were no friends or enemies, there was no embarrassment or apologies and everything hinged on who offered the biggest slice in the pie.

Ajay Vardhan Loya, their main conduit for the flow of information, was also the best facilitator to expedite decision-making in their favour. For this he had access to unlimited funds to grease palms at every level till the contracts were signed and so mired in red tape was the process that sometimes deals could spread over several years and changes of government before they materialised.

Ajay Vardhan Loya was a skilled juggler adept at managing these divergent forces and it was fortunate that by sheer osmosis his son had imbibed his acumen, because within the four walls of the House of Loya trouble was brewing.

Gajanand Loya had been serving GII for over almost two decades. A distant cousin of Ajay Vardhan Loya and a part of the Doon School alumini, he had earned the complete confidence of his Chairman and was privy to all his undercover operations. Within the hierarchy of

GI Industries, Gajanand could be described as the last of the royal Indian feudals. As the Chief Liaison Officer and most trusted man of Ajay Vardhan, his past success graph had made him a satellite power who revelled in his office, the office that gave him the unique ability and instrument to mould minds and modify opinion. He was reputed to be on first name terms with the Prime Minister who was his alumnus from the glorious Doon School. Due to his frontal and intellectual belligerence, he had been given complete freedom of conduct, by the proprietors who used his office and connections for their own advantage in the corridors of power.

Gajanand Loya's boldness was a product of his unshakeable commitment to his job. Seated on the illustrious chair of his office, with his expansive frame and markedly dismissive manner, running his private *jagir*, Gajanand had no qualms about the despotic set-up he commanded. In such a climate, where he had freed himself from a day-to-day connectivity with his proprietors, he was scarcely prepared to entertain puny little Bharat Loya, with his ancestral pomposity and public school attitude, worn on his sleeve. Neither was Bharat accustomed to being reminded of his lowly status, in the official and intellectual hierarchy of his father's domain. The clash between the two titans, whose similarities ended with their family names, was imminent.

It would destroy the classic and inherent structure of their working module, and teach them that managers and directors, even if they came from the same bloodline, were dispensable commodities, particularly those with grandiose notions about themselves and that power was the singular prerogative of the proprietors and none else.

This was no mean feat for the slight, self-effacing, bespectacled, scion of the House of Loya, whose blocked sinuses and obsessive hand-washing habit gave no indication of the volatile forces that held him together.

As the 1980s were rolling along, Ajay Vardhan Loya was facing difficult times. The slow and steady dragnet of FERA had closed in on him. The government had initiated an enquiry into the sale of a French fighter aircraft by a shadowy Panamanian company believed to be owned by a Saudi Arabian billionaire and Omar Al Fayed had been recently blacklisted by the Defence Ministry. There were strong rumours that the Loyas had an equity holding of over thirty-five per cent in an Israeli company that had sold air missiles to India. A Swedish radio had made a sensational revelation that slush money had been paid by a gun manufacturer to a secret account in Switzerland to secure a huge contract from the Indian Army and loud clamours to trace the beneficiaries and ban middlemen from the defence trade were being heard in Parliament.

Brigadier Mehta's treachery had left Ajay Vardhan nursing a bruised ego and a malfunctioning heart. Devyani, Ajay Vardhan's last paramour, could only give him emotional solace. Amba and Nupur were encapsulated in their own world of pseudo-spiritualism and were unreachable.

Rumours of all not being well between Vishal and his bride were rife. Yashoda's scandalous liaison with Mallya was being talked of in embarrassingly loud whispers, and the profits from the Loya business concerns had nose-dived to an all-time low. Bharat's arrogance and clash with Gajanand Loya was threatening to disrupt the well-oiled machinery of GII.

Gajanand Loya was conducting his morning office as usual, staring up into space, behind wispy clouds of aromatic smoke coming from his finely crafted Dunhill pipe. Orating extempore, to a secretary furiously scribbling on a writing pad, he was dictating a letter as he paused now and then to light up. In the realm of power within an Indian business set-up, there could hardly have been a parallel to him, as he officiously communicated his voice and decree, which had remained unaffected by the turbulence in the prevailing political climate. He regarded his role as indispensable, not only to the organisation he headed, but also to his associates in high places, and gloated on his superior faculties that had earned him this exalted status.

Bharat Loya had set foot on a hostile domain. A shade disappointed by the antiquated state of the office, he barged into Gajanand's room expecting a rousing and princely welcome. Gajanand Loya recognised the unannounced intruder. Displeased by the young man's arrogance, he felt the anger rise in him. He continued his dictation after a barely perceptible pause to convey to the visitor that no one or nothing was important enough to disrupt his chain of thoughts.

Bharat shuffled his feet deliberately, pulled a chair and sat down. After a good twenty minutes, Gajanand

Loya finished dictating his letter and with a slight gesture of his hand dismissed his secretary from his room. A few other people present from the staff stayed seated. Gajanand Loya peered at Bharat over his glasses with a deadpan expression.

Bharat Loya pushed his hand forward smiling, and began, 'You were not expecting me here Mr. Loya, I can see. Was there something so important that you could not interrupt when I came in? I only came to tell you that I shall be working here from now on. My chair is in my father's office and you can expect to see me every morning. As you will know soon, I am planning a few changes in the present set-up that we can discuss, which shall, of course, be for the good of us all.'

Gajanand Loya in all his years of service and much less in the last five, had never been spoken 'at' by anyone, not even by the highest offices of the land including that of the Prime Minister. And here was this slight public school greenhorn, unable to run a jute or cement factory, a failure at accounting and commerce, with a visible disdain for employees, telling him obliquely, who was the boss.

A range of conflicting emotions surged up in him. He took off his glasses and placed them carefully on the table. He swivelled his chair at an angle away from the unpleasant intruder. His posture was both repellent and hostile. And then he spoke:

'Your entry into this organisation, young man, is your own business and the prerogative of your family, but you will be well advised if you keep the ambit of your functioning and your ideas confined to your father's office, not mine. Start from the ground floor, it is good to begin at the lowest. It may not be a bad idea to extend your expertise in maintaining and cleaning the toilets. Please refrain from intrusions into my room without prior appointment, because you do understand that I keep a maddening schedule and an agenda with punishing deadlines!'

Without waiting to simulate the cloud on Bharat's face, Gajanand Loya picked up his pipe, turned the lighter upside down over its bowl and inhaled in quick spurts, as the gas flame rose and fell in the same tempo as his breath. He pretended he had not seen Bharat Loya leave the room as he punched a button on his intercom to summon his secretary.

Smarting under the insult, seething with rage, Bharat stepped out of Gajanand's office for the last time, as a blubbering under-confident, fourth-generation owner. His singed ego, the remnant of mysterious experiments in his subconscious, propelled him towards absolution and revenge. It was the only way to make amends with himself. How dare he? That too in the presence of his father's lesser staff. His childhood fear of ridicule loomed large before him as he replayed the sequence of events in a slow rewind. The mocking words pounded loudly in his ears. He sat down behind his father's desk and drafted out a circular.

31

There is something pathetic about a man who is being cuckolded by his wife, because nothing can be more humiliating than being the object of pity, one who is perceived to be carrying a morbid burden upon his shoulders. He emits an ashen aura of the terminally ill, even if he is ignorant of the duplicity around him. The cheating spouse however, radiates confidence, an air of triumph, a sort of smug insensitivity, transparent to all, but the victim.

If the suffering victim takes on a lover too, believing the sinning spouse to be either oblivious of the trespass or unconcerned, then it is quid pro quo, and the element of pity vanishes. If there exists a licenced *laissez faire* between the two, then there is no social burden and it is less unsettling for outsiders.

Bharat Loya belonged to the third category, he just did not care. Having understood the cues from all the essential changes around him, the elation in his wife's mood, her frequent trips to Mauritius and the casual visits of Jaywant Mallya, he recognised that his wife was having an affair. From inside his fractured world, he felt distant enough to grant her the lease to sleep with the high-powered shipping magnate, who was clearly lusting for her.

Yashoda's infidelity had given him a sort of extraneous energy. Contrary to what most would imagine, it made him feel perversely buoyant and free. The internalised rejection would manifest later. It would invade his professional life like a blazing inferno, to destroy anything that stood in its path. His main assault would be on the senior managerial cadres and competitors of GII whose methods did not match his. He would pummel them down or throw them out. By an atypical departure from the norm, he would morph into an unchallenged emperor, to be admired, applauded and intensely despised—a far cry from the pitiable cuckold, or the guilt-ridden father of a physically challenged child.

On a secluded beach in Mauritius, stretching in a slow curve along the shimmering blue sea and the water-drenched shores, two beautiful beings lay inside a cool and shallow lagoon. Sheltered by a natural umbrella of swaying trees and a row of sharply rising monolithic boulders, they were absorbed in a symphony of the dancing and singing waves, feeling a surreal sense of joy. The urgent rush of the deep water reverberated between the figures, who were equally distinct in their form and beauty; a pair sculpted by angels in heaven, to lie in sinful embrace on earth. Like the legendary poet-musician Orpheus, Jaywant Mallya had descended into the nether world, to bring back his Eurydice, from the dead. Both shared the burning passion of those in love—the compelling ardour of forbidden dreamers and the immortal vigour of need and desire. Breaking out of the shackles of their private worlds, each one had forgotten that they were tied down by their respective offspring, and legally wedded spouses, in their separate identities. For now it sufficed that they had each other, and they had frozen this glorious moment in their timescapes.

Yashoda lay beside Jaywant, lulled into a semi-stupor, half-covered by a luminous sheath of flowing water. Grains of wet sand sparkled on her skin that was tinged with the gold and pink hues of the setting sun. A choreographed ballet of rising and falling waves, emanated from her breast. She stared at the sea being wrinkled and pinched by the wind, and splintered by the golden sun. She counted the waves that breathed in and out upon her, as she lay on the vast, psychedelic shore. A million images of her were cast onto the water and her hair floated out like a glowing halo, around her head.

She drew a big heart on the wet sand and inscribed inside it two initials, Y + J. Then she watched the grooves fill up with froth and foam and drain out over and over, till they disappeared.

She called out to him several times between sighs and words, 'Jaywant... I love you to death my Jaywant.' In this space there was no Bharat, no Aryaman, no Aranya whispering sweet rhymes, only one single feeling of euphoria. She had moved physically through time, to flee from them all. 'I love you, I need you. You madden me Jay, you really do.'

She whispered into his ear, spilling out her rage, her despair, her loss, her love. She needed him to drive out the ghouls from her soul. Jaywant kissed her for the hundredth time that evening.

He pushed her gently onto the soft mattress of the wet sand and she held on to him, to ride into a new life, on the other side. Millions of warm fireflies lit up inside her, expanding in howls and swirls from the ocean depths, as she let go of her human form to experience a profusely, fulfilling climax. She had been granted her most temporal wish, to find a doorway out of her ruined heart into merciful adultery.

Back in the capital, in the sacred dining-room of GI House, where gossip, intrigue, innuendoes and ribald jokes prevailed, the first shock waves within the tradition-bound institution were being felt. The imminent signs of a drastic make-over were hanging like a thick cloud in the air. Various exaggerated accounts of the disastrous encounter between the two Loyas were being passed around like an easily available drug that is slightly taboo and immensely enjoyable.

While the administration had been gearing up to adapt to their new boss's whims, Bharat Loya had already initiated a drastic restructuring of the office. Ajay Vardhan's room was stripped bare and refurbished by a French interior design company. Several paintings by Indian masters came up on the walls. Expensive crystal and silver objects of art were kept around his table and rosewood wall cabinets were fitted with a large TV screen and music system.

Hardly showing signs of his genealogical brilliance, Bharat received only half-hearted support from his father who was too harassed by the FERA inquiry looming before him to intervene. But soon the industry would be compelled to sit up and take notice of the slight framed, effeminate, heir-apparent, of the august Loya family, who pushed off on a study tour to New York, after he had a company law book thrown at him by an account's director telling him to learn all the clauses.

'Like hell,' he muttered, as he sifted through his organiser, reclining on the first class window seat of an American Airlines airbus.

Just then, Yashoda had boarded a flight to her fortnightly escape into a dream world at Mauritius; and Vishal Loya was stealthily checking into a room in a suburban hotel in Bombay, with a well-known model who had been promised an exciting future at GII at the owner's behest.

Changes at Global Integrity Industries had begun.

32

'You are having an affair with that cheesy slut from Delhi aren't you Jay?' The clipped, nasal London-accent of his wife jarred on Jaywant's ears. 'I've seen her throw herself at you, the foolish bitch and melt like a candle the moment she spots you. And all it takes for you idiotic men to go berserk is fluttering eyelashes and wiggling asses. You make me sick.'

A hardened Sindhi from the upper echelons of London society, Jaywant Mallya's wife Samara was a beautiful woman with a shapely body, fair skin, large eyes and a full pink mouth. With all the trappings of a trophy wife fit for a flamboyant shipping tycoon, she had made the transition from London to Mauritius effortlessly after they were married and had settled into her husband's opulent life-style, flying frequently to holiday destinations around the globe with or without him.

Samara Mallya was a hard and practical woman for whom her French manicure and blow-dried hair mattered more than her husband or his Elizabethan poetry. Her genteel daddy's girl persona and British manner could not quite camouflage her passion for acquisitions and her obsession for wealth. Quite comfortably, she turned into a vacuous lunching lady totting rock-size diamonds, branded clothes and expensive designer bags much like the other women of her ilk.

Within the first three years of their marriage, Samara had given birth to two beautiful girls who inherited the best features from both their parents. As if on cue their romance went up in smoke immediately and the couple drifted into an open marriage and separate bedrooms.

The children were packed off to an expensive private school in the Swiss Alps where they would be instilled with a finesse and education fit for international royals.

Jaywant Mallya was silent as Samara's tirade continued. He had mastered the art of shutting out the irritating sound of her voice. Samara too had worked out a perfect formula. She ignored her husband's philanderings... and there were many... as long as she could shop incessantly and mindlessly at all the fancy stores around the world.

Undoubtedly, her husband's frequent trips to India and that Loya creature's visits to Mauritius warranted looking into, but she preferred to translate it into more jewellery and more designer wear and keep the harmony and her power to blackmail intact.

Samara felt frustrated, having elicited no reaction from Jaywant. She stormed out of his study into her own bedroom cursing loudly. 'You'll do anything for a fuck you asshole. You deserve each other.' Jaywant's undisguised lust for Yashoda Loya had not really rattled her. She was accustomed to Jaywant's ways. In fact, it had given her another chance to extract something from him. She picked up the phone and punched in a London number.

'Bonjour! this is Cartier of Bond street. Whom would you like to speak to?' 'This is Samara Mallya from Mauritius. Can I speak to Jean Pierre please? Hello Jean Pierre.... Yes thank you I am fine. Could you please have the ring I had reserved from your new collection sent to my London address right away... it was fifty thousand pounds wasn't it? Charge it to my husband's account. Oh yes, Jean Pierre, I would also like you to send me the catalogue for your limited edition of diamond necklaces please. I'm going to choose something for my birthday next month.' She laughed a short throaty laugh. 'Yes indeed my husband is a very kind and generous man. I shall certainly give him your regards... thank you Jean Pierre... and I'll be in London for the opening of the new Cartier store in spring for sure. Good bye.'

Samara put the phone down. A contented smile played on her face. She was going to be the envy of her clan at the wedding of her cousin in Hong Kong next month where all the rich Sindhis of the world were going to congregate for a week-long celebration. There would be no one more expensively dressed or with bigger diamonds than hers. She reveled in the feeling.

'He's all yours Yashoda Loya...' she snorted... 'for me diamonds are my best friend!'

Back in his study, Jaywant Mallya sat staring at the rolling ocean outside his window, musing at the shape his life had taken. Samara, his wife of seven years, the mother of his children was totally out of his physical and emotional orbit. What a sharp contrast there was between her and the demure and soft-spoken Yashoda Loya, the one woman whom he could have given up his kingdom for. How nice it would have been if he could have Yashoda by his side at all times.

The thought of the soft and feminine traits that Yashoda embodied stirred his soul and lifted his spirit. The caustic sting of the words he had just heard faded away. He knew that Samara could be silenced any time with just a fistful of diamonds. He pushed Samara's hard countenance out of his head and walked out.

Yashoda would be waiting for him at his private cottage. Nothing else mattered.

Aditya Daga was getting impatient. Try as he did he could not get through to his cousin Bharat Loya. Each time he tried to call him he met with the same answer. Almost a cold rebuff.

'Mr. Loya is busy Sir. If you could leave your number he'll get back to you as soon as possible.'

'I'm family dammit. I'm his cousin. Have you even told him how many times I've called?' Aditya couldn't hide his irritation.

'But of course, Sir. Mr. Loya has asked me to tell you he'll call you shortly.'

But Bharat Loya never did. It was a dead end. A frustrating fucking dead end. Aditya knew the Loyas were big in the arms trade and had links with all the top politicians. He did not want to let go of the opportunity that had fallen into his lap. He needed their help with the minister who was rumoured to be on their payroll. He was confident that the prospect of a large amount of easy money would get him a break-through. But only if he could speak to Bharat.

What a long way the son-of-a-bitch has come, he rued. The short, whimpering, under confident, bloody son-of-a-bitch; his *chamcha* of their childhood days had actually declined to talk to him. He seethed with anger at Bharat Loya's arrogance. But Aditya Daga was not one to give up.

33

The Loya House women were a distinct breed. Everything they did was guaranteed to shock. Nupur Loya had inherited these traits from her grandmother and her overpowering mother. She was to exist in a marriage bound by a clearly defined prenuptial arrangement, where her spouse, like her father and grandfather, would not be given the option to demand conjugal rights from his wife. Like his two older counterparts, he too would have to be content with tending to her needs and taking care of his business plans that had borne ample fruit.

Uday Nanda married Nupur Loya when she turned thirty. Actually it was a reprehensible arrangement cobbled together with the consent of Ma Amba, on the insistence of their Bhagwan Guru. Nupur, who was robotically controlled by her mother, had fulfilled much of her bodily desires in unconventional outlets, primarily Osho's ashram in Poona, and had been living with her future husband for some months, but directed by her mother, she retained a kind of aloofness in her marriage.

When Uday Nanda first met her Nupur Loya seemed a self-effacing, slightly under-confident, but sexually permissive young woman whose name camouflaged most of her flaws. Uday Nanda was abnormally smitten by her. He pursued her continuously for months, sharing wild and deviant sexual fantasies with her, right under her mother's nose.

Amba Loya encouraged this continuous physical and emotional interplay with enthusiasm. Like a devoted lover, Uday Nanda was staunchly reverential to Ma Amba, whose liberal sanction for premarital sex, he naturally perceived as approval for a prospective son-in-law. Soon he moved into their home and became a disciple of their Bhagwan Guru, who ostensibly ruled the mother-daughter duo's thinking and conduct. Had it not been for her intervention, he would have continued living with Nupur out of wedlock despite the disapproval of the conservative people around them. It was only on Bhagwan Guru's decree, that he was forced to tie the knot and walk around the sacred fire seven times, to become the son-in-law of the mighty Loyas.

Like a good Punjabi groom, Uday Nanda arrived on the wedding day with a veil of flowers covering his face, riding a horse led by his friends, dancing in frenzied abandon. The procession stopped several times before they arrived at the bride's house.

The rolling drums had reached a deafening pitch as he alighted from the horse and walked up to the platform, where he exchanged garlands with his bride-to-be. The family showered rose petals on them, but the overload of classic sexual stimuli that accompanies most Indian weddings was absent and there was no pretence of a novel encounter with a chaste, virgin bride.

Unknowingly, Uday Nanda had already turned into the caricature that would be entirely controlled by the Loyas. The sexual and emotional compatibility with his wife-to-be that he believed he had sampled had already been expended with in this gourmet liaison of his choice.

True to form, doing things differently, Ajay Vardhan Loya sat at the religious wedding ceremony all alone. Ma Amba had walked off in a huff saying, 'I will not give her away like an animal. She is my child not a cow or a bull to be given away in charity.' She had sprawled theatrically on a garden bench in full view of the spectators. This bizarre display of histrionics surprised no one.

Predictably, the magic of the moment vanished as soon as the seven mandatory circumventions around the fire were completed.

Uday moved into a separate bedroom inside the resplendent home, gifted to him by his in-laws, with the echoes of the prenuptial understanding resounding in his ears.

You can take the hand of our daughter in marriage, but it is her will that shall run in your home and you shall not have the right to either question her or try to prevent her, from doing anything she desires…

The last time Uday Nanda slept with his wife was the day before they were married. The rumour mills as usual had a field day. They played havoc with their lives and sanity, though inside sources confirmed that the couple slept in separate bedrooms, symbolic of separate identities and distinctly separate existences.

Nupur's younger brother Vishal Loya also turned out to be more than his wife Priyanka had bargained for because each of the two Loya descendants had their branded airs of supremacy and the primary disability to be in normal marriages. They formed the superior but clearly crippled rung of the social ladder, inhabiting their own secluded glassed-in worlds.

But, Ajay Vardhan Loya's only son-in-law Uday Nanda enjoyed an envious status. After inheriting a major shareholding in GII and a sumptuous cash back-up, he went on a wild expansion spree, in keeping with his progressive management background. His theoretical expertise found a platform for experiment, when he took over the Ritz Grand, a five-star hotel in the capital and tied up for the franchise of a well-known international chain, and everything seemed rosy for him for the time being.

While the entire Loya conglomerate was celebrating their relentless expansion and diversification Amba Loya was nominated to the Upper House of Parliament by the President of India for her services to society and the cause of women. Rajiv Gandhi, the clean, handsome, son of Indira Gandhi, with an attitude bred in the dormitories of the famous Doon School, was Prime Minister. A grand reception was held on the sprawling lawns of Loya House, where he was invited by GI Industries to felicitate the newly elected Rajya Sabha MP. Omar Al Fayed was seen mingling freely with the guests that included several cabinet ministers, senior bureaucrats, the chiefs of the armed forces, some members of the diplomatic corps and glitterati that spanned the industrial world. A beautiful, coloured glossy booklet was brought out by the Loyas that contained messages of felicitations from the Prime Minister, heads of international organisations, top-ranking industrialists and senior politicians.

The panoramic event turned out to be a huge success that earned for them unprecedented publicity and an enhanced social prestige. Their proximity to the Prime Minister and the ruling party was clearly established and the Loyas felt more empowered than ever before.

Undeterred by this, the Enforcement Director, R. K. Lyndoh's investigation had stealthily spread its tentacles into their subterranean world. A sudden swoop on all the offices and homes of the GII proprietors, directors and senior staff throughout the country was brewing. A five-hundred strong raiding team was waiting on full alert, and the first assault on the impervious and powerful institution was waiting to happen.

34

No one really knew of the existence of Vishal Loya the unobtrusive younger sibling of Bharat Loya till he took charge as Director Public Relations of GII. To pander to his own desire for recognition and his genetic weakness for the flesh, he could not have found a more satisfying medium. He soon assumed the self-assigned role of puppeteer in their extended world of power and wealth and bagged the natural benefits of wannabe women willing to grant favours for a price.

Priyanka, the incumbent casualty, was undergoing consistent assaults in her fledgling marriage. She was watching her dreams come crashing down. How long she would hold out, became the favourite guessing game of the chattering class.

For his part, Vishal Loya had meticulously woven around himself, a cavalier picture of a billionaire playboy, with a bounty of floozies and starlets that served to camouflage his closely hidden, sexual dysfunction. He presented a sinfully, attractive image of *the most eligible married man*. The quiet sufferer Priyanka, could have experienced no greater anguish, but silenced by personal embarrassment and good breeding, she maintained a dignity in her pain, so if any suspicion was to arise regarding the virility of the younger Loya, she was giving no evidence to substantiate it.

Priyanka soon found solace in the age-old and time-tested formula, the arms of a willing and younger cousin of her husband, who was only too happy to provide her the physical and emotional therapy she so desperately needed. The quid pro quo restored their mental and marital balance for the time being.

Aryaman Loya was growing up a spoilt and difficult child. Like most privileged children and all handicapped ones, he was undergoing his private ordeal in a broken home. He had stopped fussing about the prolonged absences of his mother and father, but his dependence on Paula had grown to pathological proportions.

A state-of-the-art set up was created to educate him, and the best facilities that money could buy, were made available to equip him to deal with the adult world, despite his visual impairment.

Although he did accompany his parents on occasional trips within and outside the country, he never felt totally at ease without Paula. Like all mixed-up adolescent boys, he too had his share of tantrums, that were most often attended to by Paula and ignored by the others. The constriction in his throat always worsened after a hysterical episode and gradually eased up, on its own. The doctors had dismissed it as nothing, so no one gave much importance to it and he began to treat it as one of his other abnormalities that was there to stay.

Aryaman was taken on a trip to Mauritius by his mother, when Paula left for her month-long annual holiday to the United States. It was the first time he would be without her, in a new place.

Aryaman had learned about the sea and its salinity. He could taste the salty air and feel the droplets of water on his skin, as he breathed deeply inside the private beach house, in which they stayed. He could sense the enormity of the volatile and restless water body. The restlessness crept into him too. He had become acquainted with the stranger whom he addressed as 'Uncle', who always gave him a lot of attention.

Aryaman just could not bring himself to like him. His mother was never herself, when this uncle was around—she was not herself these days at all, or she was absent altogether. He didn't know which he preferred. His sister Aranya and he had been brought there, to spend their Christmas holidays that year.

His father was away in New York. Nothing new. He was always away. He wished Paula had not gone. He ached to be with her or with his Dad in New York—closer to Paula. He had begun counting down for her return, even before she had left. She had promised to come back soon. No one could ever take her place—not even his mother.

Aryaman reclined lazily on a chair, listening to the pitter-patter of falling rain that beat a rhythm, with the music playing in the background. He tried to sleep.

The incessant rain resounded for miles around the solitary beach house. It pulled up the waves in a tantalisng striptease and pounded the sand with a passionate zeal. The dark sky was silhouetted with the twinkling lights of the quaint island in the distance. A limitless expanse of water stretched to the line where the sky kissed the earth.

Yashoda stared out from the window of the cabin. Her eyes travelled rapidly forward, to the endless end. Her gaze profiled the sea that was being carved into crevices by the spears of rain. A cloud rumbled in the distance and the music of falling rain filled the sky.

Jaywant Mallya stood for a long time behind her. Then he stretched his hands and gently touched the nape of her neck. She swirled around to face him. In the air saturated with sea-spray that had wafted in through the open windows, he kissed her—tasting the salt on her lips and breath. He kissed her neck and breasts and took her into his arms, away from her body and conscious thoughts, into another plane.

Yashoda grabbed his shoulders greedily as she closed her eyes and commanded everything in her mortal world to shut up. She pulled her T-shirt off over her head and stepped out of her jeans. Her luminous skin and deep glowing eyes had never looked so beautiful before.

In the adjoining room, Aryaman tossed and turned restlessly, as the horrible constriction in his throat came up again and Aranya had curled up in bed, to watch a *Tom and Jerry* show.

Far away in Delhi, Vishal and Priyanka were out celebrating Christmas separately and Amba Loya and Nupur were in a spiritual retreat at an ashram in Haridwar, enjoying their own liberation.

More than ten hours behind them in Washington, a crisp winter morning witnessed Bharat Loya scouring the plush office of Dextron Systems, the largest manufacturers of missiles and submarines in the US accompanied by Omar Al Fayed. He had a folder marked TOP SECRET tucked under his arm that contained classified documents from the Indian Ministry of Defence.

Twelve hours later, a door bell rang simultaneously, in fifteen different homes and offices of the GII to announce the arrival of the most dreaded raiding teams from the Directorate of Enforcement, under the aegis of one R. K. Lyndoh.

35

In the last three years, during which the country had witnessed the brutal assassination of ex-prime minister, Rajiv Gandhi, and three general elections in 1989, 1990 and 1991, the political climate had become highly unstable. The Congress government brought in by a cynical and apathetic public, was hanging on a fragile thread, that could snap on the slightest jerk.

This instability had sent nervous tremors into the foundations of the economy and a radical and strong governance was the need of the hour. Limping on the crutches of corruption, nepotism and selfish power mongering, the nation had come to a complete standstill. Anyone who had a stake or a contact in high places could strike anywhere and vandals and dacoits were having a field day. At such a time, the sudden swoop down on Ajay Vardhan Loya's establishment seemed a trifle incongruous.

The raiding teams however, seized a number of incriminating documents from their various targets that were enough to construct a foolproof criminal case against the Chairman.

The Directorate of Enforcement issued a summons to Ajay Vardhan, to present himself for interrogation at a stipulated date, where it was proposed to impound his passport and, if necessary, arrest him which was well within its purview.

Ajay Vardhan Loya's in-house experts were put on high alert, to devise ways to protect him. A list of people in high places who were beholden to him and could be of help, was drawn up.

Even as Brigadier Mehta gloated over the first successful salvo fired at his adversary, savouring his dish of sweet revenge, Amba and Bharat came rushing back to Delhi, to provide moral comfort to the persecuted man, and furious activity was underway in the Prime Minister's Office, to salvage the honour of Ajay Vardhan Loya.

Within the next twenty-four hours, Ajay Vardhan suffered a debilitating heart attack and had to be admitted to the All India Institute of Medical Sciences at Delhi.

This served two purposes. The overt one was to be treated at the Coronary Intensive Care Unit, for his life-threatening condition. The hidden but more crucial one was to evade the horrific interrogatory session by the Directorate of Enforcement, that could hold credence as evidence admissible in a court of law. Life for everyone connected with the GII came to a grinding halt.

Until the time Bharat Loya had barged into the sanctum sanctorum of the Chief Liaison Officer, the last bastion of the autocratic nabob at GI House it had a history of dated administrators, shut up in formidable ivory towers. Back from his short stint at the US, he was all set to shatter the moulds of convention—to grab it by the scruff of its neck and shake it up. The impenetrable teak doors of the cabins that housed the august old-timers, were awaiting their demolition in an orchestrated drive by Bharat Loya, perhaps, to assuage his public spurning, the stinging insult by Gajanand Loya, that he was not willing to forget in a hurry.

'Profits first and ideals afterwards.'

'We'll give the customers what they want—freebies, cuts, bribes or even bare bodies. What the hell!'

'What difference does it make as long as we sell goddammit!'

'We are in the business to make money—let someone else sell ideals.'

His one-liners reverberated down the newly refurbished building of GII, a renovation that had now moved far beyond the masonry and woodwork.

Bharat Loya believed that only young yuppies of the new age could run the company efficiently. He was determined to get rid of all the insufferable old stuffed-shirts who were redundant in his scheme of things and highly expendable. Predictably, Gajanand Loya was shown the door after he was caught in a compromising position with one of his junior colleagues, whom he had been desperately pushing for seniority and some evidence of misappropriation surfaced. That provided the management, the lever to push him out, without the ceremonial bugles of farewell that he deserved. He was immediately replaced by a young and energetic fresh face, parachuted in from Paris, to occupy the illustrious chair.

The ever-eager Maharashtrian, Phillipe Chitle, with a high degree of intellect and a fashionable fluency in French, could not have been prepared for the assault on his ego, that he would undergo, before he moulted three times over, to become the perfect entity. A faceless, mindless, spineless, robotic, genetically mutated organism, who possessed only an auditory sense organ and motor responses, voice-trained to respond solely to the MD. The MD, who loathed employees who had notions about themselves, had begun his exercise in demonstrating once and for all, who was the boss.

Within a few months, the dividing walls between administrators and the lower staff were taken down. This sent ripples of horror within the entire organisation. Outsiders and weather pundits scoffed at the recklessness of this assault, believing, that those whom the Gods wish to destroy, they first turn mad.

Within the GII set-up, all those who held these radical changes in contempt, were given the option to leave, or were sacked. The profit graphs from all the companies slowly began to climb, even as the conventionalists sneered and the perpetrator's dictatorial violence continued, unabated.

Egos had never been so brutally savaged before, but from that cataclysmic churning, there emerged a whole new attitude to the business of brokering and networking and if their trade was surprised by Bharat Loya's sudden business acumen, it was going to be set back even more by his next move.

Meanwhile, in a discreet bureaucratic reshuffle two persons were appointed to very crucial posts in the Ministry of Defence. They were known cronies of the Loyas and had been enjoying their largesse for a long period of time. Their children as also the children of some top military brass were studying in the United States at the Wharton Business School and the Massachusetts Institute of Technology on fully paid scholarships from their generous benefactors.

This set the stage to clear the pending proposal for the purchase of a highly sophisticated combat aircraft from a particular Russian company that had its links with Omar Al Fayed and the mighty House of Loyas.

Ajay Vardhan Loya had taken a quiet back seat. Debilitated in spirit and body, by the relentless investigation of the Enforcement Directorate and his coronary condition, he took refuge in his expert advisory team and the business was left entirely to Bharat Loya.

An appointment was set up for consulting the world's best cardiac-care centre in Cleveland, at Ohio. All government formalities were completed including the mandatory clearance from the Reserve Bank that sanctioned the foreign exchange for his treatment. Three first class tickets, with a special request for a low-calorie vegetarian meal, were reserved on an American airline, for a date, four weeks after Ajay Vardhan Loya's heart attack.

On the legal side, several petitions were filed in various courts. An urgent application for anticipatory bail was moved in a sessions court in Delhi, which was denied, but a subsequent one in the High Court granted some relief, when it ruled that the Enforcement Directorate could only arrest the accused, after obtaining a clearance from a specially constituted medical board. The fact that the medical board had been chosen by none other than the petitioner himself, was no secret.

Another petition was moved in the High Court, alleging that the enforcement officer's investigation was vexatious and motivated, and that there should be an immediate injunction on the proceedings, to prevent undue harassment of the ailing Chairman of GI Industries. Another interim petition obtained a favourable ruling, by which the Directorate of Enforcement was restrained from interrogating the accused, except in the presence of the approved medical committee.

While Ajay Vardhan Loya began packing his bags to leave for the United States away from the horrific spectre of interrogation and arrest, the Directorate of Enforcement had tied themselves in knots over this unexpected setback.

Now Ajay Vardhan's departure for medical treatment stymied the investigation process, indefinitely. The underlying gain was to avail of a clause that stipulated filing of a charge sheet within a year of seizing of evidence—six months had already lapsed for the case to close.

But there was more flak to come onto the morally upright and incorruptible Lyndoh.

36

In a completely contrasting and illusory world preparations for a grand celebration were underway. The capital was agog with the homecoming of the victorious Indian Cricket Team that was returning to a jubilant nation with the GI Gold Cup—a prestigious international trophy sponsored by the Loyas.

Wah! Wah! India! The slogan had never rung louder before. The city of Delhi laid out its best red carpet to receive the victorious eleven. Television crews, camera men, newspaper reporters and thousands of star-struck Delhites, lined the streets, waving flags and banners to greet them. The roads were festooned with colourful streamers and lights, alongside a barrage of posters and hoardings put up by the official sponsors, the GII. Floral gateways were constructed at several points along the route, from the airport to India Gate, through which they would be driven in an open carriage, with the pomp and regalia akin to that of the Viceregal days.

The front pages of all the national dailies were splashed with snapshots of glorious moments of the matches and individual profiles of the players. All the

Merchants of Death

important magazines scrambled with each other, to write about the magical victory. Messages of felicitation from the Prime Minister and President took up prominent positions on the front pages and grand receptions were scheduled as part of the salutary ceremony.

Dozens of corporate houses were ready with contracts that would take the winners into their exciting world of commercial advertising. Soft drinks bottlers had found the face of the year, to sell their products, and a host of jewellery, apparel and watch manufacturing companies had zeroed-in, on their brand ambassadors. Indeed 'India's Eleven' had struck the jackpot. By their astounding victory they had stepped into the ultra-glamorous hall of fame, with a bounty of riches and glory, lying at their feet.

There could have been no greater testimony to the fact that cricket, wealth and glamour go hand in hand together. As the official sponsors, the Loyas held a grand reception for the team at the Ritz Grand hotel where a bevy of filmstars, media personalities, politicians and the capital's glitterati were in attendance in full force.

Large hampers filled with choicest liquor and exotic foods were doled out to the winners as Vishal Loya circulated among the guests. Clinging on to his arm was a budding starlet, his choice date for the evening. In the backdrop a gigantic TV screen was showing replays of the final match and the historic victory.

As the photographers and TV crew jostled for space in the mega-star event there were hushed whispers about the political and underworld links of the chief of GII, Bharat Loya, who was conspicuous by his absence.

His highly visible brother Vishal Loya however was in a trance as he held the statuesque woman who looked like a Botticelli painting close to him and watched the screen distractedly. Shouts of jubilation and cheer deluged his senses...

He was transported into a celluloid dream, where he pranced around an artificial lake filled with floating candles and pink lilies, dressed in a satin shirt and tight fitted white satin trousers, that bulged around his crotch, singing a song to his heroine adorned in a snowy white net and lace gown, looking like an ethereal maiden, descended from heaven. She was wearing pink roses in her long cascading hair and her rose-bud lips parted in synchrony, as she mimed the words of the song with him... she was blowing him kisses... winding her willowy arms around his torso, tripping and dancing in tune with the music...

Vishal Loya was stirred with joy and pride. The delirious pleasure of being able to display the trophy on his arm and the joyous anticipation of the night ahead, made him heady. She was his, to do as he desired. She had to do his bidding, in a night full of kinky sex. She was eternally beholden to him. Had it not been for him, she would have still been struggling in the shady bylanes of her home town, seeking cheap thrills, amongst thousands of her ilk, hoping to strike big. Thanks to him she had managed a break in a big banner film of Bollywood with a mega-star cast and he was not going to let her forget the favour.

A smartly attired military band began playing a lively tune. The security men on duty had a hard time, controlling the screaming crowds.

Vishal Loya snapped out of his reverie. He held his princess by the hand, as she stepped onto the floor. Hundreds of bulbs flashed to capture the magical moment. The unending waves of applause and the jubilant shouts drowned out all else.

A little while later, Vishal Loya led the lady towards a black sedan waiting outside the hotel that whisked them away to an unknown destination. The barely-clad starlet wrapped her arms around him and tilted her head to one side as he kissed her on her parted lips. She moved her hands teasingly onto his crotch in a gentle rubbing motion. Vishal pulled down her bustier with a firm tug and buried his face in her sumptuous bare breasts. 'No panties like you promised...' he whispered into her ear as he pushed up her dress and went down on her.

Far away from the glare Bharat Loya sat holed up in his office, basking in the glory of their publicity campaign, strategising his next move. The pleasures of new flesh were not on his agenda. That was an area he had left entirely for his kinky, younger brother.

37

New Delhi
March 1991

Phillipe Chitle had been taught a brand new lesson. He had learned that although he was the Chief Liaison Officer of GII, his very office had been restructured to that of a nominal figurehead. He was supposed to obey the will of his boss implicitly, and accept the ridiculous role that had been assigned to him, if he desired to retain his chair. At the behest of his supreme commander, he was often summoned to the sacred office on the eighth floor, with his pen and notebook, to the high-culture sessions of the distinguished first family and their special guests. Like a performing animal at a circus, the suave new French-speaking convert, was made to dance a verbal jig. He had to spout words and phrases in his adopted language, to regale the visitors, till they tired of him or their meal finished, whichever was first. After all, he was getting a whopping salary from them, and was duty bound to give them their money's worth.

Every week, serious meetings were held in the boardroom at GI House chaired by the MD who was an impatient stickler for rules. His staff, officials and backroom boys were aware of his finicky demands.

No cologne please. MD hates strong smells.

They were expected to always carry pens and notepads to record every word he uttered, because he never repeated instructions. These sessions were held to review the past week's events and announce future strategies.

The directives that emanated from the august boardroom were religiously recorded by the mindless robots, who stood at attention, taking them in, for hasty implementation.

Gradually, changes became perceptible and the sales figures began an upward march. Plans for expansion and diversification began slowly taking shape. In the pipeline were proposals to start a domestic airline and also buy up equity in an international airline. To establish their presence in all leading metros of the country, plans to set up a chain of hotels were also taking shape.

By the year's end the Loyas wholly owned the domestic airline Beetle Air, that zig-zigged across the nation bringing its competitors to their knees in a crazy price war. Bharat Loya had achieved the impossible. Each week, as the balance-sheet registered a galloping growth in profits, he drove his point home. The Loyas had made flying as cheap as railway travel by creating a new structure of low fares that soaked up a huge portion of the market.

All these competitors were stopped dead in their tracks, with the presence of this swashbuckling new giant, with bottomless pockets and infinite money power.

A whole new breed of young and energetic sales personnel, were employed for the services of Beetle Air, the office of which was located on the refurbished ground floor of GI House. They were assigned ambitious sales targets, with attractive emoluments, spanking new cars, generous house allowances and fully paid holidays abroad. Anyone who failed to meet his target, was thrown out mercilessly, stripped of even the shirt on his back. The elements of fear, insecurity and persecution were fully exploited by the management, to keep them permanently on tenterhooks, but the revenue collections showed, that the formula worked.

For every one man who was booted out, there were ten queuing up to take his place. A few senior managers who felt marginalised or humiliated, attempted in vain, to meet Ajay Vardhan Loya but couldn't get past the doctors and medical staff that protected him, so they either resigned in a huff or waited in terror, for their certain execution.

A particularly frightening story had been doing the rounds. A sales manager was rudely interrupted by the MD, while he was having lunch.

'What are you doing gorging free food off the company, you oaf, while your division has not met its target?' he thundered.

The poor simpering bloke, all but choked on his free meal, and tendered his resignation, reeling under the public insult.

True to form, Vishal Loya took charge of the collections, and his elder brother retained his role, as unchallenged policy-planner and de facto Chairman, to replace his father, while his application for grant of a licence to start international operations for Beetle Air was awaiting clearance in the Ministry of Civil Aviation.

No one cared that the whole of Delhi was agog with the rumour that the Loyas had acquired their airline from the illegal kickback earned on one single defence deal.

In the midst of all this frenzy, the last thing Bharat Loya had time for, was a call from his cousin, Aditya Daga.

38

In the waning hours of his tenure, just thirty days before the general elections, the Prime Minister was huddled in his office with two trusted colleagues. They were examining a file that had been cleared by the Cabinet, allowing the transfer of five hundred crore rupees to a particular company in Russia. The recipients were manufacturers of the highly sophisticated fighter jet Sukhoi-30. They were to hold this amount as a security deposit towards the purchase of thirty aircraft till the next government was formed.

The Russians had been assured that as soon as the new government was sworn in, the balance amount of approximately six thousand crore rupees would be paid to them. All the three men present were confident that they would be back in power in a couple of months to execute the clauses prescribed in this mega-contract.

Unfortunately what followed was a disastrous defeat for the Congress Party and no one could say if the new government would honour the commitment to acquire for the Indian Air Force what was deemed to be the most lethal combat aircraft ever made. But there was one closely guarded secret. The said aircraft was merely a drawing on paper and the Russians had cleverly managed to wrangle from an unsuspecting Indian public the funds to develop it by colluding with the Minister in question.

That left the field wide open for hordes of middlemen who had been edged out of the race to start lobbying afresh with their contacts in high places and negotiate the deal between the Russia and India that smacked of political will rather than operational needs. Of course the front runners were none other than the invincible Loyas.

A fear psychosis had taken root in the hearts of the GII staff. The plush work environment, comparable to any state-of-the-art corporate house of the world, had some conspicuously missing elements. There was no job security and the employees could not afford any self-pride. Bharat Loya, the relentless butcher, revelled in playing ducks against drakes. His policy of divide and rule, turned them all into a bunch of grovelling humans, petrified of their own shadows. No one trusted anybody. The two brothers had their own favourites, not necessarily harmoniously inclined towards each other. They were equally vulnerable to the changing fancies of their eccentric bosses, who had their own distinct behaviour patterns.

Bharat Loya was ruthless to all. From the Corporate Directors down to the peons, he was a democratic sodomiser, whose act of sodomy was uniform, only the penetration depths varied. Vishal however, was the character straight out of *Alice in Wonderland,* which meant that if he didn't like your face, it was, *off with your head!* No reasons were assigned and no one dared question the decision.

The work schedules were punishing and for every one rupee that GII spent on their staff, they extracted a hundred rupees worth of sweat, blood and tears.

By now Phillipe Chitle had been assigned a more crucial job, that of troubleshooter for Ajay Vardhan Loya, obliged to move heaven and earth, to help him out of his mess, or even become the courier of bribe money to political high-ups, if the need arose.

But, there was more to celebrate in GI House. A forty-nine per cent share had been cornered by the Loyas in a foreign airline and they had acquired two hotels, one each in Srinagar and in Goa.

In Srinagar the magnificent heritage property, that had shut down after the surge in militancy, fell into their lap because they managed to outbid all the other hopefuls in the race. The two hundred room hotel that had provided the backdrop for scores of Indian films had been the holiday destination for most of India's elite. It was refurbished in barely six months and the Loyas made it their private resort for networking where they would often ferry important friends over a weekend and entertain them in royal style.

Once again the drawing-room socialists and the city's gossip-mongers were found lamenting the fact that the Loyas were flush with ill-gotten wealth from defence deals which they had used indiscriminately to acquire these hotels.

But for Bharat Loya this was no deterrent. His tactical expansion and diversification campaign had indeed made him the man to watch. Profit graphs of Beetle Air soared to unprecedented levels and it soon became the preferred carrier connecting every major city of the country.

Strategically at this time, the Loyas used the outreach of their power to unleash a blitzkrieg in the media, to malign the role of the Directorate of Enforcement in the FERA inquiry against their ailing Chairman and garner public sympathy for him. This was as far away from the truth as it possibly could be, but because the written word is gospel, they managed to create a sizeable lobby of sympathisers among the masses, to give credence to their lie.

In the meantime, violent convulsions were being felt in the political arena. The golden period of economic liberalisation, during the five-year tenure of a highly astute, erstwhile External Affairs Minister Narasimha Rao who had assumed the office of Prime Minister of India at a very crucial time, had come to an end. The farcical general elections that followed, failed to keep him on the chair. A grievously fractured mandate could not throw up any party that could form the government with a clear majority. After a great deal of bickering and heckling, the single largest party, the Congress, supported by some smaller parties in a United Front coalition, propped up a humble, unassuming, but highly ambitious farmer from Karnataka, H D Deve Gowda as Prime Minister.

Even as the staff of GII ritualistically grovelled at Bharat Loya's feet, another eighty-year old, far away from GI House, was grovelling at ex-Prime Minister Rao's feet for a different reason. The ex-Prime Minister, nominated the octogenarian Sita Ram Kesri, to the post of President of the Congress Party, supposedly to act only as his rubber stamp. Kesri however, brutally stabbed his mentor in the back by denying him a bona fide ticket to contest the forthcoming general elections, because some cases of bribery and corruption had come up against him. Rao retired, a sad man, thereafter to write his autobiography in a valiant battle against the threat of fading.

Rajiv Gandhi's widow Sonia waited for a while in her self-imposed exile, before throwing Kesri out, to take over the reigns of the comatose Congress herself. A horde of desperate partymen prostrated themselves at her feet for their own survival and the grant of a fresh lease of life for the disintegrating party, amidst an indignant uproar from all right-thinking and patriotic Indians.

But before that, the owners of GII obtained a welcome breather with Deve Gowda heading the coalition government. The Finance Minister and his canny Revenue Secretary who had survived tumultuous political upheavals, to retain plum assignments as an indestructible satellite of power were also beholden to them.

With such a powerful lobby of loyalists on his side, Ajay Vardhan Loya was confident, that nothing could go wrong and Lyndoh would be mowed down, for having dared to touch him. The Party President, their old faithful ally, who had been receiving their largesse for a sustained period of time, would prove his allegiance to them by twisting the Prime Minister's arm, to get Ajay Vardhan Loya off the hook. He would also help them clinch the biggest ever defence contract in the history of independent India.

But there was just one hitch...R. K. Lyndoh!

39

Even as Bharat Loya's success story resonated around the country, baffling all the watchdogs of corruption and the sharks of the arms trade, he was fast losing touch with himself. Every few months he retreated to an ashram in Haridwar, to take refuge in silence on the banks of the Ganga and listen to the whispers from beyond. He tuned into a cosmic energy, to help him slay the demons that stemmed from his own neurosis. A deeply tragic figure, he sought to recharge himself, to be able to survive in his temporal world. He cut himself off from everything, to step into his private penitentiary, to make amends with his bleeding soul that he had exposed to no one. But his noisy inner street just would not let him be in peace. The screaming cries of Oedipus Rex, the painful memory of that self-imposed tragedy, and thousands of those hissing serpents, did not stop haunting him.

Staring out at the devilish dance of the waves on the immortal river that flowed down the tresses of the mighty God of destruction into the restless ocean, he was hurtled into a space and time, beyond the frontiers of his mortal shell. For a fleeting moment, he felt freed from the shackles that bound him to his earth, away from his wife who had fled to the arms of another man, from his helpless son's infirmity, for which he blamed himself, from the deviant love for his mother that emanated from deep within his flesh, from his father's wasting body, his uncaring wayward brother, his sister, and his innocent little daughter. He felt freed from the bondage of pain. It dulled the agony in the depths of his soul, till the nagging whispers drowned the melody from the celestial spheres and scraped his wounds, bringing him back into the field of the earthly forces that held him together.

He felt no desire for anything. Even the primal force of his libido had fused with the energy that drove him to worldly success. The myths that proliferated around him were far away from the truth. No one knew the real purpose of his spiritual retreat. His razor-sharp mind never slipped when he came back to work as the tyrant, who only understood servility and sales figures but the spiritual break could do little to check his fast greying hair and ashen skin.

At home there were equally tumultuous changes. Yashoda had become even more distanced and stayed most of the time in Mauritius. The two children were habituated to their surrogate parenting by their respective governesses. Ma Amba's new guru, Sri J Radhakrishnan, had initiated her into a new life. His Soul Search programme had given her a fresh purpose and direction. Nupur in 'copy mode' was blindly doing her mother's bidding, with no attachment to Uday Nanda or commitments to her marriage and Ajay Vardhan Loya was scurrying for cover between his Intensive Care wards and convalescence rooms, from hospital to home, tended by his old-time faithful Devyani.

De-linked from outsiders and ostensibly from each other, the Loyas were still bound to their material world, in pursuit of a common goal. If it was peace they sought, they were scarcely going to find it on the paths they had chosen, to get out of their private hells, while the silver spoon gathered dust waiting to claim its next casualty.

40

In the heart of the capital, the Director of Enforcement, R. K. Lyndoh sat in his office in a sombre mood. He was reflecting on the unsavoury events that had transpired a few hours back. A thick pile of newspapers lay on his table. He had read the headlines, highlighted in fluorescent pink, several times over.

Directorate of Enforcement on a fishing expedition to get something on Ajay Vardhan Loya.

This was one more in a flurry of highly publicised articles in the national dailies splashing the state of the deteriorating health of Ajay Vardhan Loya. The conspicuously placed story had a certificate from his doctors in Cleveland, stating that the Chairman of Global Integrity Industries was dying. There were some other detailed health bulletins, related media reports and strongly worded statements from leading industrial houses, condemning the action of the Enforcement Directorate. They had lambasted the role of the Director, in trying to kill Loya by sending him harassing and intimidating summons for interrogation. The horrific death of an international biscuit baron in judicial custody a year earlier, had made investigative agencies cautious and given interested parties a timely edge, which they were using to whip up mass hysteria against the FERA authorities that were threatening to arrest one of their ilk.

Lyndoh jogged his memory. The Chairman of GII, if he remembered correctly, had dodged more than fifteen such summons, by repeatedly getting himself admitted to different hospitals, on the pretext of a precarious heart condition. Their orchestrated campaign to cast aspersions on the ED office and delay proceedings on the grounds of ill-health, was clearly a case of overkill.

Even though the High Court and Supreme Court had found no substance in those charges, the superefficient, troubleshooting Revenue Secretary, had lost no time in calling a meeting of the ED officers, to voice his concern at the adverse media publicity, nicely on cue.

It had prompted the Finance Minister, to urgently summon Lyndoh to his office that morning, with all the pertinent files relating to the matter. That was all very well. As Finance Minister, it was well within his purview to demand any files because he desired to monitor them personally, but in this case, there was a distinct conflict of interest.

Lyndoh frowned. The bad taste lingered on. He was an upright servant of the people of India. The solemn oath to his office was the only religion that he knew. In keeping with the tenets of his philosophy, he rebelled against this brazen travesty of justice. Never in all the years of his service had he been compelled to defy orders from his superiors.

He knew that both the Finance Minister and the Revenue Secretary were shamelessly protecting Ajay Vardhan Loya, whom he had almost nailed and who had brazenly greased the palms of all the officers below him.

Lyndoh's chilling words echoed down the corridors of the Finance Ministry.

'Sir, I can apprise you regarding the Loya matter as you desire, but I cannot hand over the papers to you. I believe there is a conflict of interest here, because you have represented the Loyas in some legal matters earlier. However, if you give me a written order, to that effect, I shall be happy to hand over the file to you.'

The polished and eminent Minister of Finance, was staring at his own unmasked image, right in the face. He was stunned by this insubordinate refusal. How could he deny the undeniable, or admit that there was much more than a conflict of interest here? How could he say that he was only discharging his duty that stood at sharp variance with an upright officer, attempting to discharge his? Clearly, their confrontation had exposed the duplicity that lay therein.

Lyndoh felt a renewed sense of pride. His righteousness was his greatest strength and he would stake his life for it, no matter what.

He summoned his secretary to reiterate his earlier orders. There were confirmed reports that Ajay Vardhan Loya was booked on a flight to the United States that night. There was no way he was going to let him get away.

Just as the Minister sat fuming in his office, with the sound of Lyndoh's words mocking in his ears, his indomitable Revenue Secretary sat across the table, devising ways to salvage his boss's ego, and eliminate the insolent Director of Enforcement.

A few hours later, a group of officers from the DOE, set off for the airport in an innocuous looking white Ambassador. They were armed with a paper that carried an order, directly in contravention to the unwritten decree of the honourable Minister, a corrupt and self-serving leader of the world's largest democracy, who happened to be their boss.

If anyone believed that the responsibility of carrying out illegal orders had been settled at Nuremberg, they were in for a surprise!

41

It was thirty minutes past the hour of midnight. A spanking, metallic gold, Mercedes Benz pulled up at the International Departures terminal, at Delhi airport. The occupants, a middle-aged couple, were being escorted by the dapper and suave young man, in charge of public relations of their multicrore conglomerate. He was there to see off the boss who was travelling to the USA, on a critical mission. They were greeted by a smartly dressed, alert travel agent, carrying two first class boarding cards, wearing a small, white laminated identity card, attached to a chain around his neck. It was a special permit to enter the baggage check-in area; a privilege he had been granted to facilitate a comfortable, no-wait, trouble-free departure for his important passengers, who were not accustomed to being pushed around by strangers, in long queues at crowded airports. All formalities completed, the special passengers only had to go through the mandatory immigration and security check, before they would embark onto the waiting aircraft.

The two privileged travellers proceeded with their boarding cards to the immigration counter. The man was wearing a dark lounge suit and had an overcoat hung carelessly over his arm. His companion, an average built woman in a floral chiffon sari, walked alongside, with an air of authority in her step. She held onto the man's elbow as they stopped to be frisked in front of a metal detector. They would be the last passengers to board the flight, but they were in no hurry. Both of them were looking forward to a comfortable nap on the improvised super-luxury seats of the first class cabin, on the American airline.

'Please step this side Sir.' A sharp commanding voice startled them. 'Can we see your passports please?'

The two stepped aside, annoyed by the sudden intrusion. They saw a group of four plainclothes men waving a paper at them officiously, blocking their path.

'Sir, we are officers from the Directorate of Enforcement. We have orders to search your bags. You are hereby restrained from leaving the country. Please step this side Sir!' One of them flashed an identity card.

The Chairman of GII held tightly onto his companion's arm. He felt a wave of terror overcome him. His heart hammered inside his chest as if it would burst. His face turned ashen, as blood rushed down from his head and he crumbled onto a chair, clutching his heart.

'Call Bharat,' he rasped, as Devyani threw down his overcoat and cradled him in her arms to break the fall.

'Someone's head is going to roll,' she mumbled, as she glared at the plainclothes men, ferociously.

In the hour well past midnight while most of the city had retired into peaceful slumber, the slick GII Director had activated more than a dozen people from the highest office of the land. It was a desperate measure to rescue the panic-stricken couple, detained at the last checkpoint at Delhi airport.

Within a span of barely ten minutes the enforcement officers received a startling phone call. The caller introduced himself before he boomed in a commanding voice.

The Prime Minister desires that Mr. Ajay Vardhan Loya whom you have just detained at the airport should be released immediately and be allowed to proceed as per his schedule. DO NOT, I repeat DO NOT search his bags or put him through any humiliation. Just let him go. Do you understand? Make no mistake, this is an order from the Prime Minister and nothing should go wrong.' The crisp and authoritative voice was that of a very senior bureaucrat who was known for his proximity to the concerned ministers. The two hapless men, only performing their duty in earnest had no option but to let the fleeing couple go.

'You too Mr. Secretary!' they chorused in shock.

The held-up American aircraft taxied out onto the runway, after an inordinate, three-hour delay. Two rattled but triumphant passengers, settled into the front row, super luxury seats, fastening their seat belts. They were finally flying out to a safe transatlantic haven, away from the clutches of Lyndoh. The rest of the passengers on board, had no idea, that during that unexplained delay in their departure, the country's top machinery had been shaken up, to rescue a very important fugitive from the FERA authorities, who was flying out with them. Indeed not one, but many heads were going to roll. It was Lyndoh's turn to fume.

42

On a humid Saturday morning, in an ornate drawing-room in Lutyen's Delhi, an intense discussion on metro-spirituality was underway. The newly initiated disciples of Sri Radhakrishnan were holding an interactive session, narrating their inner experiences, under the aegis of the distinguished Ma Amba. This was a regularly held convention that helped them to tap into their inner voices. It was a programme designed to create a societal shift for a city trying to look at itself in a mirror. They were being taught the tenets of a nouveau-spiritualism, which was about simplicity. It was about creating inner pathways into their troubled souls, a greater high than snorting coke or downing Ecstasy could procure. It was about breaking patterns, to create a novel and richer quality of life.

Ma Amba as usual orated graciously.

'...The day will come when after harnessing space, the winds, the tides and gravitation, we shall harness for God the energies of love. And on that day for the second time in the history of the world we shall have discovered FIRE...'

She ended her session by urging her followers to believe in her. 'Follow me, have faith in me, I shall lead you to Nirvana...'

None of the people present had any way of knowing that she had turned away a horde of charity seekers from her door just that morning. 'Ask me for love, don't ask me for money,' she had said smilingly. Her prime teaching spelt detachment from the material world as the only way to attain supreme bliss.

Amba Loya was seemingly cut off from the turbulence that had threatened the peace and stability of the country. As long as her private coffers were secure, she didn't care what happened elsewhere—and her preachings rarely translated into practice.

After the current political upheavals, that had unseated the Prime Minister and replaced him with another candidate, who was a staunch supporter of the Loyas, she felt back in control. With the new Prime Minister they were safe, and the goose that laid the golden egg had been given a fresh lease of life.

Suddenly Uday Nanda found his stock rising high. He was put solely in charge of the crisis-management committee, to rescue his father-in-law and save the clan from ruination.

Socialite evenings can have eerie undercurrents. At a cocktail reception hosted by the Loyas to celebrate another anniversary of the Ritz Grand hotel that coincided with Beetle Air being declared the best airline of the year by a global organisation of travel and tourism, Priyanka Nanda was listening to a mindless drone from a group of women sporting designer apparel and flashy jewellery. They were holding forth on the joys of extra-marital sex. A reed thin beauty with streaked hair and tight jeans, strolled down in stiletto heels. She had discarded the slow, subtle art of flirtation and replaced it with quick direct strikes. She could flash skin and seduce with her sharp intellect with equal elan. She was a crisp and captivating woman of the millennium, the star of the city's smart set.

Priyanka was amongst a hundred odd partygoers of the capital, that included a few ministers, bureaucrats and industrialists. She tuned out of the inane sounds that came from there. The vacuous rhetoric, punctuated with giddy laughter and clinking glasses, made her feel distanced and alone. Painful musings on her life came rushing back to her. The duality of her existence had become insufferable. Society perceived her to be the envied wife of a billionaire, whose coveted family name she carried, but the emptiness it had brought her, could not be compensated for. Her kinky husband, who was reputed to be a vagrant philanderer, always in the company of a particular beauty queen, and sometimes seen with other toothpick-shaped models, was not what he seemed to be. Her societal accolades were as fake as false eyelashes, and her secret lover could not promise her a future with him.

The revolution of Indian attitudes on sex and the open licence to sleep with multiple partners was not something that she could easily fight or accept. She was tired of the anxiety, denial and distrust that hounded her marriage. Even as she pretended to be unaffected by it, a conformity remained emblazoned inside her heart. Overtly, she belonged to a generation of sexual liberals—a squad of cheerleading women, for whom G-spots were as important as their jewels. As the good wife or the good girlfriend, she was not supposed to be inhibited—but her conflict was deep and searing. As the new-age, voraciously sexual woman, she could allow herself multiple sex partners and many of her associates talked openly about their intimate sex life, in and out of bed, but she actually did not know what she wanted. Neither her husband nor his family, cared about her emotional needs.

The sexual gratification she had been getting from her husband's cousin had lost its sheen. She found herself repeatedly despairing at the hollowness of her life. Many times she contemplated getting a divorce, but there were some major obstacles. Her brother's peculiar marriage to her husband's sister, was the greatest impediment of them all. She knew that the two were not happily married, but the power of wealth had intoxicated him and made him emotionless. She saw Vishal surrounded by some scantily clad women with his arm snaked around someone she did not recognise. She turned her face away in disgust.

A group of men and women huddled around the bar were talking loudly. Some words filtered through.

'What's with this kinky couple?'

'I believe Vishal is being blackmailed by that new screen bimbette. He's got her pregnant.'

'Nah! He couldn't have. He's totally gay. Likes his ass taken. He hangs out with the masseurs from the hotel. I know one of the guys, he does my massage too. He's been telling me wild stories about him. He likes to be tied up and all that kind of crap.'

'But I saw him last night with a really hot woman at Annabelles, he was almost doing it to her on the floor.'

'God knows what the truth is but it seems that Patil chick is demanding fifty crores to abort the kid.'

'Feel bad for Priyanka.'

'It's okay yaar, she's getting laid by that cousin of his. They've been seeing each other for quite a while now.'

'What fun, all in the family. Incest is best.'

These bloody Maarus are completely depraved. Stop at nothing, do they?'

'The guys have the balls and the bucks. They do what they please and the rest can fuck off. Wish I had that kind of money.'

Their raucous laughter was drowned in the music from a band that had been flown in from Trinidad especially for the evening. A few couples began gyrating on the floor and the lights dimmed between psychedelic flashes.

Priyanka had heard the vile rumour. The scandal had reverberated, like a newly released porn-film in the capital, and finally came to her, grossly twisted out of shape.

A newly crowned beauty queen and actress of Bollywood, was rumoured to have been impregnated by Vishal Loya, from whom she was demanding a fifty crore rupee settlement to end the affair. Priyanka was snowed-under by a spate of overblown tales, all pointing to her husband's sexual indiscretions and bestiality. She had found public justification for her affair with his cousin, who was also stuck in a three-year old boring marriage and the perfect chance to opt out, but it pained her to see the four-generations old Loya family being brutally savaged by foul-mouthed rumour mongers, who gobbled up and regurgitated the delectable fare, viewing her both in pity and contempt.

Priyanka envied men who played the field and had an easier time. She would have liked to come to the defence of her estranged husband, like a dutiful Hindu wife, but she was deeply disturbed by the cruel joke being played on her.

No one knew better than her that Vishal Loya was incapable of what was being spread by vicious gossip mongers, and she could prove it, but that would mean opening up a dirty Pandora's box. She would have to testify that her husband suffered from a near total sexual dysfunction and that he was addicted to kinky and abnormal sex. She would have to blow the tailor-made cover around Vishal Loya's nonexistent virility. Shamefacedly, she would have to admit her own demeaning position in a loveless, sexless marriage and the compulsions that kept her in it. Her own, not-so-secret affair with her cousin-in-law would be out in the open. She would have to confess, that as the younger daughter-in-law of the illustrious House of Loyas, she was not willing to become a repository of hypocritical values and feigned chastity, and that orgasms did figure high in the hierarchy of her needs.

Priyanka's plight was a thousand times worse than her older sister-in-law Yashoda, who had a powerfully placed lover and ostensibly good sex. She also carried the title of the eldest daughter-in-law of the House of Loya and was the mother of two legitimate children. Above all, she had the courage of her convictions and despite her blatant transgression her status at home had remained intact.

Priyanka felt demeaned. She could not figure out how to get out of her hell. Tears welled up in her eyes as she fumbled her way to the exit.

43

After several attempts, Aditya Daga did get through to Bharat Loya.

'Aditya Daga to see you Sir.' The intercom in Bharat Loya's office came alive with the voice of his secretary.

'Is he alone?'

'Yes Sir.'

'Send him in.'

Bharat Loya settled back into his chair. He closed the cover of the file in front of him marked 'CONFIDENTIAL' and pushed it into his drawer.

Aditya Daga entered the office of his cousin confidently. There was a spring in his step and a smile on his face. He stretched his hand towards Bharat who remained seated as he shook hands with him.

'How're you doing Bharat? It's been ages…'

'You look just the same. Where have you been?'

'Nature's been kind to me I guess. It's good to see you Bharat after all these years. You know how it is in this city. No one meets anyone unless it's an occasion or a party. But you have been making waves I can see.'

Bharat's face was deadpan as Aditya continued with his praises.

'Wonders you have done man. We are proud of you Bharat. Who could have thought...?'

'So tell me, what brings you here Aditya?' Bharat cut him short. There was no inflection in his voice.

'I've been calling you for the last fifteen days. They don't put me through, your guys here. Been wanting to discuss something very important with you. You know there's this Slovakian company that manufactures air missiles and fighter planes. They have a huge presence in the international market. They did well at the Paris Air Show last month and will be participating in the Defence Expo in Delhi this year. Seems they had good relations with the last Defence Minister and they managed to sign a few contracts. The greedy bastard got a whopping commission, some two-three hundred crores they say. They are now being edged out by the Russian Sukhois I'm told. Theirs is the lowest bid in the tender and all they need is a push from the top. Their chief's in town. He's a nice and reliable kinda guy. I've known him for a while now. A real man of honour. Time tested and tried.' Aditya rambled on. 'I can bring him over to the house if you like. And we can bind them whichever way you want. They are offering a clear ten per cent to get the job done.'

Bharat's face slowly contorted into a frown.

'We may be able to squeeze another two-three per cent out of them,' Aditya added quickly, 'if we get them the contract. Six thousand three hundred crores is the projected cost in the first phase buddy. And we can net a cool...'

'Now just a minute, will you hold on there Aditya.' Bharat shot up from his chair fuming. 'What the fuck are you talking about? I know nothing of the arms trade. That's not our business for God's sake. Now if you'll excuse me please. I have a really busy day.'

Bharat was striding briskly to the door. Aditya was dumbfounded. He followed him out sheepishly smarting under the insult.

'The lying son-of-a-bitch, the lying fucking son-of-a-bitch. Not in the arms trade! Hah!' he cursed as he heard the door shut behind him. He could've sworn that the icy, robotic man he had just been snubbed by was not the Bharat Loya he had known since his childhood.

Bharat Loya tilted back his swivel chair and pressed a button on the intercom. The frown on his face had not eased.

'Don't put any calls through to me,' he said stiffly.

The cheeky intrusion had annoyed him. His mind was racing ahead onto far more pressing matters. He had only one hour before his meeting with the new Prime Minister who wanted to discuss a long pending proposal for the grant of a licence for an international airline to the Loyas. But before that copies of some vital information from Air Headquarters had to be forwarded to Moscow in time for the visit of the Indian Defence Minister scheduled for the next month.

'Fuck you, Aditya Daga, you can go to hell you fucking no-good upstart'!

44

The new Prime Minister had realised his life's ultimate dream. Taking advantage of the contradictions in the United Front coalition he had been victorious in a neck and neck race with a sly wrestler belonging to a backward class of Uttar Pradesh, to assume the highest office of the land. Ostensibly he had assumed his office as head of a government committed to root out corruption. But the truth was that he had a serious obligation to the powers that had propped him up for the post. It hung over his head like the sword of Damocles, to remind him that he was duty-bound to a cause that was completely antithetical to the oath of his office.

The prevailing confusion before his coronation had helped a few very important citizens, in gaining crucial time for some ominous matters. Serious inquiries against them were heading towards fearful outcomes. The undertaking of the Prime Minister's Office to protect them was his *fait accompli*. He had to exhibit a high degree of tolerance towards their right to loot and protect those law-breakers, who were being persecuted by a handful of upholders of an outdated moral code.

Within one week of assuming charge, the Prime Minister convened a high-powered meeting with the Finance Minister and Revenue Secretary. The people in attendance had a singular agenda, their absolute commitment to safeguard the interest of some specific persons who were being hounded by the Enforcement Directorate.

Predictably, one of them was the mighty Ajay Vardhan Loya who had been charged with serious breaches of FERA to the tune of millions of dollars.

The minutes of the closed-door meeting outlined the powers of the PM to say whatever he desired to civil servants, who could not under any circumstances contradict him; and to demand appraisal of the goings-on in crucial matters, to ensure that no investigative agency could decide any case in which he had an interest, without his knowledge and consent. The meeting was also an oblique warning to the civil servants, of the price they would have to pay, to survive in their chairs. Thereafter he would have to publicly assert that people guilty of scams would not be spared, but in truth, the ones who would be in his line of fire were those who had persecuted them.

The meeting brought to the fore the stark truth that the PM's continuance in office depended solely on the will of some ruffians and goons.

While the echoes of the Prime Minister's newly enunciated, anti-corruption policy, resonated down the corridors of the PMO, in a house not too far away on Prithviraj Road, his jubilant allies were popping champagne and far away in Cleveland, a couple had just begun a romantic, candle-lit dinner, to celebrate what promised to be their final retribution.

45

Bharat Loya's *alter ego* had lain dormant in its embryonic stage for years. It emitted a raging force that destroyed anything that stood in its path, leaving behind a deadly holocaust, through which emerged an intensely hated, but exceptionally successful man who did not have the time to think, or to feel the pangs from his tormented soul.

Pursuing his surreal God through celibacy and truth, and his greater God of wealth and success, he lashed out at his competitors and subordinates with a canny and methodical madness.

Yashoda had packed her bags and moved out to the serene shores of Mauritius into her lover's nest, in the quest of her own identity. The exploration and acceptance of her individual sexuality had helped her to recognise the strength of a new mantra. With Jaywant's masculine, red-bloodedness she had discovered the relationship between herself and her needs that she was hitherto ashamed to admit. She was no longer tied down to hypocritical alliances, unlike her sister-in-law Priyanka and resolved to live life on her own terms.

As the shock of forbidden sexuality sprang out of the closet, their marriage became a public casualty and the choicest morsel on the gossip mongers menu, it was time for both the concerned men, Jaywant Mallya and Bharat Loya to conduct a reality check.

The nineteen-year victim of this break-up, Aryaman, cried bitterly, when he learned that his mother was not coming back. His diseased insides shrivelled up and the uncomfortable constriction in his throat worsened. He felt a burning sensation in his eyes all the time, which did not go away even after lubricating them with medicated drops, but when he was with his computer, his only solace and best friend, he felt he was freed of all his problems.

Amba's angry outburst after Yashoda left, fell on Bharat's deaf ears, for Yashoda's desertion did little to change their lives. In any case, she had always been independent and free. He decided that he should allow his truant spouse the cooler option of extramarital sex, but not at his expense, so he totally choked her cash supply.

The ex-Prime Minister who had been unable to sack R. K. Lyndoh, paid a heavy price. He had much explaining to do. He had to come to the public defence of Ajay Vardhan Loya. He had to justify a midnight call from his office to the officers of the Department of Enforcement at Delhi airport. He had to explain the reasons for his obstruction of duty despite explicit orders from the Enforcement Directorate to detain Loya and frisk him. He had to dutifully proclaim, that the chairman of Global Integrity Industries was an honourable and wealthy man, who had enormous stakes in the country and that he would return after being treated for his dangerous heart condition at Cleveland. He had to also strongly condemn the DOE for trying to harass Loya needlessly.

Rarely in the history of power abuse had a government been so thoroughly exposed. Daily press releases from the PMO carried strongly worded statements against the Director of Enforcement, who was supposed to have given selective leaks to the media regarding Ajay Vardhan Loya, and privately there was wholehearted support from the PM to contain and muzzle Lyndoh if he did not go easy on Loya.

Almost immediately the Central Bureau of Investigation launched an absurd inquiry into the antecedents of the Director of Enforcement. They summoned his income tax and service records of the last ten years and put him under strict surveillance to frighten him into silence. The press played havoc with this news and some keenly analytical newspapers, who still believed in their dated fundamental democratic rights, reported and condemned the government for showing unwarranted favours to Loya, and taking undue interest in the completely perverted investigations into the antecedents of Lyndoh. A shocking report of Intelligence Bureau officials, barging into the office to raid the Director of Enforcement was also splashed prominently, in the same newspapers a few days later. The writing was on the wall.

It was the first time in the history of India since independence, that one agency of the government had been unleashed upon another, in a blatant mockery of the basic laws of democracy. Indeed, the KGB had come piggy-back riding into the corridors of the Prime Minister's Office.

Soon after, a series of crucial meetings were held by the concerned ministry to consider ways to revoke FERA and grant reprieve to the high-profile offender.

Meanwhile, emboldened by the events transpiring at home, Ajay Vardhan Loya and Devyani had boarded a flight back to Delhi.

46

New Delhi
31 December 1999

Another mega-celebration had been planned by the Loyas on the eve of the new millennium. In keeping with the rest of the world, GII was also preparing to bid farewell to 1999 with a dazzling sound and light show for the citizens of Delhi to mark a new beginning of a new and historic day. All the inmates of Loya House, inhabiting their secluded worlds, spinning within the centrifugal force of their private lives were preparing to welcome the new millennium with varying shades of enthusiasm, in tightly compartmentalised zones.

Amba and Ajay Vardhan, Bharat and Yashoda, Vishal and Priyanka, Uday and Nupur, the segregated casualties of a dynastic curse, impervious to the pain of human emotions, were being driven along with a velocity that would not slacken even when they said goodbye to the nineteen hundreds.

Ten minutes before the zero hour a helicopter circled over the brightly lit domes of the President's Estate, and then moved towards the illuminated arch of India Gate, the grand war memorial that stands proudly in the capital, as one of the last symbols of the British Raj. Below, three flaming torches flickered wildly in the cold December air as the helicopter boomed its way overhead, showering a mixture of floral petals and confetti on the august monument. The lawns on either side of Rajpath were jam-packed with men, women and children, frantically waving multicoloured flags in the air. Some faces were painted with bands of colourful stripes on their foreheads and cheeks, in keeping with the spirit of the occasion. The buildings of the North and South Blocks that house the high-powered offices of the government, were outlined with millions of yellow fairy lights that created a golden aura around the whole of Lutyen's Delhi.

At the same time pair of helicopters were seen circling over Connaught Place. The circular shopping centre in the heart of New Delhi, that had been built by the imperial rulers had also been lit up with fairy lights that silhouetted every curve and line of its historic structure. All roads leading to the Central Park were cordoned off, and no traffic had been allowed into the inner circle after six o'clock that evening. Giant poles that had been erected around the park at regular intervals were festooned with hundreds of luminous streamers, of various lengths that glowed in the dark and fluttered wildly in the breeze, dancing to a joyous tune, to herald the beginning of a new millennium.

Thousands of spectators, wearing heavy winter woollens in bright colours, had collected at the venue to witness the heavily advertised show. Jantar Mantar Road had also been given a similar make-over. With scores of policemen directing the traffic to alternate routes, it had also been spruced up and cordoned off earlier that evening. All street vendors, peanut sellers and unsightly hawkers were shoved out of sight, and no dilapidated buses with dented bodies, peeling paint and streaks of dried vomit below their windows, were allowed on the illumined pathway that led to the august GII building, where the celebrations were to be held. Every inch of its facade was lit up with laser and fairy lights, doing a psychedelic dance in tune with a popular rap song. There were rock bands equipped with powerful speakers waiting on high alert, for a signal to begin their fusion music, in synchrony with each other. The people of Delhi arrived in hordes, to watch what promised to be an unprecedented display of hi-tech gadgetry for their audio-visual pleasure, sponsored by GII, to usher in the first day of the millennium with a novel gift to the citizens of Delhi. The display of lights, music and fireworks was to match in its grandeur, the opening of an Olympic Games ceremony.

As the clock struck the midnight hour, a hushed silence fell on the massive crowds assembled there. Six helicopters circled overhead and paired off into the direction of the venues. A fiery burst of vibrant colours flashed simultaneously over Rashtrapati Bhawan, Connaught Place and all its radial roads.

The aerial kaleidoscope of colours and patterns, scorched the winter sky, through the fog and mist and a thunderous applause broke out which was drowned in the music that came alive as the fireworks began.

Fusion rock bands reverberated their musical rhapsody, through powerful mega-wattage speakers, for miles around the capital. The rap symphony rocked the jubilant crowds at Central Park and the sprawling lawns on either side of Rajpath. Its rhythm matched the laser light show in the sky, pounding the senses of every mortal present there, stirring up a momentum of pure sensual delight.

A cloudburst of rose petals and confetti rained down on the cheering crowds. The children screamed hysterically, jumping up in the air to catch the fluorescent floating snowflakes, dancing wildly to the music, throwing balls of rose petals and confetti at each other, in jubilation.

Another helicopter appeared just a few minutes later, over GI House and a transparent capsule that had been illumined with neon-blue lights was lowered from it. The luminous object that looked like a flying saucer descended in slow motion outside GI House. Inside it were seated a star couple that had the spectators awestruck. Amidst riotous applause, blaring music and a fresh cloudburst of confetti and flowers, Vishal Loya and a young starlet of Bollywood fame, landed softly on the deck that had been cleared for them. The younger scion of the House of Loyas, beaming with pleasure and anticipation of the night ahead, lead the snow-white princess to the brightly lit main entrance that had a wide mutlicoloured tape tied across it. Thunderous applause amplified by a musical score resounded for miles around, working at a feverish pitch, to roll out a brand new experience to the people of Delhi on the first day of the new millennium.

Just past midnight, Bharat Loya stared out of his office window. He would see the changing shapes and hues of light and colour, bouncing off the pink monument in tune with the musical rhythm that reverberated through the walls and floors of GI House. It animated every nook and cranny, flushing out the cobwebs of gloom, dispelling its darkness. Shades of incandescent yellow, flaming orange, glowing fuschia, acid green, electric blue and royal purple painted patterns on the walls of his room, weaving a three-dimensional tapestry of a magic world that had come alive on a palette of colour, on the stroke of midnight.

He turned around to look at the framed blow-up of his son. An icy chill gripped his heart as he clutched the edge of his table and keeled over heavily onto his executive leather chair.

47

At GI House Phillipe Chitle's elevation to Chief Liaison Officer had caused severe heartburning to a particularly disgruntled K V S Raju who had been hanging on hope, chasing the carrot at the end of the stick for a long time. The son of an eminent poetess and the descendant of a royal family of Travancore, Raju's antecedents were by no means humble. His family, that owned a chain of hotels in South India, had sold out to the Loyas, with the condition, that all three sons would be accommodated in directorial positions within GII. Raju had been waiting for his turn patiently, while managers had been constantly picked out and soared up to senior positions over his head, in the last few years. Each time he thought the assignment came to him it was yanked away and awarded to someone else.

Phillipe Chitle was no super hero and in no way worthier than him. Smarting under the insult of having been superceded for the fourth time, K V S Raju was a rumbling volcano waiting to erupt.

Meanwhile the application for the grant of licence for an international airline to the GII, that had been gathering dust in the Civil Aviation Ministry, was expedited in record time, and a massive exercise to remove Lyndoh from the Enforcement Directorate was underway. The Prime Minister's obligation to the powers that had placed him on the highest chair of the land was never more transparent.

This Prime Minister's tenure lasted for just about nine months, during which, despite his best efforts Lyndoh could not be put into a straitjacket. After his stormy term, the already impoverished nation was saddled with another general election, the third in a period of less than four years, after the Congress withdrew its support from the coalition and the government fell.

Sonia Gandhi emerged from her self-imposed exile, to take over as party president, bulldozing all her rivals, to present a new face of her party, to an exhausted and highly frustrated electorate. Her nomination led to a spate of violent protests from within and outside the ranks, and snowballed into an unprecedented, histrionic display of pseudo-nationalism and insulted national pride. The rabid right-wing opposition was apoplectic with rage, at the thought of a white woman heading the very party that had been instrumental in driving out the Imperial rulers from India, half a century ago. Simmering resentment from within the ranks found expression in a belligerent Maratha, Sharad Pawar, himself a fierce Prime Ministerial aspirant, who broke away to form his own party. Most of his party men, who subscribed to the traditional, sycophantic bootlicking culture of the Congress, were unwilling to stick their necks out to support him and he found himself totally isolated. Subsequently, amidst strong public outcries and secret lamentations, Sonia Gandhi defeated her fiercest rival, an old-time Congressman Jitendra Prasad and assumed the office of president of the oldest party of independent India.

Unfortunately for her, despite the high blitz of publicity that followed her as she blazed the campaign trail with her daughter during the elections, the Congress could not muster a clear majority from the people's mandate and their numbers reduced to an all-time low.

Atal Behari Vajpayee, the president of the right-wing Bhartiya Janta Party, was sworn in as Prime Minister of the National Democratic Alliance, supported by a hotchpotch coalition of as many as twenty-two political parties. Diverse in form and thinking, they came together to form the next Lok Sabha, and how long they would endure, became the favourite guessing game of all political pandits.

Riding on this motley bandwagon of the National Democratic Alliance, headed by Vajpayee, was a volatile Tamilian woman politician, Jayalalitha, reputed to be a tough bargainer and notorious rabble-rouser. But when the newly formed Lok Sabha convened for its first parliamentary session, it was Sonia Gandhi who sat in the front row, occupying the second most important chair in the House, as Leader of the Opposition in a highly fragile coalition government.

Predictably, the external rumblings being felt throughout the country, had their repercussions within the GII establishment. A crucial job was assigned to the

French-speaking Chief Liaison Officer. Neatly packed suitcases containing five crore rupees in large denominations, had been delivered to his office for a very precise and highly secret mission.

K V S Raju was on full alert. With his ears always tuned to the ground he had kept careful track of Chitle's movements. He had full knowledge of the reason for and date and time of Chitle's appointment with a newly appointed minister in the PM's charmed circle. He had recorded it meticulously in his own little black book. He picked up his phone and punched a number to the lady in Chennai.

48

Undeniably, the Loyas' manic obsession for the acquisition of wealth was only surpassed by their cold insensitivity to those who were devoid of it, or were in some way dependant on their mercy. Their hypocritical values and cruel behaviour had become the subject of many gossipy tales. Rumour had it, that Anuj Vardhan Loya, the insolvent and dissolute uncle of Bharat, was strictly forbidden to set foot in their homes or offices. His two sons, Vivek and Piyush, the last vestiges of an extinguished family, were untraceable. There were unconfirmed reports that Vivek worked as a part-time crooner in a seedy suburban hotel in Bombay, and the last time anyone had seen Piyush was on a railway platform in Old Delhi, waiting to board a train. Totally infuriated and disillusioned, Aditya Daga had broken all links with his childhood friend, and no one shed a tear.

Surprisingly, a house in a prestigious colony of south Delhi, that had been leased to GII for one of their erstwhile managers by one of Bharat's distant cousins, had been restored to its owner. The widowed septuagenarian, who had fallen on bad days had put in a plea to return the property to them. But it was not mercy that had impelled them to vacate her premises.

'You have no right to live in South Delhi if you cannot afford to. Tell your mother to sell the house to us. We can donate five thousand rupees from our charity trust for her if you like,' Bharat Loya said.

The indignant son of the widowed woman shot up from his chair enraged by the insult. 'Don't talk like that. We just want our house back. GII can easily rent another property.'

Bharat Loya leaned back on his swivel chair. He picked up his calculator and did a quick calculation.

'Let me see, GII has paid you at the rate of fourteen hundred a month, almost five lakh rupees in thirty years. If you refund that five lakhs to us, you can have your house back, but just remember, we are doing you a favour. You would have had to shell out much more had it been anybody else."

Even as the bearer of five crore rupees in neatly stapled bundles of crisp hundred rupee notes, made his way down a tree-lined avenue of Lutyen's Delhi to the house of a GII director for a top secret mission, Ma Amba and Nupur were seated bleary-eyed in an adjoining house on the same street, amidst a congregation of their disciples. They had just completed a practical interactive demonstration of the omnipotent cure to all internal and external strifes, the *Divya Pranayam,* a controlled breathing technique for emotional and spiritual upliftment.

At the same time flying high on his success formula, Uday Nanda had wrapped up a contract to take over another hotel in Agra and Vishal Loya was scouring the beaches of the French Riviera with his new found mate, another seductive starlet of Bollywood for a possible partner in a *menage-a-trois*.

And far away from the capital in Bombay, dozens of blue candles had been lit in a plush Malabar Hill flat. In the ornate interiors done up in ocean colours of azure blue, aqua green, turquoise, coral, ivory and gold, a short, squat, bespectacled man in his sixties, hyperventilating with the surge of endorphins in his clogged veins, had taken his paramour into his arms. Eight perfectly carved briolettes that were suspended from a double row of the finest Belgian-cut diamonds, crafted by Van Cleef and Arpel were caressing her bare cleavage. The fragrance of his favourite French perfume, emanating from her throbbing pulse points snaked up his flared nostrils.

49

Barely forty-five days after the Congress was voted out of power, the Russian Minister of Defence came calling. He was armed with copies of a contract signed by the previous regime which had committed to the purchase of their high-powered fighter jet the Sukhoi-30, in lieu of which a sum of five hundred crore rupees had already been advanced to them.

While the nation was gearing up to receive this very important dignitary, all the sharks of the arms trade were on full alert and feverish networking had begun in the strangest of places. Hawkers had set up shops in almost every neighbourhood. Any and everyone began trumpeting their links with the concerned authorities and all kinds of enticements were being flung around as bait to the sellers. So much so that even the household staff of some high-ups in the cabinet turned into fly-by-night arms agents in order to grab this multi-billion dollar opportunity that was floating around.

The Russian Defence Minister, a retired general from the army was well versed in the mechanism of the Indian polity. Intelligence sources had done all the groundwork for him. Omar Al Fayed's associates were uppermost in his mind. He knew that none other than the Loyas could get the job done.

The newly appointed minister, who was ignorant of the nitty-gritty of his office, gave his Russian counterpart no assurances to honour the said contract.

'I have just taken charge,' he ventured, on the side of caution, 'I need some time to look into the files and only then will I be in a position to decide. I shall have the secretary examine the papers and communicate to you as soon as possible.'

Meanwhile, Ashish Kumar Sinha, a slick member of the Upper House of parliament had taken charge as Political Adviser to the leader of a vital coalition partner of the government. Being an operator with the savage cunning of a wild predator, he had immense persuasive powers and connections that cut across party lines. Expectedly, he had become the fulcrum for all activities inside the defence ministry. All top posts in the ministry were manned by his men and he became the *de facto* minister in charge so nothing moved without his knowledge and approval.

Sensing the favourable opportunity to crack the easily corruptible Sinha, Bharat Loya approached him with an offer that he couldn't turn down. But before that he had followed the conventional route to the minister. Without mincing words the minister had said, *'Kaam ho jayega Loya ji, baki baat aap Sinha ji se kar lijiye. Woh aapko sab samjha dengey.'* He was rubbing his thumb back and forth on the side of his index finger as if he were counting invisible notes in the air. The implications couldn't have been clearer. The minister had cracked.

Sinha sat in his plush office in the presidential suite of a super deluxe hotel in the heart of New Delhi wiping the dial of his gold Rolex wristwatch with a soft tissue. He was waiting patiently for the emissary of the Russians. He had conducted similar exercises several times in the past but this time it promised to be a different ball-game. Loya was an old acquaintance of his from Culcutta who would not have given Sinha the time of the day some years ago. But today he was in a position of control. The minister's call in the dead of night had geared him up for what lay ahead.

'Loya ko aapke paas bhej diya hai Bhai. Kas ke nichod lena usey. Bahut paisa hai haram ke bacchey ke paas. Aur Russi toh note chaapne ki machine sath laye hain. Kursi hai jab tak apni pooch hai ... baad mein to yeh log pehchanegey bhi nahin. Aap toh khud samajhdaar hain ...'

Sinha was prepared for some tough talking. After all he was in command of a mega-market which gave him supreme bargaining power. The anticipation had sent his pulse into a frenzy.

Bharat Loya was no novice at the game. He was brief and came straight to the point. The offer was a clean seven per cent of the six thousand crores to be spent by the Government of India on thirty aircraft in the first phase of the agreement. They were willing to deposit the payment in any currency anywhere in the world the moment the signatures had been put on the contract.

At his slimy, oily best Sinha clutched his heart that was somersaulting at the thought of the lucre that had suddenly and effortlessly fallen into his lap. But he had learned to be a tough bargainer.

'Ten or nothing.' He dug in his heels. 'Don't be so selfish Loyaji. *Hamaara bhi to khayal kijiye, sab aap hee khaa jayengey to kaise kaam chalegaa?*'

The deal was struck at ten per cent but with one rider. Loya would have to manage the Leader of the Opposition so that they posed no impediment to signing the contract.

'They have to be brought into the loop,' Sinha blubbered. We don't want to be facing any untoward inquiries later. *Mahilayen pesh kijiye naa Loyaji; aaj kal aap ke paas koi filmstar vilm-star nahin hai kya? Aisey thodey hee kaam ho jaayega.*' He grinned lecherously.

The rest was easy. The Leader of the Opposition had a nephew who had gained notoriety as the most effective and powerful extra-constitutional authority in the last regime. As confidant and legatee of an erstwhile Prime Minister, this wheeler-dealer who was rumoured to have earned thousands of crores when his uncle was at the helm of affairs, was no stranger to Loya.

Seven days later...

In the central hall of parliament it looked like any other day. The regular hum of the country's most privileged people could be heard outside. The Lok Sabha had convened for a usual morning session. A notification had been given to the Speaker by the Leader of the Opposition to designate time for him to raise a motion during the zero hour.

Merchants of Death

From the front row of the Opposition benches at the assigned time, an extremely self-assured octogenarian, a man of great oratorical skill and lofty principles, rose to move a motion to an almost full house. With his head tilted to one side, his right hand stretched out in front of him as he spoke fluently in his mother tongue. The sheer force of his rhetoric should have been enough to drive the point home for when he spoke, people listened.

'For our military strength and the security of the nation, it is vital for us to modernise our armed forces. It is imperative for our national interest to acquire the highly sophisticated combat aircraft, the Sukhoi-30 from Russia and all parties must concur on this decision.'

Amidst a muffled thumping of tables the august leader sat down. Not a whimper was heard from any of the benches. It was indeed a historic moment.

A battery of stenographers seated in the well of the house typed away furiously and mindlessly as they are wont, to record the proceedings of that routinely ordinary day. Some members absorbed the leader's words, some ignored them, some listened to them inattentively and some simply snored loudly in the back benches ignorant of the chain reaction that had just been set into motion. Only four people were deeply stirred by this fiery display of patriotism.

A Cabinet Minister of the coalition government sat straight-faced in the front row of the seats assigned to his party. He had a hard time concealing his triumph.

High up in the distinguished visitor's gallery two pairs of eyes were watching the proceedings with great concentration. Bharat Loya heaved a quiet sigh of relief. He glanced at the person seated beside him. On his otherwise deadpan face there was a hint of a smile that did not travel to his eyes. The man beside him smiled back. His uncle had kept his word.

Sitting among the elders in the Upper House, Sinha was restless. He glanced at his wristwatch. He almost tumbled over his fat belly when he realised that the zero hour had passed. He was going to be a very rich man.

Four weeks later on a special flight, meant for senior officials of the Defence Ministry, Bharat Loya, Ashish Kumar Sinha and his party supremo the Central Cabinet Minister left for Moscow. The contract worth three hundred billion dollars for the purchase of the Sukhoi-30 that had incubated in the files of both the countries for a long period of time was finally concluded.

Far away in the lush surroundings of his villa in the French Riviera, Omar Al Fayed thumped his chest that had swelled up with pride while Bharat Loya waited in the wings to collect and distribute the loot to the baton-holders in the relay.

Twenty-four hours after the Leader of the Opposition moved a motion in the Lok Sabha, following a long chain of events that had ignited his patriotic zeal, a senior director of Credit Suisse was contacted by Bharat Loya with a peculiar though not unprecedented request. The director, Bernard Hoffman, familiar with the constraints of such clients, flew down to Delhi for a vital parley with two high-profile, very senior politicians in the Ministry of Defence to prepare the grounds for opening a numbered account. They urgently needed to avail of these services because they were expecting a huge kickback from a source in Russia.

In a sprawling ministerial bungalow in Lutyen's Delhi, the Cabinet Minister and his slick protege, Ashish Kumar Sinha, held a closed-door meeting with Bernard Hoffman and Bharat Loya. All the four people in attendance had a common agenda. All four of them had full faith in the Swiss banking system and its code of secrecy. All four of them were privy to a secret that would lie secure in the vaults of an age-old and trustworthy institution in Zurich and all four of them were going to benefit from the transaction that had necessitated this action. The formalities were duly completed and they parted ways to await further developments.

Everything had been meticulously looked into and all tracks covered. Even if there were to be an inquiry any time in the future, nothing could possibly be traced back to them. The Minister had no links whatsoever with any bank in Zurich. He had never been to Switzerland in his entire life!

It was altogether another matter, however, that enticed by the prospects of a huge bounty, Switzerland had come to him!

50

In the winter of 1999 a long overdue divorce petition was filed in the session's court in New Delhi, on grounds of mutual consent. The two petitioners, Vishal Loya and his estranged wife Priyanka had already completed the nine month period of separation required by law in such matters.

Priyanka Nanda returned to her father's home after a fourteen-year, stormy and unconsummated marriage, finally breaking out of the manacles that had kept her within the formidable House of Loya. The younger scion of the Loyas ended his farcical commitment to her, after shelling out an officially announced alimony of twenty crores—less than half of what was rumoured to have been paid to silence the Bollywood starlet, who was allegedly carrying his illegitimate child. Priyanka, a sadder and wiser woman reverted to her maiden name and maintained a stoic dignity in the face of the break-up. She never uttered one word against her depraved spouse, nor did she fall prey to the temptation of savaging his decadent family, and no one had any way of knowing whether the sum she received from the Loyas, was in truth twenty crores, or just an inflated figure floated around by them for public consumption.

For a while, the city grapevine sliced, chewed up and regurgitated the morsel of gossip even as the divorced couple were spotted separately at the same parties, till Priyanka Nanda gradually faded away from the limelight, as a 'has been'. Vishal Loya continued his reckless and mindless philandering around the globe, surpassing in ostentation and glamour, his one-time flamboyant uncle, Anuj Vardhan. Their uncanny similarities were disturbing.

Aryaman Loya had grown up to be a good looking boy. Understandably, his physical impairment coupled with parental neglect, had turned him into an over-demanding and rebellious teenager, who had frequent episodes of hysterical behaviour. Paula, his surrogate mother, had finally quit the job and gone back to the United States, leaving him emotionally crippled. Two young men in their twenties were brought in to replace her, possibly because his father imagined that the adolescent boy needed to be in the company of men his own age. Both of them were educated, well versed with computers, smartly groomed and familiar with their job of keeping the only male child in the fourth generation of the House of Loya happy, comfortable, entertained and occupied.

Even though he was now out of his teens, Aryaman's juvenile behaviour continued to worsen. He would fling his things around in angry outbursts and stop eating. At times, he would lock himself in his room for hours, ignoring the knocks on his door, beseeching voices and urgent pleas from his caretakers to let them in.

Aryaman felt neglected and pressurised and that made him gloomy and angry. The two men constantly accompanying him could not give him the solace he needed. He had no patience for his younger sister either and rarely responded to her tender love and caring; neither did he find the occasional appearances from his father or grandmother any source of comfort. Bharat Loya began examining the prospects of sending him to the United States to a special institution equipped to deal with the handicapped. Even with the best resources at his disposal, he knew he did not have the power to bring his mother back to the miserable child.

Far away from their raucous surroundings, living in an illusory world, Yashoda was in the throes of an insane and delusory romance. The tranquil beach-house in Mauritius where she had been living for over a year, provided the perfect backdrop for her to marry the man of her dreams, who had just made his intentions known to his wife and children.

As soon as the fourteenth Lok Sabha convened its monsoon session, R. K. Lyndoh the redoubtable officer who had performed his duty in the face of overwhelming odds, was shunted out of the Enforcement Directorate. He was replaced by an additional secretary who had the backing of a charming and energetic fixer from the PM's inner coterie. Unknown to them, two persons, K V S Raju of GII and the grand lady in Chennai, had zeroed in on their common enemy. The two highly disgruntled elements with completely dissimilar backgrounds and mutually exclusive missions were ready with their ammunition to mount their offensive.

The delusory and grandiose lady considered herself a vital and indispensable ally to the National Democratic Alliance, so she not only demanded the treatment that one would give to a spoilt child, but she also knew exactly how to get it. The Department of Revenue was proving to be grievously troublesome for her. It had raised her hackles by resisting the wholesale transfer of revenue officials in Chennai, who had the audacity to close in on her for serious evasions of income tax. She knew that Lyndoh had been wrongfully removed from the DOE by senior officials of the department. She also knew exactly who was the slick troubleshooter from the cabinet, the blue-eyed boy of the Prime Minister, who had accepted five crore rupees from the Director of Corporate Affairs of GII for the job.

Even though Lyndoh's removal suited the lady just fine, as he had been aggressively investigating some FERA matters against her as well, she had hit upon the sure-shot means to embarrass the government and blackmail them into letting her have her way. Or else she threatened to withdraw her support from the NDA, with the frightening prospect of another election that not a single Indian wanted to face.

The letter from Chennai to the Prime Minister was brilliantly crafted. The lady had made specific allegations that a gentleman in the PMO, had had a series of meetings with a particular arms-dealer on whose insistence the Enforcement Director had been sacked. The letter was followed by a series of TV appearances, accusations and denials from both ends, and the press had a field day.

Clearly, the government had chosen the wrong issue on which to challenge the lady because she had raised enough of a stink to put the Prime Minister in an awkward spot over her real concerns, which were blanket amnesty from FERA and the income tax authorities even though it was no secret that she was far from being unhappy over Lyndoh's removal.

Meanwhile, Ajay Vardhan Loya returned triumphantly from another of his frequent medical visits to Cleveland, on the eve of the presentation of the fiscal budget in Parliament after the Minister declared that FERA was being repealed; and the government maintained a studied silence on a request from the Enforcement Directorate to take the Chairman of GII into custody for mandatory interrogation, as per the Supreme Court orders.

No one could stop the clock that was racing speedily, as all clocks are wont, towards expiry of the time limit for the completion of investigations.

Indeed Ajay Vardhan Loya had reasons to rejoice. He was going to be a free man.

But for the salvo fired by the grand Lady from Chennai.

51

The GII group had every reason to gloat over their achievements. There were corporate houses that enjoyed greater credibility, but under the aegis of their MD Bharat Loya no other corporate house was a match for their aggressive growth and modernisation and indisputably they reigned supreme.

By the turn of the century, the successor of Ajay Vardhan, Bharat Loya had acquired the reputation of being the most successful arms dealer of the subcontinent. As the representative of the powerful cartel of the international broker-cum-oil-sheikh Omar Al Fayed, he had surpassed his father and cleverly survived the onslaught of the political turmoil within the country leaving his competitors far behind in the race. The three hundred million dollar contract that had been recently signed between the Russians and the Government of India for the purchase of the Sukhoi-30 had established indisputably that Bharat Loya was indeed the leader of these merchants of death. From gunrunner to druglord to arms supplier of the underworld to chief facilitator of the defence forces, he stood as the warlord at the apex of a multi-billion dollar empire much of which lay stashed away in secret vaults in Switzerland.

But on the face of it the Loyas were clean. Their airline Beetle Air owned the largest number of passenger planes in an ever-expanding fleet. It had flights to almost every corner of the country and had recently begun operations to London and New York. Their spanking new aircraft and super quality service had made them the most popular carrier and they had soaked up a huge market share of the business. In keeping with their diversification plans, GII had acquired another chain of hotels in the South that were undergoing massive refurbishing in order to meet with the demands of the growing economy and their other industries of the North-east had also shown profits in the last year.

The situation as it presented was that the face of Global Integrity Industries and its allied concerns was singularly and undeniably that of its abstruse forty-five year old owner and Managing Director, Bharat Loya.

The cannon fired by the lady from Chennai hit the bullseye! In a landmark judgement, the Supreme Court ordered the immediate reinstatement of R. K. Lyndoh to his post as Director of Enforcement. The restoration served as reassurance to the believers of the doctrine, that the wheels of justice grind slowly but surely. It sent nervous tremors into the corridors of the Finance Ministry and the House of Loyas in Lutyen's Delhi.

The errant officer of the highest rank from the Ministry of Finance was finally given the boot. The shifty officer had to face a drubbing on his own turf. The dirt wantonly thrown up over the persecution of an honest officer to protect Ajay Vardhan Loya had landed squarely on his head. But he began a hasty damage control, assuring the prime accused who faced imminent arrest, that this was only a temporary setback, and that all Loya's loyalists and friends were working on a war-footing to resolve the crisis.

His empty words were drowned in the loud and ominous sounds of a slow and steady death knell.

52

For all her spiritual evolution and worldly renouncement, Bharat Loya's sister, Nupur Loya, was a flamboyant young woman given to all the vagaries of feudal living. With a sizeable equity holding in Global Integrity Industries, she frequently forayed into the offices, running amok with her grandiose refurbishment programme. Known for her keen passion and wild extravagance in the art circles, she regularly splurged on creations of famous artists that caught her fancy. Vibrant and erotic life-size canvases depicting the nude human body in homosexual or pornographic illustrations, and several expensive paintings filled up the wall spaces of conference rooms, hallways, corridors and landings at GI House. The famous dining room also came alive with several canvases by renowned painters.

Nupur was rumoured to have marched into famous art galleries in New York, where she picked up an astounding number of paintings at phenomenal prices like a royal eccentric of an earlier time. With hundreds of thousands of dollars at her disposal, she continuously pandered to her compulsive whims, if only to demonstrate the power she wielded within the establishment.

Those days another new visitor had been seen frequenting GI House. A special manager, a young and dynamic employee was assigned the job to chaperone the young man as long as he remained on the GII premises. Aryaman Loya, the young prospective owner of the company, was being subtly projected as the super whiz-kid of the IT generation, competent to take charge in the future, lest anyone believed that his handicap should pose a hindrance to his succession.

The tall, fair, well built, young man, with a strong resemblance to his mother, glided around confidently on the arm of the manager in his ancestral domain, revered, indulged and acknowledged by the staff and employees, and the exclusive section of software development and programming was made out to be his personal fiefdom.

Except for the perceptible lack of eye contact from the heir-apparent to the House of Loya, nothing in Aryaman's behaviour betrayed the torment that was eating into the vitals of the visually-challenged young man.

In the heart of New York city, a deluxe flat in an upmarket building on Fifth Avenue, was being spruced up for its high profile owner. Confined to his hospital bed for a prolonged period, Ajay Vardhan Loya was preparing to leave Delhi for the last time, a disconsolate, lonely and panic-stricken man. The unforeseen changes around him, within and outside his home had left him with no option.

His medical file, now bursting at its seams, contained enough evidence of his deteriorating heart condition. The triple bypass surgery, performed by the super-skilled team of cardiac surgeons at the Cleveland Medical Centre, had not been able to stall the progression of his disease. His prolapsed mitral valve had become almost dysfunctional. He was suffering from respiratory stress and severe debility. The official committee of his doctors and a medical advisory board had testified that his life-threatening condition entailed a highly advanced valve-replacement procedure, that could only be performed at Cleveland, and any government authority that should deny him the permission to leave the country would be in effect signing his death warrant.

Ajay Vardhan Loya was acutely depressed. All hopes of physical and emotional respite had vanished. The fear of death and arrest loomed large before him. The memory of a rebuff from the Prime Minister gnawed painfully at his diseased heart. Some weeks ago, at a public function to be held in the capital by an international organisation where the Chairman of GII was to be felicitated with a Lifetime Achievement Award, the Prime Minister had declined to share the dais with him, and for all his cunning machinations, the old-time friend of the Loyas from the Finance Ministry had not been able to get him any reprieve. The writing was clearly on the wall.

Ajay Vardhan Loya had been deserted by all his friends in high places. Even his own family had no time for him. Racing on the superfast track of their mercenary and selfish lives, no one had even a moment to spare for the dying man, who had indeed outlived his utility. Only Uday Nanda, his devoted and dutiful son-in-law who had singly handled the FERA cases stayed unflinchingly by his side, giving him the moral and emotional support he desperately needed. Of course, his old-time faithful and adoring Devyani, his crutch in a world bereft of human values and emotions, the epitome of sacrifice and commitment, stood solidly by him, never leaving him for even a second, not even when her husband succumbed to a massive cardiac arrest on his wheelchair all by himself in Bombay.

53

On a smoggy, cold grey winter morning in the heart of Delhi, a fair, buxom woman seemingly in her late forties, barged into the Darya Ganj Police Station, weeping hysterically. Her face was distorted with rage, her hair was dishevelled and her blouse had a jagged tear down the front, that she made no attempt to cover with the shawl that hung untidily over her shoulders. Her exposed body under her torn blouse looked inflamed and swollen, and long red welts that could have been nail marks, showed signs of possible physical assault.

The Station House Officer, a lumbering, six-foot tall Haryanavi, with an ugly, protruding belly that showed years of gastronomic abuse, leered sloppily at the outraged woman, who staggered into a chair opposite him sobbing loudly. Not for a fleeting moment was he flustered by the occurrence that he regarded as an everyday feature in the police station. He tilted his head upwards and looked accusingly at the harried creature to size her up. His gaze was characteristic of a man whose gender bias perceives female victims as evil doers, who have only got what they deserve. He opened his thick *roznamcha* that was frayed at the edges, and turned to a fresh page with a laboured flick of his knotty weather-beaten hands, to register the first complaint of the day. In an illegible scrawl, he began reluctantly scribbling on the yellowed pages of the register in Hindustani.

The complainant alleged, that at 10.00 hours that morning, Bharat Loya, the MD of Global Integrity Industries had summoned her to his office, where he molested her and attempted to rape her. Pointing to her exposed flesh and torn blouse, she broke down and wept piteously, saying that she had been badly bruised and injured in the struggle, while trying to save herself and get away.

Mechanically recording her accusatory words that were punctuated by loud teary outbursts, the SHO paused just once in a while to look up at the woman sitting across him. A case under sections 354 and 375 of the Indian Penal Code for molestation and attempt to rape was registered, and after receiving a matter-of-fact, verbal assurance from the beefy man in uniform, the woman settled her hair and clothes and left the police station, satisfied that she had set a process into motion that would serve to avenge her.

The perjury and blackmail in her First Information Report should have been transparent to any discerning individual, but such is the nature of the law and the working of the police force, that the complaint would have to be taken cognisance of, and properly scrutinised.

Forty-seven year old Brinda Gokuldas, five feet three inches tall, weighing over seventy-five kilograms, with a hardened face, revealing the brutal side of survival, hardly looked the suffering victim of sexual abuse and assault by a superior. Known in political and bureaucratic circles as a serial accuser and dangerous blackmailer, with a history of mischievous cases of extortion, she had been charged with the murder of her husband twenty years ago. The Air Force Officer had met with a gory death under suspicious circumstances, after falling off the balcony of his tenth floor flat in an inebriated condition. She had been let off due to insufficient evidence that failed to indict her for culpable homicide.

Managing Director Bharat Loya, five feet seven inches tall, weighing all of sixty kilos in his puny frame, was the most visible and established celibate of his high-powered world. Given the fact that he had easy access to scores of nubile beauty queens and starlets, queuing up at his door, he could scarcely have fallen prey to the temptation of molesting a dowdy female employee. He would have to cough up a hefty price for the one thing that even his worst detractors could not accuse him of, a perversely insatiable libido.

For sixty-four year old Amba Loya, the *de facto* Queen Mother of the House of Loya—life was on a roll. Sitting at the apex of the mighty industrial empire, that was being run super-efficiently by her ruthless elder son, she had long donned the mantle of an enlightened spiritual guru. She had cast herself into the enviable position of unchallenged supremacy in her material and spiritual world, by presenting a unique fusion of characteristics, grossly antithetical to each other. The power she wielded at that level and her hypocritical and hidden Janus face, created an aura of mystery that compelled most people to question themselves about which one was the real Amba Loya. Even past sixty years, her creamy translucent skin and lucid eyes retained their youthfulness and despite her carelessly donned, inexpensive saffron attire, her body showed no signs of ageing or fatigue. Her tireless spirit, the driving power of success, the charisma that she marketed to an audience ever-hungry for elusive dreams, and the carnal bond she shared with her son that most perceived as vile and sinful, had empowered her immensely.

'Touch me and you will attain nirvana,' her oft-repeated and vain words had any number of takers from among a goggle-eyed following, that had fallen in love with the perfectly groomed icon, who had surpassed the best of image manufacturers at their own skill.

Embodying all seven of the deadly sins—pride, jealousy, anger, sloth, greed, gluttony and lust, she cruised along the years of her highly visible glamourised life, as an irresistible enigma. Sitting on a tidy pile of treasured jewels that she inherited from her mother-in-law, grabbed off her deceased sister-in-law, and carefully collected from bankrupt estates of erstwhile Maharajas, she was rumoured to be in possession of a king's ransom worth of treasures that she regularly flaunted.

She was often seen sporting curious oddities as pendants around her neck. An intricately carved figure of

Ganesha in yellow topaz with a long rock crystal tusk curling downwards embellished with precious stones; a giant-sized rectangular Colombian emerald engraved with verses from the Gita; or an irregular, natural pink coral in the shape of a lotus encrusted with diamonds, suspended from a string of *rudraksh* beads, were some of her adornments, that could neither be replicated nor evaluated. With an artist's precision of line and form, she constantly put together her own unique creations that left most people awestruck.

Completely contrasting with her intense passion for acquisitions, were innumerable and horrific legends of her blatant niggardliness. Her household was a guarded fortress where food, rations and fruit were carefully padlocked in the pantry and store. Not a single morsel could be consumed without her approval. Often, perishables would lie rotting in her locked larders and then thrown away—but never given to the servants. The servants were allowed a meal of only one seasonal vegetable and coarse rice or grain, and the leftovers from the food prepared for the family were thrown away, rather than given to them. Every drop of fuel used in her fleet of cars had to be accounted for and registers maintained for recording meter readings and mileage. No one could incur an extra expense of even ten rupees without her sanction. House guests were denied afternoon meals as per the rules of the house, as no food was cooked at lunch.

A family of relatives with two young children, who chanced to stay at Loya House, got the worst dressing-down when their children finished a quarter kilogram of

Merchants of Death

tomatoes with their breakfast sandwiches, for which the head cook nearly lost his job.

The only person who was spared this meanness, and had free access to the services of the house as well as Amba Loya's treasures, was Nupur. She had the licence to walk freely in and out of her mother's vault. Her childhood memory of Kanupriya's horror at being denied tomato sandwiches by Amba, one of the many bitter grudges that the suicide victim carried to her grave, had long been drowned in the tempo of her younger cousin's high-speed mindless existence. Indeed the only worthwhile memory left of the depressive mother and her three children, was Rajshri's bag of jewels that now lay locked in a drawer inside the family vault in Amba Loya's custody.

But Amba rued the loss of the twenty crore rupees that the Loyas had given as alimony, to Priyanka. She was relieved that Yashoda had exited quietly, and that her desertion was unlikely to leave another gaping hole in their pockets. She fretted about the current state of affairs in the FERA matter and its dismal outcome, with Lyndoh now firmly back in the saddle. With all their clout exhausted, the Loyas would have to devise some other means to escape the arrest and prosecution of Ajay Vardhan Loya, and the thought of forfeiting their bounty stashed away in Credit Suisse terrified her.

That fear was far greater than the fear of death. Amba stopped in her tracks. If death was the only way out then death it would have to be.

54

No one from the family accompanied Ajay Vardhan Loya to New York. He boarded the Virgin Atlantic flight from IGI Airport, one hour before midnight, in the last week of September, disregarding the ominous signs of departing on a Wednesday, which most Hindus believe to be inauspicious. His soulmate, Devyani, wearing a turquoise blue sari to pander to his passion for the colour, walked imperiously by his side. She was pushing a Burberry overnighter with one hand and lightly supporting his elbow with the other.

For Ajay Vardhan Loya, Devyani had stood the test of time. Baptised in the fires of life's trials and tribulations, she had never wavered in her duty or love, staying always beside him when he needed her.

A surge of emotions overtook the feeble sexagenarian, as he crossed the immigration barrier to leave his homeland, a despondent, disillusioned man.

The Chairman of GI Industries—now only a titular head, had lived an envied and glamorous life. He had tasted the supreme power of being able to walk into the Prime Minister's office at any time that very few people

Merchants of Death

could have boasted of. He had possessed everything material that he ever desired, and had indulged in the wildest carnal fantasies that could have been perceived of by a mortal. Never in all the sixty-five years of his life had he known the feeling of having being denied anything, yet as he crossed the last checkpoint at the airport, into the dimly lit, accordion-like tunnel, that connected the waiting lounge to the cabin door of the aircraft, he felt a deep, hollow emptiness within.

A slow-moving, action replay of his entire life, rolled past—his childhood as the adored first born of Draupadi and Baldev Das, his youth as the heir-apparent of an autocratic, doting mother, his post-marriage years as the much sought after industrial supremo who had the ability and the means to command any woman to submit to his will—all of it came rushing back to his mind. His own bonding with his distant but dutiful father, the sharp, business acumen, he had inherited from him, the crafty, manipulative, techniques he had imbibed and then passed on to his son—the son, who had done him proud.

The thought of Bharat gave him a warm glowing feeling, but then, something jabbed him. It was the sharp throbbing pain of an ageing parent, whose children just don't care or don't care enough, and the cruel rejection of his beautiful wife, whose body had not been touched by the erosion of old age and who continued the pursuit of her esoteric ideals in an illusory world. He had never shared a normal conjugal relationship with her. The mechanical birth of their three children, had failed to strengthen the bond between them, in either flesh or spirit. He felt defeated and alone.

He knew that in the peculiar realm inhabited by his wife and son, there was no room for him. The thought of their unnerving and consanguine chemistry, deepened the pit in his stomach. A perverse jealousy invaded his conscious mind, a strong resentment for his child, who had surpassed him in every conceivable manner, having usurped his position even in the love for the most important woman in their lives—a love which was nothing, if it wasn't Oedipal.

The memory of his adored grandchild, tugged at his soul. The cruel accident that had snatched away his vision, filled him with endless waves of remorse. The state of disarray in the marriages of his three children was disturbing. Nupur was not a good wife to his reverent son-in-law. Priyanka had been a disaster and Yashoda's forthcoming marriage to Mallya was a cruel betrayal.

When the flesh is weak and wasting does the mortal mind undergo a process of penitence that is both depressing and debilitating?

Ajay Vardhan Loya—the frail, diseased and persecuted fugitive, whose only hope for survival lay in the hands of the skilled cardiac team at the Cleveland Medical Centre—strapped himself into the extra wide seat of the first class cabin, trying to fight the terrifying demons from his past. The faces of several women from his past—crippled and bedridden Nayantara Jaipuria, Rashmi Mehta, Sunita Aggarwal, Preeti Jhawar, Mukta Loya, Kumkum Jindal and a host of others—flashed before him till he stopped at Devyani. A serene look of contentment radiated from her. A floral fragrance permeated his senses and mildly eased him. She leaned over the armrest, smoothened his hair, caressed his cheeks lightly and nestled her head on his shoulder.

'Don't worry. All will be well. I am here and will never leave you, no matter what!' she whispered.

Those words, that had been said hundreds of times before, failed to reassure him that night. The loud droning sound of the propellers reverberated in two hundred and eighty-six pairs of ears, as the 'Fasten Seat Belts' sign flashed, and the plane taxied onto the runway. A chilling and grim Wednesday, bade farewell to the high-profile fugitive. It would give credence to the irrational superstition, that it was indeed ill-omened and he would never be back.

By now Bharat Loya was an established master of marketing gimmickry, and he constantly churned out new ideas, to expand his outreach and profits. Each day, newly devised techniques rolled out of the MD's office, that were translated into practice by bands of young men and women sporting bright orange T-shirts with the Beetle Air logo at every traffic light, doling out gift hampers and credit vouchers that could be redeemed at famous shopping centres in the capital. Weekly lucky draws with bumper prizes were sponsored by the company in popular shopping areas, and gifts ranging from spanking new Mitsubishi Lancers, to refrigerators, to high-end plasma TV sets, to computers, to motorcycles, were generously distributed to lure more and more customers into their fold.

Each week beaming, smiling photographs of winners shaking hands with, and accepting prizes from, glamourous celebrities, stars, cricketers and popular icons, were prominently splashed on the front pages of the newspapers, instilling hope in the minds of millions of hitting the jackpot. Indeed the collective gambling instinct of human beings, the enticement to get free air-tickets, complimentary rooms at five-star hotels and to strike lucky on a public platform of fame, had never been exploited more cleverly before.

Similarly, in the smaller cities, lucky draws with generous prizes were organised *en masse,* bombing all other regional and national competitors out of existence. Not able to withstand the merciless onslaught of the rolling juggernaut, many of them had to shut shop.

Despite the stigma of being the most influential wheeler-dealer of India with links to Bombay's underworld and the international mafia Bharat Loya's clean front of airline owner and hotelier came strongly to the fore. This provided him with convenient opportunities to entertain and oblige the people who mattered, an art that the family had mastered over four generations and no one could question the source of his limitless funds. Some people however became wary of the enticements being offered by the Loyas at the Ritz Grand hotel which had become their networking base. They became apprehensive of using its facilities for their illicit sojourns because a strong rumour had spread around the city that some of the rooms were wired to closed-circuit TV cameras that were used to record the murky goings-on in there regularly.

But stories about Bharat Loya, who was hated intensely and criticised bitterly, were lapped up greedily by those who mattered. He had become truly indestructible.

Soon after Ajay Vardhan Loya left for Cleveland, a prime space was reserved on the front page of all the national newspapers to publish a daily health bulletin of his progress. Cleverly worded and detailed reports about his failing health, were strategically marketed by then with the specific intent of garnering public sympathy.

Amba's puzzling presence in Delhi and not by her ailing husband's side warranted some clarifications. As usual, her prime tenet of practical detachment from the world was on full display, and marginally helped to settle public discomfiture, and life for the Loyas rolled along at breakneck speed.

55

London
December 1999

Ashish Kumar Sinha was stark naked. He opened his eyes and tried to focus slowly in the dim light of his surroundings. A dark green damask curtain loomed before him as he threw off the soft duvet of eiderdown and stretched hard like a cat. He felt good. It took him a few seconds to realise that he was sprawled on a plush king-sized bed in a suite at the Dorchester Hotel. He massaged his eyes with his palms and tried to focus once more. The mist of a cold London winter had frosted up the window-panes outside his room making them translucent. It made him feel horny all over again.

Sinha lay spreadeagled on the bed for just a while longer soaking in the euphoria of the previous night that had lingered on. These white women really know how to please a man, he thought. He would have the time for one more sinful night on the weekend before he returned to Delhi. These were the fringe benefits that came with his position. His fetish for sex with white-skinned women had never been ignored by the Loyas. He made a mental note. He must remember to ask for the same woman again. Her huge luscious breasts, creamy thighs and tight ass were addictive. Sinha was in seventh heaven reliving the climactic moments of the last evening, when a sharp ring of the alarm snapped him out of his reverie. He jumped out of bed clumsily almost tripping over his pot-belly and padded into the shower. He could not be late. His flight to Zurich was to leave in just a few hours.

As Political Secretary and most trusted aide of the Defence Minister he was on a top secret mission. He had been informed by Bharat Loya that a certain transaction had been completed by his associates in Russia and he needed to go to Zurich to complete the last formalities. The anticipation of what lay ahead was almost as invigorating as his one-night stand. It came with the thrill of unearned lucre, a bounty that was way beyond his imagination, all of which was coming to him and his boss. He scrubbed his podgy flesh vigorously with a scented bath-gel and hummed a tune. In a few hours from now he was going to be a very rich man, a multi-billionaire. He drooled as he drew innumerable zeroes in air slicing the shrapnels of water that fell on his body. He had last seen so many zeroes in his primary school books when he was learning how to count.

He stepped out of the shower and sprayed himself with a strong body mist. He pulled out a dark grey flannel suit from a hanger in the closet and put it on. He knotted a bright silk tie and looked at himself in the full-length mirror. The image pleased him. He had to keep the sombre dignity of the office he held. He glanced at this wristwatch, grabbed his briefcase and dashed out to the lift. Outside the hotel a smart black Volvo was waiting to take him to the airport.

A few minutes after the clock struck eleven a speeding taxi pulled up on Paradeplatz in front of the august grey building of Credit Suisse in Zurich. A short plump man in dark flannels carrying a briefcase scurried into the main entrance where he was greeted by a security officer who escorted him in. The smell of freshly brewed coffee snaked up his nostrils. He looked around barely concealing his feelings. He was overawed by the power that emanated from the bricks and mortar of one of the largest banking operations of the world—the squirrel-nest of billions of dollars stashed away in secret funds of some very important people. He smiled at the thought that he would soon become one with this elusive, distinguished gang of the rich, powerful and corrupt elite that needed a safe haven to keep their ill-gotten lucre outside their homelands.

'Good morning, Mr. Sinha, I am Maria, the secretary of Mr. Bernard Hoffman, our Senior Director.' The cheerful voice of a tall woman in a black business-suit and pencil heels interrupted his thoughts. He was struck by her comely figure and slender legs and began to strip her instantly in his mind's eye.

'Please take a seat, sir. Mr. Hoffman will be with you in just a moment,' she said in accented English flashing perfect pearly-white teeth.

'The lucky son-of-a-bitch—must be ramming her every night,' Sinha thought with a twinge of jealousy as he smiled at the curvaceous twenty-something woman. He picked up a newspaper from the table and eased his bulky frame into a wide leather chair. He began tapping his fingers impatiently on the handrest staring out of a window that overlooked a dark forest. He did a quiet replay of the events that had transpired in the last seven days. Had it not been for his craft this contract would have slipped out of their hands.

The Senior Director, a seasoned old-timer in his sixties had finance interred in his bones. 'Welcome to Zurich Mr. Sinha. It is good to see you again. We are very pleased to have you here with us. Did you have a pleasant flight?' Hoffman's deep voice belied his age. They shook hands and sat down across a sleek glass table in the steel and leather lounge reserved for special clients.

'We are grateful that you have chosen our bank to handle your finances, sir. You shall be glad to know that in accordance with the instructions you gave me when we met in Delhi, everything is in order. I suppose you are familiar with the rest of the formalities,' he said. 'May I have your passport please. I shall not keep you very long. All the clearances have been done and the money has been credited to your numbered account as desired by your honorable Minister and you. You shall have to fill in the names of your nominees on our papers for the record. I shall just reiterate some rules and procedures for your information. I take it that you understand that the same apply to the co-beneficiary of this account. Needless to say that the bank takes full responsibility to maintain total secrecy of your transactions and pledges never to disclose these details to anyone other than your authorised nominees. In the event of your death your nominees shall be entitled to operate the accounts and inherit the monies held therein. If your account is not operated for a maximum period of ten years and we do not receive any communication from your nominees then presuming that the original account-holders are dead we undertake to search for and identify your respective nominees at our expense, to apprise them of this account and to take future instructions from them. Please be assured, this pledge of secrecy is as sacred for us as it is imperative for you.' Hoffman handed him a leather folder. 'You can go through these papers while I make copies of your passport and your authorisation. You need to fill out some details on the forms that are in there.'

Sinha broke into a sweat. The morbid word 'death' sent a chill down his back. This was not the time to die. Life had just begun. Thank you Mr. Hoffman,' he said uneasily. 'Perhaps I need not remind you that no statements, records or correspondence with regard to these transactions shall ever be sent to India.'

Hoffman clasped his hands. 'Don't worry Mr. Sinha,' he said 'ours is a relationship of trust. We are one of the oldest banking institutions in Switzerland with a history that spans over one hundred years. And like I said, secrecy is both our God and our religion. We have an impeccable record as you may have been told by Mr. Loya and there has never been a breach to date. Trust me, even if a gun is held to my head I shall never reveal the details of your holdings to any one who is not part of this pact.' Hoffman's voice had dropped to a barely audible whisper. He spoke with an air of reassurance and confidence that had a calming effect on Sinha's nerves.

In a few minutes Maria walked into the room with another folder. She handed it to Sinha mechanically and left. Sinha flipped open the cover of the file which contained a sheaf of very officious looking documents that had the imperious logo of Credit Suisse stamped on them. The neatly stapled papers confirmed the transfer of two hundred million dollars into their account. Sinha made a quick calculation. That bastard Loya is richer by fifty million dollars he thought.

Sinha steadied himself and mopped his brow. Indeed they had struck the jackpot. It all seemed so simple. He began dreaming of a much-awaited holiday in Las Vegas with its lure of sex, gambling and enticing women in all shapes and sizes. Yes, that was a holiday that he was going to enjoy like never before. He felt his spirit lift instantly. He picked up the receiver of the phone beside him and punched in an international number.

'Mubarak ho Bade Bhai, kaam ho gaya,' he said in a loud voice typical of Indians talking on long-distance calls. 'I have instructed the bank to keep all the papers in a special locker assigned to us. Yes, I shall bring back the keys with me when I return. I am booked on the flight back from London on Monday morning. No, no, I have not forgotten the Rolex watch, yes I know you don't like

the steel one, yes of course gold it shall be. *Kaho to puree dukaan ley aaoon, bhai, ek ghari ki kya baat hai!'*

Sinha stood up and almost embraced Hoffman shaking his hand vigorously. 'Thank you for everything, Mr. Hoffman. We are going to have a long and meaningful relationship I can see. And by the way, you have a very sexy secretary. Please say goodbye to her too.' Sinha winked lecherously.

'Good-bye, Mr. Sinha. I hope to see you again soon. Do give my regards to Mr. Loya when you see him and have a safe flight back.' Hoffman led him to the door with a wide smile. He was used to these oily, raunchy politicians from India. He had been dealing with them for as many years as he could remember.

Back home in New Delhi, the jubilant Minister of Defence, his partner-associate Bharat Loya and one relative of an ex-prime minister had just accomplished an unprecedented feat. They had acquired for the Indian Air Force a non-existent fighter aircraft, the Sukhoi-30 from Russia for which they had paid a staggering two billion dollars from the national exchequer. This was the single largest defence deal in the history of the Indian military. For the beneficiaries, it was time to rejoice.

56

Ostensibly, death did not come easily to Ajay Vardhan Loya. Having been in severe cardiac distress for a prolonged period of time and even after a triple bypass and valve-replacement surgery, his only chance for survival lay in a transplant of his heart, which was barely functioning at twenty per cent. The risky wait is at the best of times much too long, and many prospective recipients have known to succumb to cardiac seizures before donor organs can be made available; therefore, death was a foregone conclusion.

The morbid announcement of Ajay Vardhan Loya's end made front page news in all the national dailies that featured the concluding saga in the four-month long build-up, over a period of several days. A deluge of obituaries, condolences, lifetime achievement portrayals and milestones from birth to death, occupied prime space on the front pages. The offices closed down as a mark of respect for the passing away of the third generation owner of GI Industries and several condolence and prayer meetings were held all over the country, in the memory of the deceased luminary.

Bharat Loya was the only one from the family, who went to New York to complete the last rites of his dead father. Most people expected him to bring the body back to India for its cremation. The rest of the clan—Amba, Nupur, Uday and Vishal went into silent retreat and hordes of mourners and relatives who came calling, were turned away from the door as they wished to see no one.

The following day, an announcement was made to the public that Amba Loya was indisposed, and all concerned were to stand by for further announcements about the post-death rituals. The eager mourners, friends and family members awaited orders from *the holy Troika*—in a scramble to score brownie points with the soon-to-be coronated Sultan, Bharat Loya.

R. K. Lyndoh had been rendered powerless. He was fully aware that the Loyas had pulled off the most foolproof hoax imaginable, and that he had indeed been trounced by a rotten and corrupt system.

Brigadier Mehta finally gave up.

'The son-of-a-bitch is not dead,' he hissed.

Ajay Vardhan Loya's mortal remains came back to his homeland inside an urn packed in a cardboard carton, as part of his son's baggage. As he flew silently eastwards, Bharat Loya's mind went blank. The eighteen-hour journey that he had traversed back and forth innumerable times, felt longer and different that day. It was not grief he felt—it was numbness. There would be no major shift in his life with his father gone. He stared out of his window, over the fluffy bed of white cotton clouds rolling along.

The wisps of smoke gave way and then came back together again. He saw them dissipate on impact, as the aircraft pierced through. He saw various configurations of birds, sheep, feathers and the form of a woman. The sound of the droning engine made him drowsy, Life is like these clouds he thought to himself. Nothing changes—it only restructures itself to stay where it is!

Amba Loya had not accompanied her son to bring back the remains of her dead husband. 'It's too cold in America,' she had said in chilling words that pierced far deeper than their import warranted, and no one had noticed that Devyani did not return to India, the grieving widow—perhaps, the only one who was devastated by the pain of a final parting.

57

New Delhi
January 2000

A short, squat, middle-aged man in a white khadi kurta entered the presidential suite of the Ritz Grand hotel. He had receding salt and pepper hair, a round face and a visible pot-belly that protruded like a large melon. His thick jaw was framed by lines that stretched from the sides of his nose down to the corners of his mouth and deep frown-lines formed a triangle between his brows that made him look mean and angry.

The room was panelled in dark wood with soft beige sofas and deeply cushioned armchairs. A champagne bucket with a bottle of Dom Perignon tilted over round chunks of ice had been placed on the coffee table with a large silver bowl filled with strawberries. There was a full bar stocked with the choicest liquor on one side of the room.

The man settled into a sofa and reached out for the remote control. A feeling of deep contentment overcame him. The management was familiar with his habits. They had not overlooked anything. He flicked the buttons on the remote control till he came to a channel that was belting out a raunchy number from a Hindi movie. A sexy starlet was performing an item with vulgar gyrations and pelvic thrusts. She had her navel exposed in the shot and the dimples on her lower back glistened with sweat as she moved provocatively. Her barely-clad bosom also jiggled in rhythm to the popular rap song that had been riding the top slot on the charts for many days. These Bollywood beauties have bodies made of rubber, he thought as he glanced at the time. She should have been here, he had only two hours. The song had made him horny and he was becoming impatient.

A soft knock on the door startled him. A young woman looking flustered appeared and plonked herself beside him.

'I am so sorry. Don't blame me,' she said. 'You should do something about the traffic. It's your government, but I'll make up for this.' She winked teasingly and flashed a wide smile. Her full red lips parted as she kicked off her boots and stepped out of her tight jeans and undid the buttons of her shirt revealing a black satin G-string and a lace brassiere. She waltzed to the bar in a deliberate swagger. 'Come and get me,' she cooed.

By now the man had torn his clothes off. He pounced on the woman, lifted her off her feet and carried her into the bedroom. He lay down panting, stark naked as his belly flopped over loosely on both sides of his abdomen.

'Make it long and good like you always do ... ' he whispered as she sat astride him. She had not removed the last of her clothes. She stretched out her hand, picked a cube of ice from the bucket and took it into her mouth. She began to lick his stomach slowly drawing tiny circles on his skin with her tongue.

'You do look like that Shetty woman from the movies my *jaan*,' he sighed. His eyes rolled upwards as he felt an ecstatic icy cool sensation on his groin that travelled down his thigh...

Bharat Loya lifted the remote control and pointed it forward. He clicked a button. The monitor on his office wall spluttered and died. He had seen this man in action many times before. The cabinet minister was a regular at the hotel. He was addicted to afternoon sex with this particular woman, whom he had handpicked from a dossier compiled by a highly reputed agency of Bombay. She was the highest paid call girl in their circuit. And she was all of twenty-one.

The Presidential Suite was one of the many that had been fitted with a closed-circuit camera. It recorded this afternoon sojourn of the cabinet minister in lurid detail. It would be tagged, dated, catalogued and put into the confidential files of the management for future reference.

Bharat Loya leaned back in his chair.

'Make sure nothing goes wrong in the Presidential Suite. I don't want any goof-up behind the scenes,' he said into the intercom.

Peering gleefully over his glasses at the motley group of monitors mounted on his private office wall he had seen many specimens of humanity at their ugliest; debauched men and women in various stages of undress who had morphed into naked oysters, big, fat, lean and small, grunting with sounds of carnal pleasure. For Bharat Loya this was a periodic travel back in time. The words of his favourite childhood verse came alive....

> *'I weep for you,' the Walrus said:*
> *'I deeply sympathise.'*
> *With sobs and tears he sorted out*
> *Those of the largest size*
> *Holding his pocket-handkerchief*
> *Before his streaming eyes.*
> *'Oh Oysters,' said the Carpenter*
> *'You've had a pleasant run!*
> *Shall we be trotting home again?'*
> *But answer came there none—*
> *And this was scarcely odd, because*
> *They'd eaten every one.*

Indeed, the galloping giant had swallowed up each one of them—the stuffed shirts, the mocking critics and the entire gamut of a woebegone system that he had turned into his private checker-board.

That should settle the motherfuckers,' he muttered as he walked out briskly. He forgot he was small, sickly, underweight, and emetic...

58

Aryaman Loya understood death. He understood its finality and permanence. He understood its reality, as much as he understood the irrevocable truth, that he was visually impaired. But something was amiss in the death of his grandfather which he, like the rest of his clan, had been expecting for a while. In measured doses, he had been absorbing the transatlantic news of the ebbing life of his *Dadaji,* but something was seriously amiss. He couldn't understand it.

When the news of his death finally broke, why did no one grieve for him? Why was his father the only one who went to America? He thought he would bring the body back but he did not. He cremated him there, all by himself. Why? Why was no one by his side when he passed away, except Devyani. Why not his grandmother? But his *Dadima* never stayed where *Dadaji* was. She was always on her spiritual tours, lecturing people on the art of higher living. Perhaps, she had stopped caring about anyone's dying, or perhaps, she thought she would never die. But Aryaman knew that no one could cheat death.

He knew that for a fact; that people died and disappeared forever into an unknown realm, from where there were no comebacks. The thought of death comforted him. A dead man couldn't think, or weep, or feel pain. It didn't matter if he could see or not—it was all the same. A dead man would feel no sadness or joy—it was all the same. Like a feather floating from the sky—a numbness—a lightness, a weightlessness and a permanence—he knew he would get there some day. But something was not right here. Aryaman knew his grandfather had come back as ashes inside an urn. But why was no one sad? No one was allowed near the urn to offer flowers or pay their last respects to the mortal remains of the dead man. Something was seriously wrong.

An old director of GII, one of the few who had been allowed to come to see them had been cut short, mid-sentence, by a cold rebuff from his father. 'If it's my father's death you want to condole, please don't, Mr. Jha. If it's anything else you can go ahead.' The pregnant pause that followed felt like a million tonnes of ice and snow had avalanched on poor Jha's head!

Bharat continued. 'Have some *idlis* they are hot, the cook makes them really well.' Jha had left the room without saying a word. The *idlis* were untouched, unlike his soul, that had never been more rattled before.

Aryaman Loya knew something was seriously wrong. He knew no phone calls were being entertained and streams of mourners had been turned away, except for one hour on the evening of the thirteenth day, when his father conducted a brief farcical meeting. It could well have been an AGM of the company.

The solemn and eager mourners came in droves. They would. It was the correct thing to do, but something was seriously amiss. His father distributed Ferrero-Rocher chocolates at the meeting.

'Have these,' he said. 'The body is dead and gone, but the soul never perishes. Why grieve for something that we know has to come to an end? My father is not dead—he lives in me, my mother, my son, and in all of you here. Only fools weep for the dead.' Aryaman heard his father intone the sounds of a familiar shloka from the Gita.

'Vasansi Jeernani Yatha Vihaya
Navani grahnati naro parani
Tatha sarirani vihaya Jirnanya
Anyani samyati navani dehi'

He understood the meaning of those words. Just like you would discard an old garment, the soul also discards the body to get a new one, he had been taught.

Aryaman felt a chill down his spine. He felt deeply disturbed.

Then his grandmother floated in. He could not see that she was in pristine white and her salt and pepper hair formed a soft frame around her bewitching face, but he could feel the power that emanated from her like a strong current. She sat down on the raised platform with her eyes closed and after what seemed like an endless pause she began to speak.

Her voice was hypnotic, musical, soft and enchanting.
'Jinka naam hi Ajay ho unko mrityu nahi jeet sakti; unke liye kya shok.'

(Why should you grieve for him, who cannot be defeated by death?)

Deep resounding chants from the Gita, came alive in the background and Amba went into a trance. An unnerving silence followed. A few stifled sobs and coughs interrupted the swaying musical rhythm, as dozens of boxes of the round chocolates, the size of small golf balls, wrapped in crinkled gold paper, with a tiny round sticker on top were passed around like holy bread. Each one solemnly picked up a piece. Some were seen staring at it disconcertedly.

A half-empty box came round to Aryaman. The strong aroma of chocolate hit his nostrils, as it stopped in front of him. He picked up two pieces, one in each hand. He slowly unwrapped the crinkled gold paper. *'You are not supposed to bite it. Just put the whole chocolate into your mouth and feel it melt Baba.'* He remembered Paula's words. He remembered his favourite chocolates as creamy, crunchy and fulfilling. He put the delectable morsel into his mouth. It filled up his oral cavity. It stuck to his palate. His lips puckered up and curled tightly around it. He moved it from side to side, from one cheek to the other tantalisingly and he felt a constriction in his throat. He licked his fingers and closed his fist tightly around the other one.

The musical chants from the Gita played on. The other voices began to fade away. Aryaman had still not finished sucking the chocolate, which had melted down to the nut in the centre. He tried hard to not let his teeth bite into it. He savoured the taste of the sweet syrup drop by drop on every pore of his mouth and tongue.

The holy bread had to be swallowed whole. It was the flesh of the father in heaven. You were not supposed to bite it.

He gulped and bit hard into the crunchy mass. He felt as if he had eaten the forbidden flesh of his forefathers, the body of crucified Jesus, the ultimate act of beastly cannibalism. But something was seriously amiss, and someone had cheated death.

Aryaman stood up and rushed out, away from the vicinity of his clan. He couldn't bear to stay there any longer.

Something was seriously amiss. And someone was cheating death.

His throat felt like a thick rubber band had tightened around it.

59

Geneva
May 2000

Around a sleek conference table in a compact room panelled with dark brown beechwood, felled in the forests of the Canadian Tundra, five men of diverse origin had congregated as guests of Omar Al Fayed. These were the chosen few who had each proven their worth to merit entry into this private club of billionaires. Bharat Loya from India, Uri Orlov from Russia, Pascal Durrand from France, Abu Karzen from Palestine and Lazzaro Mancini from Italy sat on chairs covered with rich ivory silk listening to the impassioned speech of their flamboyant host in surroundings that rivalled the homes of the world's most ostentatious royals of an earlier era.

'Friends we are gathered here today for a very special reason. It is a day of rejoicing. It is a day for celebration. It is a day to thank Allah for his gift of divine blessings. Today my friends, I am proud to tell you that we, the cartel of Omar Al Fayed have been rated among the top eight arms cartels of the world and that we have in the last year sold weapons in excess of ten billion dollars. Of the five major war zones on this planet, we my brothers are present in all. Today we have come together as a family, to applaud and enjoy the fruits of our toil and to discuss future plans so that each one of us can carry forward this mission with greater zeal.

'Before we proceed I want to say a special word of thanks to the youngest one present among us. Bharat Loya is more than a son to me. His father, God bless his soul, and I were old friends. For this boy I had a dream. I wanted him to be big; bigger than any other man in this business in India and today I can say with great pride that Bharat Loya has surpassed all the other rivals by his finely honed skills and has clinched the largest ever arms deal for us in his country.'

'Hear! Hear!' the muffled sound of thumping tables could be heard as Bharat Loya suppressed a smile.

'Our prospects are getting better by the day in the Indian subcontinent. The situation is like never before. India is surrounded by hostile neighbours. The tension on her borders is fast on the rise. The insurgency within has touched an all-time high and our links with the underworld are wide and deep, so it looks like we are going to be in business for a long, long time.'

'Hear! Hear!' All eyes were on Loya.

Fayed rambled on. The war on terror has worked well for us in the rest of the world too. Our friends in the White House tell us that the Pentagon is secretly preparing to invade Iraq to put Saddam Hussain on a leash and that should surely give our business a big boost. Uri Orlov and Pascal Durrand have spread their nets across the length and breadth of Europe and North America. The Islamic insurgents in most of the pockets there are dependent on us for their supply of arms. Central Asia and South America are being superbly managed by Lazzaro Mancini. The crafty fox has sold ten thousand AK-47s to Peru just last month and in some places he has even sold weapons to warring factions on both sides. Well done, Lazzaro!' Mancini stood up and bowed in acknowledgement. 'If I may say so, today our cartel has the power and money to buy out a large part of the Third World.'

'Hear! Hear!' the five men thumped their fists on the table in approval.

'But friends, there is some bad news from Angola. Our associate Viktor Falcone is dead. He was brutally murdered last month for not heeding my advice. I had told him never to break tradition. He accepted diamonds in exchange for a consignment of AK-47s in spite of my repeated warnings. I have told all of you never to alter the old and established code. Money in Swiss banks is the safest and the best. We don't want to risk our lives for petty greed do we? His body came back home badly mutilated. They had stabbed him forty times and cut off his genitals.' Fayed's eyes clouded over and he bowed his head to say a silent prayer.

A smartly dressed steward appeared with an ornate trolley laden with an array of drinks, caviar, fruits and exotic cheeses. He wheeled the trolley around, stopping behind each guest, taking orders, pouring their chosen drinks into Baccarat crystal glasses. He placed crested gold cutlery beside porcelain plates individually painted with a motif of crossed swords in gold. Each guest was served generous helpings of firm, white, well-rounded grains of Almas over crushed ice and flutes of chilled champagne. The only one who did not partake of the royal feast was Bharat Loya.

Uri Orlov spooned up a tiny heap of the world's most expensive caviar with a long-stemmed spoon of gold, onto a thin crust of toasted bread and took a large sip of the champagne. Try the Beluga, it's exquisite,' he whispered with his mouth full into Mancini's ear gesturing to the steward for a refill. He knew the taste of this rare and exotic delicacy. He knew it was sold for an exorbitant price out of 24-carat gold tins. He also knew that it had been fittingly named Almas, the Russian word for diamonds by the company that processed it in Iran. This caviar is surely meant for the gods, he thought as he sampled the delightful taste of his favourite food.

The sight and smells of the rich spread had lifted the momentary gloom. The sounds of clinking crystal and metal scraping porcelain could be heard around the table. Orlov looked up and forced himself to concentrate on Fayed who had begun to speak again.

'Did you know my friends that there are half a billion people with firearms on this planet, which makes it one in every twelve. For us the challenge is, how can we arm the other eleven? And after that you know what shall happen to us my brothers, we shall inherit the earth because everyone else would have shot each other dead.'

Fayed broke into a throaty, boisterous laugh as the imagined spectacle was drowned in large infusions of alcohol. He stood up and raised a toast. 'To our global family, to our brotherhood, to our growing trade, to the Gods of War!'

Bharat Loya had tuned out.

A 'Fasten Seats Belts' sign lit up to the sound of piped music. The fresh whiff of a subtle Bvlgari fragrance filled the cabin as the aircraft began to descend. Bharat Loya looked out of the window. From thirty thousand feet in the air he could see one tip of the large wing-span of Fayed's customised private jet furnished with 24-carat solid gold fittings, and a separate prayer room, where this high-powered meeting was being held. The plane sliced through heaps of snowy white clouds that spread over and caressed the purple-blue slopes of the Swiss Alps. It gradually descended, circled and made a smooth touchdown at Geneva airport. Each one of the five participants were carrying back with him a parting memento from Omar Al Fayed as a token of his friendship, a bullet cast in 24-carat solid gold.

Far away in freezing temperatures of forty degrees below zero at a remote airfield in Siberia, a very senior officer of the Indian Air Force had flagged off two SU-30 jets aboard a huge Antonov cargo plane headed to India.

In Karachi, a car bomb had exploded outside the US consulate killing over forty people.

In Srinagar, a series of bombs had gone off simultaneously in crowded market places of the city, leaving a deadly trail of blood and carnage and over seventy people dead.

In Kandahar the ruling regime of the Taliban in collusion with the Pakistan Intelligence Services, the ISI, was carefully planning the hijack of an Indian Airlines plane in order to secure a huge ransom and the release of a dreaded Islamic terrorist lodged in an Indian prison.

In another part of Pakistan the decapitated head of a US journalist was found half a mile away from his brutally butchered body after he had gone missing for a couple of days.

In secret hideouts in Afghanistan a terrorist outfit by the name of Al Qaeda headed by a man of Saudi origin was rigorously training suicide squads in the name of *Jihad*. A close relative of Omar Al Fayed, he was planning to launch multiple strikes on vital targets all over America.

In a school in Kansas City, a fourteen-year old boy had gunned down sixteen of his classmates and two teachers with a .9 mm semi-automatic rifle.

And in Washington, a cartel of highly influential gun-manufacturers had stalled a bill in the US Senate that sought to introduce a ban on the sale of firearms in the United States of America.

60

At the Fifth Avenue flat in New York, a short, squat bespectacled man, with ashen skin and grey, receding thinning hair, was sitting alone by the fireside, on a rocking chair. He was staring at a pile of newspapers strewn on the floor. Each one had a deluge of reports, screaming headlines, lifetime achievement profiles, family photographs, portrait shots and reverential obituaries on the death of the illustrious Ajay Vardhari Loya, the third generation owner and Chairman of the Global Integrity Industries of India. He had read and reread the reports several times over. A lifescape of events and memories, in words and pictures were sprawled out in front of him like the careless strokes of a mad artist's brush. They stung his eyes that had dimmed with macular degeneration and progressive glaucoma, common in people with coronary-artery disease. He took off his gold-rimmed Armani glasses and wiped them in a laboured movement of his knotty fingers—a futile effort to clear the blurred vision of his ageing eyes. Then he picked up one of the newspapers to read it for the hundredth time that day. His mind was flooded with shades of varying emotions that swamped him. Waves upon waves came flooding in—fear, regret, anger, frustration, impotence, debility and utter helplessness. *Death was the inevitable end to the human body, the soul never perishes,* he had been taught all his life.

He felt defeated, disoriented and alone. Neither dead nor alive—diseased, ailing, weak and dying, his life slowly ebbing away, like the blood oozing out of a slashed wrist. With each ejection of the failing heart, life being snuffed out. But was it? He lifted his arms up and down and then moved them in a circular motion, small concentric circles and then bigger ones, clockwise and anti-clockwise, exercises for the neck. He breathed in a long laboured painful inhalation, a gush of air filled up his lungs. He rose and went to the window.

Fourteen floors down was the street below. He felt like an ant staring at a skyscraper, but in reverse. He felt that millions of souls were leaving their bodies and flying away in a strong tornado—a thick, circular, dark and lethal column of smoke. He felt a constriction around his heart and began to hyperventilate. His flared nostrils spread out even more to accommodate a larger volume of air.

A thick file of facsimiles, copies of messages from Omar Al Fayed, Uri Orlov, Pascal Durrand, Abu Karzen, Lazzaro Mancini and from other luminaries and friends around the world to condole the passing away of the doyen of Indian industry fell in a thud onto the floor. It startled him and his breathing came in sharp rasps. The short, bespectacled man felt no grief at the death of the man that the world mourned. He felt a sinister chill prick his spine. How could he grieve for himself?

The shrill ring of the phone pierced his senses. It startled him. Tiny beads of sweat had formed on his brow. His pulse raced dangerously fast and he felt his head swirl. The loud, droning, ringing sound invaded his ears like a stereophonic rhapsody. The persistent caller just would not stop. He was hyperventilating like a jogger on a high-speed treadmill. A strong gust of wind from the window, flapped open the cover of the folder on the floor. A grim black-bordered obituary, jumped out at him and struck his senses. The black and white picture of Ajay Vardhan Loya in his twenties, smiled fiendishly back at him. And then, a whole seascape of images and faces—Bharat, Vishal, Nupur, Uday, Amba, Aryaman and Aranya flashed like photo slides being changed rapidly on a screen, all of them smiling fiendishly at him. His gaze settled on the face of his ever-faithful paramour, Devyani. He tried hard not to think of Lyndoh.

Yashoda, encapsulated in her ethereal, rosy, blissful world of a surreal romance, also learned of the death of her estranged husband's father. She felt no emotions at his passing away. An unknown death in a street accident would perhaps have moved her more. In the larger scheme of things, becoming insensitive to human suffering or pain was not conducive to spiritual upliftment, but detachment was.

Yashoda had moved on. She had amputated the limb that connected her to the grim years she had spent with the man she married, bearing his children, succumbing to being bullied by the Calcutta Empress. She had finally overcome the greatest impediment that pulled her back—the bond between a mother and her children. She had found the all-empowering pull of a fulfilling love, fused with lust—the outlet for emotional gratification in the arms of a celestial being—the harbinger of all the beauteous feelings created by god for mortals; a presence that left no room for anything else in life. She eagerly awaited the glorious moment ahead, when she would officially tie the knot, to the archangel of her dreams. She was feeling too powerful to let even a shred of regret penetrate her realm of euphoria. Yashoda picked up a pen and paper and scribbled a note to her son. It would be the last time she would have any earthly communication with him.

Priyanka Loya had attended the thirteenth-day mourning ceremony for Ajay Vardhan at Loya House, a serio-comic display that had once again rattled her. She sat quietly and unobtrusively in the back row, not letting her mind drift too far away from the present. Her gaze travelled absently, onto the faces of the family of her divorced husband—a clan to which she had once belonged. It seemed another lifetime—far back in her past. She saw Amba—white, serene, lucid, syrupy, hypocritical and evil; she moved on to Bharat—hard, matter-of-fact, unemotive indecipherable, the entity with no melting point; then Nupur—cold, distant and detached; her ex-husband Vishal—callous, icy, contemptuous, with a strange deadness in his eyes;

her brother Uday—calm, together, contented, authoritative and officious; and Aryaman—she stopped at him.

The blind boy sat with his head tilted to one side, leaning towards his sister, as if he were straining to catch the hollow words being orated by his father and grandmother. Priyanka saw him clutching an empty gold wrapper of a Ferrero Rocher chocolate tightly in one hand, and another whole unopened one in the other. She saw him sucking diligently at the one in his mouth. She saw his expressions change from distant apathy to pure joy. She saw his throat muscles twitch as he swallowed the melted chocolate and saliva, painstakingly. She saw him slurp, lick his lips in delight and swallow again. She saw the familiar brown liquid spilling out, soiling the sides of his mouth.

She saw him wiping it on his sleeve and begin sucking at it again. The fresh brown mark on his sleeve, the colour of dried blood, disconcerted her. She saw him fidget from side to side, his expression changing rapidly. All his senses had become one single sense of taste, savouring the delectable and juicy chocolate. And then, all of a sudden she saw it—there was pain. His face contorted like he was being gagged. His neck rolled to one side and the furrows on his brow deepened. Beads of sweat glistened on it. The knuckles of his hand turned white as he tightened his fist onto the unopened chocolate.

A torrent of emotions surged up. She felt a painful lump forming in her throat. The two round chocolates that lay carelessly untouched in front of her, dimmed out of focus as she felt tears prick her eyes and come flooding down her face, unchecked.

Priyanka wept uncontrollably, like a child. She couldn't understand the unnatural outburst. She had held back perfectly well for a long time.

Indeed it is the holding back of tears that is more painful than the release.

It was not the death of Ajay Vardhan Loya that had precipitated it. She regretted being present at the ludicrous condolence meeting. She felt a twinge of envy for her sister-in-law Yashoda and for the departed soul. 'How lucky are those that no longer live,' she said to herself.

She had not seen Aryaman get up abruptly and run out.

The sight of the macabre, gold-wrapped round chocolates revolted her. The loud chants from the Gita drowned out all else.

61

Bharat Loya felt a humiliating blow. He had to shell out a huge sum of money to Brinda Gokuldas, to withdraw her case that charged him with attempt to rape and criminal assault. He had to pay a hefty price to buy peace, from the rabid, frothing, scorned ex-employee, who had hit him where it hurt.

That unsavoury Monday morning had seemed like any other. The neatly typed letter sacking a redundant employee, who had far outlived her utility, had been placed the night before on her table. The brief four-line missive, informing her that her contract had been terminated, and that her services were no longer required by GII, should have been adequate to settle that. She had been summarily instructed to surrender the keys of the Mitsubishi Lancer that went with the job and was told not to be present in office the following day.

Brinda Gokuldas had ambled into her cubicle humming a popular tune. For the forty-seven year old woman, life was on a roll. She wielded enough political clout to be able to get whatever she desired.

The plum job of Public Relations Officer at GII had given her an unprecedented flurry of benefits including a generous salary, entertainment allowance, house and travel allowance and the licence to hobnob with the who's who of the city as the company's authorised representative. It also gave her the leverage to avail of huge personal advantages, from the people she happened to meet in that capacity—a privilege that she exploited without restraint. Compounded with her ever-willingness to grant sexual favours, life for Brinda Gokuldas was indeed on the upswing. With the benevolent minister, who had helped her in this placement, still in his chair, nothing could alter that status and by the time it did, she would have latched on to her next milking cow. Brinda Gokuldas tore the letter into shreds and stomped into the lift that led straight upto the eighth floor. It was a blatant defiance of the unwritten decree, that no one but the summoned were allowed there. Brinda Gokuldas had overcome many bigger obstacles before. She barged into the MD's room like a raging bull.

Bharat Loya had just settled into his executive leather chair. He was going over his notes for the quarterly meeting with his board of directors, scheduled for the forenoon that day. His sharpened wits honed to perfection, he couldn't wait to embark on the solo ceremony that was his instant Viagra. He was shocked to see the middle-aged woman barge into his private sanctuary shouting hysterically.

'Who has ordered this dismissal?' she screamed, waving the torn bits of the white envelope in his face.

An angry tirade followed, punctuated with weepy outbursts and the rabid woman lurched forward, as if she would strike him. Bharat Loya was paralysed. The sheer suddenness of it had unnerved him. He was too stunned to even summon security. He stared at her, tearing up her clothes, roughing up her hair, and slapping herself hard a few times, in utter disbelief. He saw a nasty red weal come up on her half exposed breast.

'You are going to pay for this Bharat Loya. No one messes with Brinda Gokuldas.' The screaming echoes receded with her garrulous frame as she heaved herself out of the door of the MD's office.

It had cost him a ridiculous assault on his moral character, a sum of ten lakh rupees, and the Mitsubishi Lancer, to settle with her. The rapacious tiger, who had confidently stalked the jungles, for trophies to stay his hunger for power and one-upmanship, had been humiliated and humbled like never before on his own turf.

Bharat Loya, the Managing Director of Global Integrity Industries, who owned the Ritz Grand hotel chain and Beetle Air had become the most powerful arms-dealer in India and virtually an invisible man. His name hardly ever appeared in newspapers and his photographs almost never. He gave no interviews, never responded to letters, faxes or emails and if his name was ever mentioned to other hoteliers or airline owners, they became shifty and evasive.

There was no question that Bharat Loya was anything but the most influential and best-connected man in India, but the reason no one ever saw him was because he did not wish it, and what Bharat Loya wished for, unconditionally happened. The thin, nit-picking, gauche, socially maladroit nerd, with his gawky unprepossessing wire-framed glasses, had a strange deadness about his eyes. He seldom appeared at parties other than his own, never touched alcohol, was strictly vegetarian and the most visible misogynist India knew. The network of his detractors circled the entire nation. Its membership of sacked employees, embittered competitors, aggrieved and sullen colleagues crossed ideological and intellectual frontiers, a class of victims of a singular catastrophe, each with a story to tell.

Characteristically, he could not tolerate integrity; in fact he was afraid of it. He subscribed to the maxim of the school of fear, *the more fear you instil in the people who work for you the better the product.*

Predictably, the roster of his antagonists had accelerated with the growth of his empire. He was scathingly distrusting and cynical about his employees and even more about their motives. Being genuinely of the opinion that money can change everything, he used it both as a panacea and a weapon. When he really wanted someone, he paid what it took to get him, but if a face no longer fit, it was ruthlessly axed. He was charming at a one-to-one level, but never forgot anything, giving the illusion that he was always watching. His existence in a different time zone, poring over results, while the people who had achieved them were asleep in their beds, only added to his potential for terrorising them. Like a schoolmaster presiding over a large classroom of boys, he was known to have sadistically singled out and humiliated people for there was no room for failure in his scheme of things. He sometimes appeared without warning, behind an employee's shoulder to check him and if necessary boot him out into the corridor, the inviolate Gestapo formula.

The GII phobia among his peers became almost manic, and the unvarying line of his detractors, never stopped growing.

But Bharat Loya was unfazed by this. The paramount predator revelled in his field of destructive expansion. The inaccessible, unyielding and most powerful broker of death and destruction was completely oblivious of the silver spoon tarnishing in the family chest, that had not quite finished with him.

62

'... There is a long winding spiral that connects sex to super-consciousness—both empower, excite and elate. The magical fusion of the two brings about eternal bliss. The union of two mortal beings during the act of copulation that culminates in orgasm—an intensely blissful feeling unrivalled by any other known to the human senses is only a tiny mirror image of the boundless, limitless euphoria, that precipitates from the penultimate fusion of the soul with its creator—the Atman *with the* Paramatman. *It creates an energy too powerful and suffusive, too rapturous and ecstatic, to be comprehended by the limitations of the human mind...'*

Nupur Loya sat comfortably, sunken into the dark leather seat of a seven-series black BMW sedan, listening to the hypnotic voice of Osho, in the cassette playing on her car-deck. His deep soothing baritone, could have made a hummingbird stop in flight.

At forty-two, she had completely sublimated her sexual desires. In the twelve years of her marriage to Uday Nanda, she had felt absolutely no carnal stirrings towards him—or towards any other male.

She was returning from J. Radhakrishnan's workshop, on his Soul Search programme—a course, that she had attended and conducted several times. It was a skill she had perfected and internalised after having spent months together with him, trailing him around the globe on his mission—the urge to spread love and peace to a mass of suffering human beings, to kindle in them an awareness that sprang from within—a revelation of the universal truth that human beings had forgotten how to live, and needed to discover the finer art of inner engineering.

The sounds penetrated deep into the folds of her conscience. They stirred up the musical chants of words that had been tattooed on her soul.

'Manobuddhi ahankaar chittani naham
Na cha shrotrajivhe ne cha graan netre'

(I am not the mind, not the intellect, not the ego not the consciousness, I am not hearing, not speech, I am only *Chidanandarupa*—pure bliss—pure bliss—just pure bliss)

It was a chant that was to guide her along the labyrinth of her karma to her ultimate destination.

The car screeched to a halt at a busy intersection as the traffic lights turned red. Thick clouds gathered in the monsoon sky. They cast a shadow upon the surface, outlining the area where they would unleash their fury. Nupur felt an uneasy churning inside. The chanting on the car-deck continued, reaching into the depths of her soul.

'Na me dveshrago na me lobhmoho
Mado naiva me naiva maatsarya bhava'

(I am neither ill-will, nor anger, neither greed nor temptation, neither pride nor jealousy.)

'*Na dharmo na chartho na kamo na moksha. Chidanandarupa shivoham shivoham...*'

(I am pure bliss—pure bliss—pure bliss) A sudden squall followed a loud clap of thunder, snuffing out her thoughts. The car moved forward as the lights changed to green, inching towards the GI House in a snarl of traffic. It was a routine trip to the office. She thought of her own redundant status in her bother's scheme of things. He had made her sign a document, relinquishing her total shareholding in Global Integrity Industries, an act by which she had been rendered an alien, within her father's, and now her brother's domain. The cruel paradox of being the female descendant in a Marwari home, snaked into her consciousness. She was not going to protest against her summary removal from a bona fide inheritance.

Her brothers had compensated, by granting her a generous amount of liquid capital, sprawling properties in Lutyen's Delhi, a free hand for her husband to pursue his business ventures, and unstinting financial support for his ambitious enterprises. But it pained her that she had been unceremoniously plucked out of the company partnership and stripped of her equity holding. It pained her even more, that her own mother had not even uttered a murmur of protest in her favour, a penalty she was paying for being of the wrong gender. She was still allowed to function within the periphery of GII as a de-glorified interior designer—refurbishing the insides with garish, graphic, offensive and pornographic illustrations of her

Merchants of Death

choice, and she did have access to the services provided by the company albeit partially. She was indeed an alien daughter in her own parents' home, and all it took to determine that was one scrawly signature on a piece of paper—an officious, matter-of-fact, no fuss, relinquishment deed! The ugly cobra of treachery raised its head. She couldn't make it slither away. The unsparing, inexorable, theory of cause and effect would surely track them down. She recalled the unnatural deaths that the family had suffered. The numerous fiendish, inadvertent casualties. Perhaps, it was a curse that had seeped into their lives, poisoning every pore of their being—to take revenge, as it were. The accidental blinding of the first-born male in the fourth generation, Kanupriya's macabre suicide—the grisly fate of her unclaimed foetus trapped inside her dead womb; the frightful memory of Kanupriya's mother's horrific death by hanging; and then her own father's attempt to escape, to turn into another entity, untraceable, unrecognisable, like a caterpillar to a butterfly, but not quite.

'Ashes to ashes, dust to dust,' death screamed at her piercingly. 'You can disguise yourself as a tiny micro-spore of algae in a thermal geyser at 1000°C but I'll hunt you down,' death screamed at her piercingly. 'I'll hunt you down.' The screams hung around her like thick cloud.

She reminded herself that she needed to make her periodic call through to New York to check on the wellbeing of her kin.

As her car pulled up outside GI House she stepped into the bustling foyer, like a nocturnal creature. She rode up the lift with the chants still reverberating in her senses. A voice boomed somewhere between her temples. The painting you ordered has been delivered to the office Madam. Where do you want it to be placed?'

The haunting chants followed her.

'*Na me mrityu shanka, na me jaatibheda,*
Pita naiva me naiva mata na janma
Na bandhur na mitram gurur naiva shishya
Chidanandarupa shivoham shivoham...'

(I am neither fear of death, nor division of caste; I am neither father, nor mother, nor birth, nor friends, nor relations, nor gurus, I am pure bliss—pure bliss—pure bliss)

A violent clap of thunder followed by a heavy downpour thrashed the ground outside that hissed as it soaked up the acid rain. The ground floor was bustling with an electric energy. Two floors above in the ceremonial boardroom, Bharat Loya was conducting his well-rehearsed and perfected solo performance, like an authoritative schoolmaster, at the quarterly meeting of the board of directors. The aroma of freshly brewed coffee and chocolate bourbon biscuits, permeated the ducts of the central air-conditioner, throughout the building.

Just then, in a distant corner of the capital, Uday Nanda had handed a pair of gilded scissors, amidst flashing bulbs and TV cameras to a Bollywood starlet to inaugurate a new wing of their ever-expanding chain of hotels.

Conducting herself in her private arena of unrestrained power, Amba Loya was seated on a raised dais in a lotus position, at a Soul Search workshop, in a mansion in Lutyen's Delhi. The icy cold feel of the metal keys to her vault, digging into the bare flesh of her waist comforted her.

Two hours away from the Indian air space, Aryaman Loya was on a flight to New York accompanied by his uncle, and at his destination, thousands of miles across the Atlantic, on Fifth Avenue, in a fourteenth floor flat, a couple whose passions had not diminished by the relentless advances of old age and coronary disease, lay locked in embrace, on pure satin sheets of ocean blue, that felt soft and sensuous on their naked skin.

63

Aryaman Loya's problematic behaviour had kept getting worse. The introductory session at the GII office, that had purported to project him as the future heir and the sensational whiz-kid of computers, could not cure his anomaly, because deep down inside, Aryaman was stubborn and over-demanding. Bharat decided that sending him away from the family, into a more independent and challenging environment would be beneficial for him, and thereby the most feasible option. A state-of-the-art, software programming institute was identified in New York and Aryaman was packed off with Yashoda's brother, who had over the years developed some rapport with the introverted child. Aryaman's reluctance at being sent away, never abated even on the day of his departure. As usual, he was escorted to the airport by the Corporate Director of Public Relations, accompanied by his uncle, Chand. On that windy night, no one had any inkling, that the Indira Gandhi International Airport, would be the last to witness the final departure of the twenty-two year old scion of the House of Loyas.

In Delhi, things were running smoothly. The company profits had soared. Its growth rate was a relentless march against the basic laws of probability, and it had turned all cynical speculation on its head.

The equity holding of Nupur Loya in GII had been revoked without any trouble, and the ugly Brinda Gokuldas episode had been sorted out, with a dent in Bharat Loya's purse that turned out to be smaller than that to his pride.

Vishal Loya's public image was taking a drubbing, but he wore the armour of success and his mother, the figurehead Chairperson of GII, was in complete synchrony with Bharat's decree, her daughter's easy marginalisation, notwithstanding.

On the outside, although the NDA coalition government did not bear a particularly favourable attitude towards the Loyas, their current scope and functioning needed few concessions from them and they still managed to get their jobs done. For the moment, all strategies hinged on upstaging competitors and devouring consumer time and money, so there seemed no imminent danger to the established standing of the House of Loya.

Swinging back and forth, between the monitoring of sales graphs and his solitary spiritual retreats, Bharat Loya had managed to strike a balance between the conflicting and volatile energies that held him together—but there was just one tiny little party-pooper lurking in the shadows—the silver spoon.

New York
October 2000

Aryaman Loya was restless. He felt suffocated as he stood by the window of the fourteenth floor flat on Fifth Avenue. His throat muscles had narrowed painfully. He took a deep breath. He felt strong currents of air rising upwards, like souls collectively leaving bodies from all over the world. He knew he could not see like normal people, but he could clearly see another dimension that normal people could not. His inner vision could discern moods and forms and thoughts. It could comprehend the fourth dimension of an unreal existence. A vacuum formed deep in the pit of his stomach. It grew bigger and wider pushing hard at the sides of his abdomen. The gnawing emptiness turned into an excruciating spasm, that stretched like a tight band from the pit of his stomach, curling upwards, right round his throat. Aryaman had been sent to New York to get away from his difficult life in Delhi. He knew his father had exhausted his patience. There was no one who could understand his needs. His uncle, Chand *Mama* was caring and kind. He had comforted him, but the deep gnawing emptiness never let him be. His visits to GI House helped him, marginally. He wondered if Paula could have made him feel better. Perhaps not. Paula had been gone too long. May be it was his mother that he needed. A cynical smile crossed his face, making his muscles go taut. He clenched his jaws together and gritted his teeth. What mother? The one who was never there! The one who had abandoned him?

Turned her back on her son to seek refuge in the arms of her lover? Perhaps, her need to be loved was greater than his.

The last letter she had written to him, lay stuffed into the inner pocket of his blazer. Those piteous, inadequate, despicable words failed to dissipate the gloom that strangulated him—in fact they had deepened it. Those empty words of a despairing and guilty woman—he had not wanted to hear—but they had been read out to him. He could feel the hurried, impersonal, disconnected scrawl of his mother's handwriting against his pounding chest. Those cold words lay frozen on that scrap of paper, close to his heart. He would not make it easy for her. He would never forgive her. Maybe Aranya could—she was more understanding. But Aryaman was not Aranya, and did not want to be. He did not want to understand his anger. He wanted to be consumed by it. He would not make it easy for her. His mother zoomed into his dark crowded head. Morbid sounds pierced his soul.

'I love you my son. Please forgive me. Someday you'll understand why your mother left you, and why she. ...'

Aryaman held his breath. His chest squeezed tight like a contracting accordion and the words snuffed out. He heard the crumpling sound of the folded note in his pocket. He was not going to make it easy for them. He felt the rubber band around his throat get tighter. His eyes felt like hot dust was blowing into them. Then he heard the voice again.

'Aryaman, this is your mother. I love you very much. Someday you'll understand why I left you. ...'

He slapped his palms tightly onto both his ears, to block out the haunting sounds of his mother's voice. There was silence.

Aryaman stood still for a long time. No one was around him. Chand *Mama* had gone for a shower. The master bedroom was bolted from the inside. Its occupants lay in deep slumber, undisturbed by the tornado that raged inside his head. He removed the crumpled note from his pocket and brought it close to his nose. The familiar lingering smell from the uterine sac, the labour room, his mother's breasts and the milk that oozed out of her when he had put his little mouth to them, snaked up his nostrils. Yes, it was the same disturbing smell that had trailed him from the uterine pouch to his mother's breast, and was now in the letters. All his receptors rolled into the singular smell that emanated from the hurriedly scribbled lines of his mother's swansong.

Aryaman pushed a chair close to the window and heaved himself onto it. He stepped onto the open sill. He groped furtively, easing himself out onto the ledge. He stood frozen like a fly on the wall, for a long time. His mind went blank. He took a deep, long breath. Strong gusts of wind howled in circles around his ears. The early morning noises of the bustling street below him, rushed up like a column of droning bees. He heard his mother's voice again.

'You fuss too much ...'

And then his father's, *'Don't be a sissy Aryaman you are too spoilt.'*

And then Aranya's, 'Stoppit Bhaiya, you are not the only one who is hurt.'

Aryaman felt the acute tightening of a thick rubberband around his throat, like someone turning a corkscrew. The taste of melted chocolate filled up his oral cavity. His sightless eyes felt gritty and dry like their inner lids had been lined with sandpaper. His hands turned clammy and ice cold. Beads of sweat formed all over his brow. He heard Paula call out to him,

'Don't bite into it Baba. You have to put the whole piece into your mouth—the whole piece. Don't bite into it Baba.'

Aryaman jumped. On his way down he heard a loud swooshing sound of air rubbing against the cartilage of his narrowed windpipe. He heard his breath resonate in tune with the loud swooshing sound. He held onto his umbilical cord, swinging on it like a high-trapeze artist; the cord that bound him to his changing universe.

Aryaman didn't calculate his steps. As he tumbled down along his free fall, he felt his vision come back. He saw a long, narrow tunnel, filled with incandescent yellow light. He recognised it. It was the one that he had crawled out of on the day he was born. He knew he would have to take the same way out. Aryaman did not have the time to contemplate. It was the getting away that he was concentrating on. As he went over the edge like a seagull taking flight, life receding like a fading echo, like a boat leaving the shore, he held on to his death tightly, like a rope, swinging dangerously in the air, the air that reeked of the raw flesh of his mother's womb. He touched the living souls of all his near and dear ones as he rushed downwards. The last one he touched before his soul shrieked out of his body was his mother. He finally tasted eternity and nothingness.

By the time Aryaman hit the asphalt street below, his mangled body convulsed in a pool of blood for twenty seconds, before it lay still. A flattened, golden wrapper of a half eaten Ferrero Rocher chocolate, lay carelessly, a few feet away from him, near a red fire hydrant.

Chand, Devyani and her sickly paramour, rushed down the lift in shock, to retrieve what was left of the bloody mess on the street.

The twenty-two years, stretched between the joy of his birth and the agony of his dying, crystallized and appended as another gruesome chapter, in the saga of the cursed dynasty, and the silver spoon baying for blood would rest for just a short while before claiming its next victim.

Aryaman Loya's suicide would be reported as an accident to the rest of the world.

64

Mauritius
October 2000

The cottage on the secluded beach was bathed in an ethereal, ambrosial, pink light. Yashoda sat naked at the edge of her bed humming a song. The words formed like pearls inside her head and bubbled up into her soul, resonating the frequency of her heart.

Strawberries, cherries and then angels kissing spring.
My summer wine is really made from all these things.
Take off your silver spurs and help me pass some time.
And I will give to you, more summer wine.

The musical notes floated around her like effervescent bubbles, light and airy. She scanned her own soft-focus reflection in the colonial full length mirror, tilted at an angle in the corner of the room. A porcelain naiad, with a peaches and cream complexion, stared back at her. The thick, dark lashes that fringed her large amber eyes, blinked playfully, as they reflected the rainbow hues from the muted pink glowing sunset of the beach in God's own land. Her statuesque form akin to the ones immortalised in Botticelli paintings, looked like it had been dipped in liquefied mother-of-pearl. It dispersed the light that fell upon it, with each quiver of her taut muscles that emanated from her breast.

An ornate diamond and emerald necklace lay on the bed beside her. It was a gift from Jaywant Mallya. She felt a warm glow, like fireflies rising upwards, inside her chest. Yashoda closed her eyes. It was a feeling of absolute bliss. She wanted to soak in every moment of this joy.

A distant memory from her past knocked at her soul. She pushed it away. She wanted no ugly tentacles to intrude upon her. She wanted to stretch this moment into an immortal time-frame, before she officially became the wife of Jaywant Mallya, the man she loved, like she had never loved before. She felt powerful and complete. The entry in her diary read:

Love is empowerment, fulfilment, satiety,
Longing, togetherness, expansiveness,
dependence, possession.
Love is passion, lust, desire, belonging.
Love is caring, living, wanting and
being—love is all this and more.
Love is pain, laughter, joy and giving,
Love is all this and more.

Yashoda rose from the bed. Her light footsteps did not fall on the floor. The little golden bells on her toe-rings jingled as she moved. The soft, feminine chimes soothed her. She picked up the necklace and clasped it around her bare, slender neck.

The ice-cold stones tattooed a painful, invisible mark on her creamy skin. She saw Jaywant enter the room. His larger-than-life image, was reflected in the mirror and filled up her senses.

Love is satiety, longing, lust.
Love is desire, belonging, caring,
Love is being and dying.
Love is all that and more!

Jaywant turned her around gently and kissed the emerald drops on her bare breasts. He took her into his arms. The weight of his body pressed down on the diamond string and pushed it deeper into her flesh. He eased her onto the bed and made love to her.

The pain and ecstasy fused together as she surrendered joyously to him, letting her mind and soul soar into the starry night sky, that stood like an umbrella over the dark and restless ocean, rolling incessantly outside her window.

Aryaman stood behind a gauzy portiere, watching his mother's body intertwined with that of Jaywant's. Her naked flesh glistened with pearly beads of sweat, as it rocked in rhythm, with the other finely sculpted body of a Greek God. He watched the two lying naked in each others arms, separated by only an icy cold string of diamonds;

the cold isotope of carbon and coal. The hard and cruel chunks dug into the delicate flesh of his mother's breast. Circles of pink light floated before his eyes that had filled up with tears. He watched them move passionately and rhythmically. A fusion of images, colours, forms, struck him. Aryaman moved into the space inside his mother's heart. He squeezed himself into it with great difficulty. There was hardly any room there for him, but he managed...

A cold draught of air pricked the pores of Yashoda's skin. She felt an uneasy churning inside. She opened her eyes and saw Aryaman's face staring down at her from the ceiling. His eyes were large pools, filled with expanding circles of pink light. She quickly turned away and moved closer to Jaywant, who lay still and spent with his back against her breast. She shut her eyes tight, pushing herself closer and wrapped her arms around him, but the large pink saucers of light swirled rapidly around the room, fully encasing her like an airtight cocoon.

Yashoda was sweating. Jaywant lay asleep beside her, a quiet contentment reflected on his face. She felt an eerie and unsettling feeling engulf her, as a gush of cold air touched her once again.

Just then thousands of miles away in New York City, the body of a young man had splattered on a hard, unyielding, asphalt street on Fifth Avenue.

Death hung around it twirling its moustache screaming roguishly—Fuck you life, I'll hunt you down. Fuck you life, I told you, I'll hunt you down.

And dozens of phones had rung urgently across the globe carrying the morbid news of Aryaman's death.

For the first time since she had left, Yashoda felt a strong tug pulling her back to Delhi, away from the man of her dreams. She felt an old wound reopen inside her. She knew it was time to leave Jaywant and that she would never see him again. She stared out silently, at the circles of pink light dancing over the restless ocean. Circles that were there because she watched them through her tears.

65

New Delhi
January 2001

After his death, Aryaman's bedroom on the first floor of the house had become a no-man's land. His neatly made-up bed looked as if he had just stepped out and would return to it like any other day. His denim blue duvet, with a smart red edging had no wrinkles on it. It had been kept intact. The red and navy Ralph Lauren cushions, stacked near the bedhead had been fluffed up, dusted and neatly placed in their positions, like they were every day. The soft, thick pile beige carpet that touched the navy edging on the fully upholstered sofa against the wall, had been thoroughly vacuumed and cleaned. Life-size pictures of Aryaman were hung all around on the walls. Silver frames in different sizes, with his photographs at all ages, in every conceivable pose and with every member of his family, were kept on the tables on either side of the bed. There were some on the dresser in front of a mirrored wall that reflected hundreds of images of the dead boy, from whichever angle it was viewed.

Aryaman's parents spent hours in that room with him, more time than they had ever spent in all his living years. His mother wrapped herself in the sheets that smelled of him, feeling the sad mortality of being the parent of a dead child. Many times she dozed off on his denim blue duvet, hugging his giant teddy bear, and when sleep wore off, the poison seeped into her again and spilt out of her eyes, soaking the pillow on which she rested her head. She tried to communicate with him in vain, to ask him if it hurt when he died, but she got no answers.

A dull ache had replaced her heart inside her chest cavity. The sequence of events, wound and rewound inside her head, over and over again, but the unchanging finality had not yet taken root. She just could not let go...

Her own voice hounded her mercilessly.

'You fuss too much Aryaman. Don't be a sissy. Paula let him be, you are spoiling him. You fuss too much Aryaman—too much—too much'.

Aryaman's death had drawn her close to her estranged husband, as never before. They shared an alien and unnatural bond in this macabre vista of a finite truth. The two of them sat huddled together, holding hands, weeping and grieving the death of their first born.

Bharat Loya felt slightly calmed when he sat inside the four walls of his son's room. The smell of the living boy was always present. Inside his wardrobe, his clothes still hung dry-cleaned and ironed like they did when he was alive. His shoes still lay neatly on the built-in shoe-racks under which the removable trays waited to collect the dirt from their soles. Bharat looked at the photographs that had captured and frozen moments from a life gone by, playing back and reliving them. He never allowed anyone to use the *death* word and he avoided looking into mirrors, for each time he did, he saw hundreds of scaly, black serpents raising their heads, amidst agonising screams of Oedipus Rex, gouging out his own eyes, asking questions, mocking him, accusing him of what he dreaded to hear.

Bharat Loya stayed in his son's room for hours, meditating there each morning, to de-link himself from the horrific reality. A reality that screamed out to say that his son was dead; that for no explainable reason, he had jumped off the open window of the fourteenth floor flat, while his fugitive grandfather slept soundly on the same floor, with his dutiful and loving Devyani.

Bharat Loya would never know, that the recurrent constriction in Aryaman's throat was his narrowed down and progressively shrivelling up food pipe; an autoimmune failure triggered off on a dreary night nine months after his birth—the terrifying moment that had robbed him of his vision—that he would never forgive himself for.

How he wished he could get just one chance to tell his son, that he was sorry and he really cared.

Bharat Loya was not willing to let Aryaman go. His memory was the only nugget of absolute truth that held him together, and now bound him to the mother of the dead son, and who had finally come back from her surreal world.

Outside, in their pragmatic world, if it was of any consolation, the Foreign Exchange Regulations Act, the dreaded FERA, had been finally scrapped and replaced by a stingless, toothless version called the Foreign Exchange Management Act—FEMA and a revenue graph of GII had recorded an unprecedented turnover of fifteen hundred crores that year.

66

Aranya turned nineteen, three months after Aryaman died. Gripped by a dismal sadness on the death of her brother, she went into a shell. The icy stupor that engulfed her blocked every pore of her being. It did not even let her cry. She had learned the harsh, brutal, truth, that when people died, they never came back. She longed to be with her brother and could not believe that she would never see him again. Even though she had never quite become accustomed to his demanding tantrums, she had shared a bond with him that shook her up, each time she saw him upset. His tempestuous outbursts that had increased after her mother had left, rattled her. She always rushed to comfort him and had got used to his unresponsive obstinate, behaviour and crying sessions. She pandered to his passion for chocolates, and never failed to bring him some when she saw him angry. But Aranya knew that at those times, nothing worked.

Aranya had watched her brother close up from inside, when Paula left. She had seen him close up even tighter, when their mother left. She had felt the same tightening around her own heart, when she heard from her grandmother that their mother was not coming back. She never believed Dadima, but the hushed whispers of the staff and servants hadn't escaped her.

'*Badi Bahuji Mauritius wale sahab ke saath bhaag gayee. Kaisi ma hai? Andhey bete or phool jaisi bacchi ke liye zara bhi taras nahin aaya usey.*'

Those harsh comments on her mother's unfeeling behaviour in abandoning her blind son and beautiful daughter had scooped out deep wounds inside her. Wounds that became more painful as she thought of her dead brother. She tried to get some solace from her father, but he hardly had time for her. She didn't expect much from him. His business was demanding and he kept punishing schedules. She had got used to long spells of his absence during his retreats at Haridwar. She had got used to being without her parents. But she was finding it hard to get used to being without her brother. Aranya felt an expanding fire consuming the inside of her chest.

Aranya had cried when Aryaman was sent to New York. She missed him immensely. She had seen the fear and reluctance on his face. After that, he never took her calls. He never spoke to her even once. In a way, she felt responsible for his bad moods. Perhaps, she had not been a good sister to him. It made no difference to her, now that her mother was back. She had turned into a stranger anyway. She hardly ever spoke and her amber eyes seemed always filled with tears. Her face had receded into the hollows of her cheekbones and a permanent frown lined her forehead, and made her look old.

Aranya was not in the mood to celebrate her birthday. She felt the expanding heaviness flow down from her head into her heart. She dreaded the thought of facing dozens of those girls and boys with their stupid conversation, chattering and eating like a bunch of monkeys.

In college they stared at her as if she were a ghost after Aryaman died; as if she was guilty of an unforgiveable crime; of being the living sister of a dead child.

The birthday party was forcibly shoved down her throat. Aranya moved around disinterested and sad. Her friends came rolling in noisily, flinging inanities at her. Each of them handed her a gift-wrapped object that she mechanically handed to her maid. One came up to her and tugged at her sleeve.

'Come on, Aranya. Don't be a spoilsport. Let's play that dancing game we learnt at the last party. Come on silly! You know you'll win the prize. You always manage to stand on the smallest paper square with your partner.'

Aranya brushed her away drifting into her own reverie.

She was in the school gym. Loud music filled her ears. She was swirling around like a light-footed dervish with a tall, fair handsome boy. She looked at him, he was Aryaman. They danced and danced till the music stopped.

A burst of applause snapped her back into the room.

After the friends went home, Aranya sat by herself in her room. The party had ended like all parties do. The servants had cleared the table of all the food. Her presents lay neatly stacked on a long table behind her. Several boxes of different sizes and shapes, wrapped in multi-coloured paper, some with silver and gold stars, red hearts, ribbons and balloons, and happy birthday messages, lay there, waiting to be opened by her. Aranya did not want any of them. She hated the thought of unwrapping each gift and then putting it away into the gifting cupboard. People gave such stupid and useless presents anyway. They always ended up in the gifting cupboard to be used and recycled on other friends' birthdays. She was sure all homes had gifting cupboards, like theirs. She ambled across to the table. She moved the boxes aside one by one, without opening them. She scanned the names scrawled on the tags—Rajat, Shreya, Karan, Mohit, Bela, Tara. She kept pushing them aside—Aditi, Priya, Rohan, Megha, Sahil, Shweta. She continued to move them away, till she stopped at a large, flat, square box. She turned it around. There was no tag on it.

The silver wrapper had cute, tiny pink kittens, wearing bells and bows on their necks. It was scotch-taped on all four sides, securely. She peered under the table. There was no tag there either. It took her some time to unwrap it. She found a neat, black leather box inside, with a brand new Leica camera; the one she had been wanting for a while. But who could have given it to her? She looked inside the box. She saw no tag there. She picked it up and calling out loudly entered Amba Loya's room.

'Do you know who could have brought me this Leica camera *Dadima?* No one even knew I wanted it, and there is no name-card on it.'

Amba looked up cursorily from the book she was reading and replied.

'Oh that! That was sent for you, by your brother.' Her cold matter-of-fact words, hit Aranya like a bolt of electricity and she felt the room swirl around as she ran out, clutching the camera close to her chest.

She flung herself onto her pink and blue Laura Ashley duvet and wept piteously. She stayed there for a long time, hugging the camera, till sleep overcame her and relieved her of her pain.

67

Aryaman's death pushed Yashoda into silence. Bharat Loya's escapes to his retreat at Haridwar became longer and more frequent. Amba and Nupur, zealously practising the diktats of J. Radhakrishnan, had discovered the foolproof joys of finer living. Vishal Loya's pursuit of women turned into a manic obsession. Uday Nanda continued expanding his business into uncharted territories. And his father-in-law, an emotional and physical refugee, was stuck irrevocably in another time zone, where he lived incognito, the life of a helpless and ailing loner, dealing with the bitter truth, that he could never return to his homeland to live like a free citizen, absolved of his economic offences, nor could he ever share the grief of his beloved grandson's death with his family, whom he so desperately longed to be with. Priyanka, although physically delinked from it, had not been spared the mental agony of Aryaman's death and she went into acute depression. But she thanked her stars for facilitating her timely exit from the ambit of the cursed dynasty—a shadow that she believed she had cast off, with her broken marriage.

At the Soul Search headquarters in New Delhi, hectic preparations were underway, for a whirlwind tour to Assam headed by Nupur Loya. She was booked on a flight with her secretary and three other workers, to conduct workshops across the North-eastern states and examine the possibilities of setting up a network of Soul Search centres and schools there.

Nupur Loya was in high spirits. She was looking forward to the tour in Assam—the seat of the greatest temple of Yogini at Kamakhya, reputed to be the abode of the most powerful goddess, symbolising female sexual power, and the largest centre of tantric worship in the country. She felt the compelling pull of its powerful female deity.

Yashoda was gripped by an acute depression that curled around her like a giant anaconda, squeezing the life out of her, each time she breathed. Her mind was teeming with hundreds of despicable snakes that constantly trembled and hissed at her. She did not have the courage to look into Aranya's eyes that were pools of sadness and despair—of questions for which she had no answers and accusations for which she could give no denials. Her mind was shut off by a trapdoor, behind which horrific memories boiled over in a cauldron. Threads of barbed wire criss-crossed outwards and lined her porcelain skin with creases that etched a grid of despondency and fatigue on her face.

Yashoda's insides had dried up. Each night she went to bed with a heavy heart, weighing her down, till she fell off to sleep, and as soon as she woke up the demons began hounding her again. She was desperate to communicate with her dead son. A friend took her to a medium, Rati Bai—a Parsi woman, who had perfected the skill.

As she drove off to keep the appointment with Rati Bai, at a seance session, to enable her to tap into the spirit world, her emotions were mixed. She was nervous and afraid. She did not know what to expect, but, the all-consuming desire to establish contact with her dead child—a victim of parental neglect and a broken home, was much too compelling for her to waver.

'The dead are never exactly seen by the living, but many people seem acutely aware of something changed around them. They speak of a chill in the air. They wake up from dreams and sometimes see figures standing at the end of their bed, in a doorway, driving past in a car or phantom-like boarding a bus....'

In a darkened room with thick blinds, five people sat around an oval wooden table, anxiously waiting their turn to receive a signal or some communication from a loved one who had died. Yashoda Loya sat nervously amidst them, her heart pounding wildly, both with excitement and fear. The wooden table, around which they sat had a bowl of rosewater placed in the centre. All the participants dipped their hands into it and patted them dry. Then they held hands to bind the circle.

Rati Bai, the medium, a thirty-eight year old woman of Parsi origin sat with her eyes closed, solemnly conducting the poltergeist ceremony. She began chanting a prayer and told the rest of them to chant Om in unison. After a few minutes, she stopped and spoke aloud to an invisible presence, asking if her guide had arrived. The guide was supposedly the spirit of her mother, through whom she communicated with those beyond—who their relatives on earth wanted to reach for.

The table wobbled eerily, in response to her question. Yashoda turned pale.

The Parsi woman opened a book to a blank page, invoking her mother to write the first line in Gujarati. She held the pen lightly, as it took on a life of its own, sliding smoothly over the words that it had formed. *Rati kem cho?* (How are you Rati?)

As the session progressed, the force connecting the people congregated there to their departed loved ones, wrote: *Good evening friends—Hello Yashoda.*

Yashoda blanched in fear. The pen moved lightly and continuously, answering questions in turn for each one present—each new response taking the shape of a different handwriting.

Finally Yashoda got her turn.

'Mom don't be sad,' the words blurred before her eyes as they brimmed over with tears.

'I can see you Mom—and all the others in the room. My sight is back. Forgive me for going away the way I did. I had no other choice. But don't feel sad for me Mom, I am happy and at peace. No, I did not hurt when I went over the edge. I came to say good-bye to you mother. Don't feel sad for me. Make Aranya happy, she deserves to be.'

Yashoda's body wracked with uncontrollable sobs. She had got her answers. She felt slightly less distraught, after having communicated with her son. She had been too overcome with emotion to ask him more questions, to ask him what he wanted them to do on his birthday, to ask if he wanted to say something to his father.

When the session ended, two hours had passed. Yashoda had tuned out when the other participants were talking. She wanted no sounds or sights to dilute the temporary relief that loosened the anaconda around her heart.

Yashoda came back when she heard the Parsi woman. 'Time to say good-bye friends,' she trilled.

All the people present, closed their eyes and said thanksgiving prayers in unison. Rati Bai called out to the invisible guide, telling her to knock the table thrice, to let them know that she had left.

The wooden table shook three times in farewell, and then stood still, as silence engulfed those who were seated there. Like the rest of them, Yashoda dipped her hands in the bowl of rosewater, before she left.

As she drove home, seated lifelessly in the back seat of her luxury sedan, she stared out of the window. She thought she saw two large circles of pink light, moving with her. They followed her gaze wherever she turned. The draught from the air-conditioner of the car touched her face and Yashoda felt a burning sensation, where her tears had chafed her cheeks.

68

Life had cocked a snook at Bharat Loya. Inhabiting two completely antithetical worlds, separated by a thin layer that divides the surreal from the practical, and the mystic from the temporal, he swung between them like a spiritual refugee, greatly empowered by the growth charts and sales figures his company registered, and charging his soul periodically in his private haven, on the banks of the Ganga. This was the refuge he sought when the flames from the raging inferno of his subconscious leapt out of their subterranean tavern, to singe his life on the surface. From one point of view, he had achieved his lifetime ambition, that had positioned him above the others as one of the world's most powerful arms dealers, the owner of an airline and a chain of hotels with a record turnover. The unrivalled growth rate of Global Integrity Industries gave him unchallenged supremacy and power. But the story had another twist in it that had emerged slowly, but forcefully in the intervening five years. Even though India had become the largest importer of weapons in the world spending close to one hundred billion dollars annually, there was increasing pressure on the government to ban middlemen and bring in transparency into arms procurement. Multiple scandals had rocked the nation over the last decade some of which were traced back to the Loyas and inquiries had been initiated against them.

For Bharat Loya, it demarcated the frightening, but real prospect of a shift in reach, power and influence—something that hitherto was his forte. Simply translated it meant a shift away from the stranglehold he had on the arms trade.

Bharat Loya could not disguise the fact, that the Loyas had suffered a progressive weakening of their links in the corridors of power. They no longer had the muscle to stall or introduce ordinances in parliament. Their old time protege in the Ministry of Finance was unceremoniously cooling his heels in an innocuous department, and the Prime Minister and his coterie, were not inclined to show any undue favours to GII or its bosses.

Meanwhile, Vishal Loya, his cavalier younger brother, the philandering and debauched Vice President of the company, with his fashionably bleached hair and tight gigolo pants, had congregated on the sprawling lawns of Tivoli Gardens, on the outskirts of Delhi, with a gorgeous ramp model, Sabrina Saif, and two thousand members of the GII family to celebrate Beetle Air being declared the number one airline of the country in the second successful year. In joyous attendance were most of the high-powered party animals of the city, and the usual Page Three wannabes, to complete the picture.

That same evening, Nupur Loya boarded a flight, with a five-member group of Soul Search theorists for a fifteen-day tour of the North-eastern states, to spread the message of life and love.

It was time for death to finally catch up with her.

69

At 0800 hours, on a densely clouded summer day, an Indian Airlines Fokker took off from an airfield in Assam for a whistle-stop tour to some remote villages in the hilly terrain of the North-east. Among the high profile individuals on this mission of Love and Life was Nupur Loya who was ambassador of this exalted and altruistic cause.

Nupur Loya was in high spirits. Her workshops had been very successful and if all went according to schedule, then in the next eighteen months, a network of at least one hundred and fifty schools and Soul Search centres would dot most of the villages of the North-east.

Nupur Loya settled back into her seat. She felt light-headed and euphoric. Flying over mountains and dense green forests always elevated her. She revelled in the divine experience that she had when she set eyes on the Mother Goddess at Kamakhya, the awe-inspiring Shakti Temple, at the apex of the Nilachal Hill, overlooking the Brahmaputra river. She had stood rooted to the spot within the powerful sanctum santorum of the temple that housed no deity, but only a black stone, carved into the shape of a *yoni*, the female genital organ, that was being perennially watered by a natural spring. She had been drawn to the legends surrounding the mysterious temple, and the Ambubachi festival celebrated in the month of June, during which the shrine was closed for three days to all pilgrims.

During those days, the goddess Kamakhya was believed to be going through her annual cycle of menstruation, after which hundreds of yards of bloodstained, white cotton fabric that mysteriously appeared from thin air were torn up into tiny strips, and distributed to the devotees as holy *prasad,* when the doors of the temple reopened. Standing in front of the carved black *yoni,* the embodiment of a universal female *shakti,* a fraction of which lies dormant in every woman, Nupur Loya had felt a powerful stirring of an energy, that worshippers of the Tantric cult have sought to harness, down the ages. She had felt her body wrack with unending waves making her feel empowered and ethereal—a feeling that had not dissipated, since then.

The aircraft roared ahead forcefully, dispersing the dense black clouds into swirling wisps of smoke, as it sliced through them. Nupur Loya looked at her watch. It had been ten minutes since take-off. In another twenty minutes, they would land at their first stop. She let her gaze drift out to the clouds that were bristling with static electricity, when all of a sudden she felt the aircraft shudder violently and drop sharply. She heard a loud, frightening noise of something colliding with metal. She saw mortal fear come up on the faces of all the other occupants of the plane.

Merchants of Death

Nupur Loya felt herself being hurtled rapidly downwards, into a death-defying abyss. Blood rushed into her head and a deafening, unearthly shriek pierced her ear drums. She gripped the sides of her seat hard, as the cocktail of screams, shouts, May-Day cries, and the terrifying sounds of breaking metal, deluged her. The last thing she heard, was an ear-splitting explosion, as the aircraft hit the dense forest floor and went up in flames. Light flared across the sky and inside her, and in that one explosive moment, she merged into nothingness, to taste eternity, and become the single awareness of *Chidanandarupa*—eternal bliss. Thousands of voices inside her from the past and the future, joined the chant of the universe. The long series of moments since her childhood, spanned out, and her sense of self dissolved into dusk and infinity, as the immortal words resonated in the sky.

'Na me mrityushanka
Na me jaati bheda
Pita naiva me naiva
Mata na janma
Na bandhur na mitram
Gurur naiva shishya
Chidanandarupa shivoham shivoham. ...

(I am only bliss—only bliss—only bliss)

She raised her arms to embrace everybody and everything, to dissolve all boundaries and fly into silent nothingness.

Heavy rain lashed down upon the wreckage of the crashed aircraft. The water pierced the smouldering debris that lay scattered for miles, around the dense foliage. All the occupants mutilated and burned to cinders, unceremoniously merged with the *panchmahabhutas*—the five elements, in a matter of minutes. The fire devoured them greedily, like a hungry animal, leaving only the unwanted parts of the bones and carcass, to be swallowed up by the rotting, mouldy, forest floor.

Shortly after, a nation wide broadcast for a missing Indian Airlines plane carrying the Deputy MD of Global Integrity Industries, would ravage the senses of a country in shock.

The undignified, uncouth, charred corpse of a once illustrious and glorious woman, would be discovered hours later, by a paramilitary search and rescue team. And Nupur Loya would become the latest link in the lengthening chain of grief and tragedy that had gripped the House of Loyas.

The silver spoon had come alive to claim another victim.

70

New Delhi
May 2001

Bharat Loya was shaving in front of his bathroom mirror, when the news flashed across the nation.

'*An Indian Airlines Fokker with fifty-seven passengers aboard has been reported missing five minutes after take-off from Assam.*'

One hour later, Amba Loya was returning after a four-day trip from a Soul Search conference in Bombay, attended by thousands of delegates and devotees from all over the world. The drama caught up with her at the Delhi airport, where she spotted TV monitors prominently running ticker tapes with the dreary newsflash.

'*An Indian Airlines Fokker with fifty-seven passengers aboard including Deputy MD of GII, Nupur Loya, has been reported missing, five minutes after take-off from Assam, since 0800 hours this morning.*'

Two hours later, Uday Nanda attending a hotelier's conference in Madras was handed a sheaf of papers and one fax message marked *Urgent*. It read:

'An Indian Airlines Fokker carrying fifty-seven passengers aboard including Deputy MD of GII, Nupur Loya, has been reported missing, since 0800 hours this morning. The pilot lost contact with ATC five minutes after take-off. Massive search and rescue operations are underway. No further details about the missing aircraft or the fate of the passengers and crew are available.'

At twelve noon, Vishal Loya had just finished his morning workout and swim. He was driving out of the Ritz Grand hotel in New Delhi, when his car radio crackled and he heard the grim announcement.

'An Indian Airlines aircraft that had taken off from Assam at 0800 hours this morning has been reported missing. The pilot lost control with ATC Tezpur shortly after take-off. Deputy MD, GII, Nupur Loya, is said to be among the fifty-seven occupants. Search and rescue operations by the army and DGCA are underway, but are being hampered by difficult terrain and inclement weather.'

Priyanka Nanda and Yashoda Loya were each in their own homes, mindlessly surfing TV channels when the news caught up with them.

'No further information on the missing plane or the fifty-seven occupants that include Deputy MD of GII, Nupur Loya, is available. Search and rescue operations have been called off due to bad weather and prohibitive terrain. Rescue mission to be resumed a few hours later. All fifty-seven occupants and crew members feared dead.'

J. Radhakrishnan had just concluded a routine module workshop in Bombay, on his holistic view of the physical, mental and emotional dimensions to create a deeper understanding of the self, when he heard the news.

'Search operations with the help of police, paramilitary and army personnel that had been called off due to inclement weather and difficult terrain have been resumed. A rescue team from Delhi which includes Uday Nanda, the husband of the Deputy MD of GII, Nupur Loya, has headed for the site of the disaster.'

Within twelve hours, the dreadful news that had leashed together the Loyas and their kin by a ghastly and suffocating cord—the fear of death blazed across the nation like a raging inferno.

'... Wreckage of the missing aircraft located. All fifty-seven occupants including the pilot are dead. The ground party that has reached the site, reports that the bodies are mutilated beyond recognition. Adverse weather and difficult terrain are making evacuation of the bodies impossible.'

The announcement that resonated over all radio and TV channels took up prime space on the front pages of all national dailies, the following day. The city watched in shock, another one in a series of terrible, freakish air disasters that had robbed the world of many beautiful and young souls.

As more pictures and details of the accident trickled in, a deathly shadow enveloped Nupur Loya's home and hordes of relatives and mourners came pouring in to commiserate with the bereaved family.

The following afternoon, a shell-shocked Uday Nanda returned to Delhi with his wife's body, mutilated and burned beyond recognition. He was received at the airport by her two brothers, Bharat and Vishal Loya, not knowing, that when he brought back the mortal remains of his wife, he had set into motion an unimaginable, drastic and seismic upheaval. The unfortunate accident would become the most humiliating landmark of his life, stripping him of his honour, wealth and status—all in one macabre stroke. It would provide a rotting testimony in this court of injustice, where the grieving widower, would be tried by the malefic forces hovering above the House of Loyas and the matrix of his own karmas, while his wife had immutably morphed into the ultimate *Chidanandarupa*, to taste eternal bliss.

71

A heavy pall of gloom descended on the Lutyen's Delhi home of Nupur Loya and Uday Nanda. It was the home that had been mute witness to many fast changing landscapes in the life of the perplexing couple; a pair that had lawfully been husband and wife, but were in truth incompatible aliens. Their paths had forked into separate spheres of functioning, their goals diverse and autonomous. Yet, they were tightly knotted to each other in this temporal vista, for a specific period of time—each one governed by the diktat of their interlinked Karmic decree.

Uday Nanda's stature crashed to ground zero, the moment his wife died. That instant, he became a phantom intruder lurking on the periphery of the House of Loyas, a vile entity that had robbed them of their beloved daughter. Her death had reduced their numbers in the lineage to four—leaving only two female descendants—one, an ageing spiritual guru and the other, a single child in the fourth generation—a position that stood perilously on the threshold of extinction.

On that fateful day, Uday Nanda lost the moral and legal right to the bounteous benefits that had accrued to him, by virtue of being Nupur Loya's husband. The aura of hostility around him was like a million volts of electricity, enveloping him in its choking grasp. It had been less than two hours, since the charred body of what had been his wife, had been ceremonially consigned to flames. The gruesome and terrifying images of the incinerated and mangled bodies of the fifty-seven passengers on that ill-fated plane haunted him. Never in his life had he imagined that he would be assigned the morbid task of retrieving and identifying the remains of the woman he had loved and married, and then catapulted by their union onto a high-powered track of stardom and success. As he sat in his bedroom, lifeless and numb, he was summoned by Amba Loya to the study. He had no inkling of the emotional ambush awaiting him that would leave him totally and irreparably shattered.

Amba Loya was seated imperiously, on a leopard skin wing-chair near the fireplace, in the wood-panelled study, dressed in white. She looked scrubbed and clean and her watery eyes betrayed no signs of what was simmering underneath. Uday felt a distinct chill emanating from her. She did not look up at him when he entered. He bent to touch her feet expecting her to embrace him and pour out her grief—to let her tears mingle with his and become one with him, in this terrifying moment of a brutal, unchangeable truth. Instead, he was greeted by an icy, matter-of-fact directive that sent him reeling with shock.

'I want you to hand over Nupur's keys, her cheque books, her jewellery and all her valuables to me, right now. You will sign a relinquishment deed in favour of Bharat and Vishal and shall have nothing more to do with any of us. The papers are being prepared and I don't expect you to give us any trouble.'

Uday Nanda felt as if someone was pressing a cold nozzle of a revolver, hard on his temples. He seemed to have been flung far away into a deep, dark well and the cold words, alternately fading and resounding, being mouthed mechanically by the spiritually elevated woman in front of him, with her porcelain skin and lucid eyes, were filtering in from a distance, somewhere far away. He felt himself step out of his body, watching an encounter between two strangers—one a murderously brutal and cold assaulter, and the other a helpless, shocked and numb victim. The tears streamed out of his eyes, everything before him blurred like an underwater image. The smiling portrait of Nupur on the mantelshelf, floated out before him and faded away. He gripped the back of a chair to steady himself. He did not see Amba Loya rise and move stiffly out of the room. Her words hung in the air like an apparition—they would haunt him for a long time afterwards. She had not even waited for the embers of the smouldering pyre of her daughter to cool down.

Only a few hours earlier, that hot, steamy morning in May had witnessed Nupur Loya's remains being consigned to the flames. Hundreds of high-powered friends and relatives, the staff of GII, and a crowd of curious onlookers had assembled at Delhi's Link Road Crematorium, to bid a final farewell to the Deputy MD of GII, whose tragic and untimely death had sent shock waves into a lazy city, dulled by the scorching heat of an Indian summer. Uday Nanda had lit the pyre of his wife, by touching a flaming torch to the logs soaked in oil. Loud Vedic chants had rent the air to drown the rising crescendo of the sobbing mourners, and finally bring down the curtain on the last act, in the drama of a life that had been closely linked to his.

'Death hung heavy in the air twirling its moustache. It danced a ghoulish jig in synchrony with the leaping orange flames that devoured the blazing cadaver turning it into ashes and dust!'

Loud voices of a macabre theory pierced the minds of every single individual. *A sinister curse shadows the House of Loya.*

Thousands of miles away, a distraught couple had huddled together in their fourteenth floor flat in New York City. Overcome with frustration and anguish, they clung to each other and wept inconsolably.

72

Three days later...

The Lutyen's Delhi home of the erstwhile Deputy MD of GII, was shrouded in sadness. A white *pandal* had been erected on the front lawns. The balmy summer air, saturated with the fragrance of jasmine, spread the essence of purity and serenity for miles around, to mourn the tragic and untimely death of Nupur Loya—the last female descendant in the third generation, of the grand House of Loyas.

A smiling, life-size, black and white portrait of the dead woman, occupied a prominent place on the podium that had been constructed for the family to be seated during the condolence ceremony. In front, spotless white sheets had been spread out, over mattresses that were joined together to cover the entire lawn, for seating the mourners.

The stage was decorated with cream and white fragrant candles, and thousands of fresh jasmine buds were threaded into garlands, that veiled every inch of the backdrop. A densely matted wreath of white roses and lilies, intertwined with white satin bows and candles, was placed before the smiling portrait, and wisps of grey smoke curled up in the steamy air from a bunch of incense sticks, that were lit in one corner of the stage. Soft chants of Vedic hymns permeated the air from the invisible speakers, sending the assembled congregation into a realm of quietude and introspection.

As the clock struck five, friends, relatives, and the GII staff and officers began trickling in, to pay their last homage to the deceased woman. While the chanting continued, all eyes were fixed on the entrance through which cabinet ministers, political leaders, press barons, filmstars and high-profile friends came in and filed past the beaming photograph and were ushered to the seats allocated for them, according to their social hierarchy. Most people who had assembled there felt a chilling sense of *deja vu*.

Dressed in chaste white, the family members had taken their places on the stage before the gathered audience. Amba, Bharat, Yashoda, Vishal, Uday and Aranya all sat with their heads bowed, a look of deep melancholy marking their countenance. When the chanting stopped, an eerie silence engulfed them.

Uday Nanda felt acutely depressed. He looked at his lucid-eyed mother-in-law who seemed stone-like and cold. He shut his eyes in disgust. He did not want to remember the disturbing incident that had shaken him up, just one hour after his wife's cremation. He steeled himself to concentrate on Amba's speech. Amba Loya took the microphone and began—she could well have been conducting a Soul Search workshop. She waxed eloquent on the impermanence of life and the futility of mourning the dead. Tears filled her translucent, watery eyes and every single person listening to her, was deeply stirred by her emotional rhetoric.

She read out a speech on the virtues of chastity, purity and saintliness that her daughter had embodied. In a choked voice, she detailed the last moments of Nupur Loya's life that had ended in service to her cause and to mankind, and the eternal joy of being delivered straight into the arms of the almighty in heaven.

Uday Nanda couldn't help feeling a strong repugnance at the duplicity of her words. He looked up once again at the mother of his dead wife. He felt a wave of sickening remorse overcome him. He noticed the familiar key that been added to the silver key-holder suspended from her narrow waist, and Nupur's six-carat, solitaire diamond on her ring finger.

Uday Nanda tuned out to avoid a recall of the unpleasant incident that had transpired between Amba Loya and him, four days ago. There was no one he despised more, at that moment. Meanwhile, in a dramatic conclusion to her speech Amba Loya directed one of the attendants to play the song Nupur had always sung, and almost instantly, the haunting chants of the immortal melody came alive in the air.

'Aham nirvikalpo nirakar rupa
Vibhurvapya sarvatra sarvendriyanaam
Sada me samatvam na muktir na bandho
Chidanandarupa Shivoham Shivoham. ... '

Uday Nanda focussed onto the faces in front of him. Amba Loya had risen from her seat and was dancing in rhythm with the tune, her eyes closed and hands thrown up in the air with pure abandon. Bharat Loya had followed shortly after, saying, 'Let us celebrate her passing over and dance with her soul'. He saw him bend forward to pull Aranya up by her arms, urging her to join them. He saw her recoil in horror with tears streaming down her face, and the dumbstruck and paralysed onlookers watched in grim silence, the grand finale in this macabre display of their novel method of dealing with grief; the enactment of the dance of death to the tune of an immortal song....

'Manobudhi ahankar chittani naham...
Chidanandarupa Shivoham Shivoham....'

73

New Delhi
March 2002

After Nupur Loya's death, life slowly limped back to normal for the House of Loya. Bharat Loya sat in his study, leafing through a clear plastic folder containing thirty-odd sheets. A pile of the morning newspapers lay stacked on his table, the front pages of which had been prominently highlighted in places. A thick, neon-green border outlined an eight inch by six inch square column, written by his old-time protégé from the Finance Ministry. It read:

> *The Government's third pro-reforms package in the year 2002–2003 is all set to be unveiled tomorrow announcing the grant of another licence for international flying operations to a liquor company in order to break monopolistic practices.'*

Bharat Loya's face froze into a mask as he reflected on the facts.

Omar Al Fayed was dead. The cartel had disintegrated. Uri Orlov and Abu Karzen had branched out on their own. Pascal Durrand had been found lying face down in a pool of blood in his villa in the south of France. He had been shot in the eye from a high precision weapon at point-blank range. Lazzaro Mancini had disappeared mysteriously from his yacht off the coast of Florida. He was last spotted gambling at a local casino accompanied by an unknown woman whom eye-witnesses believed to be of South American origin. And there were rumours of another agent from India being brought in by Fayed's successors.

At home, the government was making loud claims of having removed all middlemen from defence deals even as anti-corruption watchdogs had accused the Central Bureau of Investigation of colluding with a powerful hotelier who was known for his links with an international gunrunner.

The Delhi High Court had ordered the CBI to reply to accusations of corruption which stemmed from the procurement of a submarine from a French company with dubious antecedents and links to the Loyas.

The CBI, investigating forty-eight contracts finalised during the previous administration was planning to swoop down on the offices and homes of several leading defence agents of the country.

In a sensational expose an Indian news web-site had released a secretly filmed documentary showing a host of ministers, bureaucrats and army officials receiving kickbacks from undercover journalists posing as arms dealers. The scandal had far-reaching ramifications that led to the resignation of the Defence Minister.

In Parliament, a senior cabinet minister had raised a question about the dubious antecedents of the international carrier, Beetle Air, owned by the Loyas. It was brought to the notice of the house that the parent company was an offshore holding incorporated in the Isle of Man. No one could explain from where the initial transfer of ten million dollars at the time of purchase had been made and whom it came from. He had evidence to the effect that it had been funded by India's most wanted terrorist who had links with Omar Al Fayed.

The Ministry of Civil Aviation had finally cleared a licence that it had been dragging its feet over, to another private airline to operate in the country and unfortunately the Loyas no longer had the muscle to stall it in Parliament.

Bharat Loya was overcome by a feeling of disquiet. It was time for him to conduct a reality check.

On the home front, Uday Nanda had been ruthlessly thrown out from Nupur Loya's Lutyen's Delhi house which had turned into the official headquarters of the Soul Search Foundation as a tribute to the ardent disciple, who had laid down her life for the cause. A large white laminated board greeted visitors in the foyer with an inscription that read:

God shaped man by mixing the five elements,
Fire, water, air, ether, earth,

And man became too proud;
God created blindness to defeat man
And blindness became too proud;
God created sleep to defeat blindness
And sleep became too proud;
God created worry to defeat sleep
And worry became too proud;
God created death to defeat worry
And death became too proud;
Then God descended on earth himself
The immortal being to defeat death.

While Amba Loya was reported to be waiting anxiously in Bombay for her emissary, who had been sent with a proposal to an international beauty queen of Bollywood to marry her younger son, informed sources confirmed that Uday Nanda had moved into a two-bedroom flat in south Delhi, stripped of all his earthly possessions, and was not available for comment.

In the Calcutta High Court, a seemingly innocuous public interest litigation had been filed by a long-forgotten septuagenarian, by the name of Brigadier Harish Mehta. The petitioner claimed that the ex Chairman of GII, Ajay Vardhan Loya, was alive and hiding somewhere in the United States, under a fictitious identity, and pleaded that he should be brought back to India and prosecuted for his pending FERA offences and the fraudulent staging of his own death, to hoodwink the authorities.

Within GI House it had not escaped notice that the MD's new blue-eyed boy, a handsome, clean-shaven

Harvard graduate, had been seen hovering around him for unnatural lengths of time and whispers of late night, closed door, homosexual activity on the eighth floor, were doing the rounds.

For Managing Director, Bharat Loya, the terrifying prospect of an open combat with the government loomed menacingly before his eyes—and the cruelty he had always been ready to mete out to others, now threatened to be his lot.

He sat alone at his nineteenth-century banquet table made by Lazarus, stuffing vegetable-stew into his mouth with a silver spoon.

New Delhi
September 2002

The lone candle on the cake kept on flickering. The dancing flame had distracted Aryaman. There was a ghostly light shining behind it. Its quivering reflection projected a magnified image on the window behind. One was real and the other an apparition.

After the cake was cut, Aryaman followed his father out, clutching his arm. They rode up in silence to the eighth floor, like they had done all their lives. They entered the office noiselessly. Aryaman looked at his father's weary eyes that were deep pools of sorrow. He saw him lower himself heavily on to his leather chair and then stare out of the glass windows at the distant skyline, that silhouetted a gigantic pink sun-dial which was remnant of a long extinct dynasty. He did this all the time these days.

Aryaman sat down on the low green chair in the corner. It was his favourite place. He had been sitting there ever since he could remember. His father's room was like a vault. The low chair was warm and soft. It felt comfortable like his mother's womb. He wished he could see some signs of happiness in his father's eyes. He wished he could infuse the same joy in him that he had felt on the day he was born. He saw him sitting there under an invisible weight. A weight that pressed down on him so hard that it would not let him move—like a stake hammered through his heart, nailing him to the ground, the dreadful hand of a dark force that pressed him into himself, crying out—

'You were not there for your son ... your son ... your son!'

Aryaman screamed out the words that his father had long craved for—the words that would have made his spirit soar like it had never done. He wanted to tell him that he was alive and able to see, but his words became soundless waves that vanished into thin air. He pushed and pushed against the unyielding barrier between them, but couldn't break through. He felt trapped inside another dimension that would not allow him any grace. He crept out through a narrow crevice that led into his father's mind—the cryptic cave that held the charred embers of a tragic accident. He saw him choreograph a bitter memory from somewhere, deep inside it. He saw his eyes cloud with remorse and pain. Then he saw him pillow his head on his elbows resting on the table and cry. He hadn't done it in a long time.

Aryaman crept out into the long corridor that led to the lift. The happy painting on the far side, jumped up at him. A hundred whirling, squatting, dancing images, screeching and howling storms of colour engulfed him and turned into squares of white silence. He simulated the cocktail of sensations emanating from the well-defined strokes of the artist's brush. He sailed into the lift that moved down to the second floor.

The lights in the conference room had been turned off. The lone candle still stood flickering on the table in the dark room. It had burned down almost to the end. Droplets of wax had formed pointed icicles at the top and a mottled pyramid around its base. The quivering shadow on the window still loomed in the background. Some crumbs of the half-eaten, chocolate cake were scattered around it. He pressed his index finger on a cake-crumb that flattened and stuck to the underside. He slowly raised it and put it into his mouth. Then in one long breath, he blew the flickering candle out. He knew he didn't have the time to make a wish.

Back in his room on the eighth floor, Bharat Loya felt a rush of cold air prick the nape of his neck.